WANTON THOUGHTS

"Smile, Miss Norcrest. Your smile could light a man all the way home."

The sudden intensity of his tone held her gaze to his in a way his words alone could not have done. An expression unlike any she had yet seen softened the hard planes of his face. It thrilled her, made her shiver in the warm ballroom, ringlets of curls tickling her shoulders. Suddenly she wanted Lord Thomas's hands there instead. Even his lips.

The wanton thought startled her. She had danced with other men, even handsome men, but she had never wanted them to touch her more closely than propriety decreed. Lord Thomas's eyes had widened while she had felt herself blush from the toes up. He had become very still.

The music began, startling both of them afresh. They barely had time to do honors before he took her hand and led her around in a circle to start the dance.

"What position are we in?" Caroline asked, for she could not tell with the entire set circling.

"I do not know," he said, and suddenly they both laughed. "Ah, we are seconds."

"It would be horrible not to know what one was supposed to do," Caroline said.

"Tonight especially, I believe."

BOOK YOUR PLACE ON OUR WEBSITE AND MAKE THE READING CONNECTION!

We've created a customized website just for our very special readers, where you can get the inside scoop on everything that's going on with Zebra, Pinnacle and Kensington books.

When you come online, you'll have the exciting opportunity to:

- View covers of upcoming books
- Read sample chapters
- Learn about our future publishing schedule (listed by publication month *and author*)
- Find out when your favorite authors will be visiting a city near you
- Search for and order backlist books from our online catalog
- Check out author bios and background information
- Send e-mail to your favorite authors
- Meet the Kensington staff online
- Join us in weekly chats with authors, readers and other guests
- Get writing guidelines
- AND MUCH MORE!

**Visit our website at
http://www.kensingtonbooks.com**

THE UNEXPECTED SISTER

Glenda Garland

ZEBRA BOOKS
KENSINGTON PUBLISHING CORP.
http://www.kensingtonbooks.com

*To my mom,
for first exposing me to writing and for telling
Dad that my stubbornness would
eventually stand me in good stead. Thanks.*

ZEBRA BOOKS are published by

Kensington Publishing Corp.
850 Third Avenue
New York, NY 10022

All Kensington titles, imprints and distributed lines are available
at special quantity discounts for bulk purchases for sales promotion, premiums, fund-raising, educational or institutional use.

Special book excerpts or customized printings can also be created to fit specific needs. For details, write or phone the office
of the Kensington Special Sales Manager: Kensington Publishing Corp., 850 Third Avenue, New York, NY 10022. Attn.
Special Sales Department. Phone: 1-800-221-2647.

Zebra and the Z logo Reg. U.S. Pat. & TM Off.

First Printing: March 2004
10 9 8 7 6 5 4 3 2 1

Printed in the United States of America

Chapter One

Late September, 1814

Lord Thomas Dashley paced around the large drawing room to which he had been shown. The Red, the butler had said, and its deep color complimented the landscapes, still lifes, and portraits of antique gentlemen and their ladies that covered every wall. Thomas stared long at a picture of a dinner interrupted, bread torn, glasses knocked over, and the door open in the background.

Remembering Captain Peter Wendham's love for art, Thomas had expected nothing less than such magnificence and richness. Norcrest Manor might officially belong to the Wendhams' young half-brother, but Thomas never doubted Wendham could manage to impose his taste on whatever he had chosen to impose it upon.

What emotions had these paintings witnessed? What would they see today? Doubtless there would be anger and resentment. There had been anger and resentment when he had visited the families of Wendham's two lieutenants.

Whatever the emotion, Thomas was prepared. He had saved the most difficult visit for last.

Not, he thought, from cowardice. Few could accuse

him of cowardice, after all. His sins and defects of character, although legion, did not include cowardice. He had been saving this visit for last because it deserved to be done well. To Wendham's family Thomas owed the most serious debt.

Wendham had been his friend.

Many the night they had sat by a fire, the Spanish air soft and moist. Thomas would describe the land he had explored and mapped, its strange, sudden precipices and rolling plains, the people he had searched out for anti-French sympathies, and the French patrols he had avoided.

Sometimes he could say why Lord Wellington sent him to a particular place. More often he could not. Being an exploring officer was a strange life, one Thomas sometimes had to talk himself into accepting as necessary to the British effort in the Peninsula. He did not think he could have done it if he could not have come back into camp occasionally and have Wendham read from his sister's letters.

Thomas had craved those letters. Miss Melisande Wendham, at once witty, droll, and eloquent, would have become the epitome of perfection for him even without the sketch of her Wendham had drawn. The sketch had merely given veracity to Thomas's imagination. Imagining what Miss Wendham would say to him pulled him through the roughest days of his Army life.

He had imagined Miss Wendham urging him to give his French captors some information, any information that would give him time and opportunity to escape. He had imagined her telling him to send the French to the White Lady's Bridge. The irony still left a sickening taste that repeated deep within his soul.

What were you doing there, Wendham? Thomas thought. *Why were you at El Puente de la Dama Blanca?*

"You are the officer who knew Peter?" inquired a light voice.

He spun around, saw a slim young woman with honey-colored hair and a warm smile that flickered out uncertainly. She was not the French soldier he still expected to leap through a window at him, bayonet poised to impale him, or to shoot suddenly from the shelter of trees, boulders, or bony ridges of land. Thomas reminded himself sternly where he was, and took a deep breath.

Then he frowned. She was not Miss Wendham. Who was she?

Nevertheless, he bowed, cursing himself for probably frightening her, and said, "Lord Thomas Dashley, ma'am, at your service."

She was about twenty, beautiful in the well-tended way of the rich. In her white morning dress trimmed in lemon-yellow ribbons, she looked cool and light, like a sweet summer dessert. "I am Caroline Norcrest. You are waiting for my sister Melisande?"

Thomas bowed again, hiding his surprise. Wendham had never mentioned a second sister—well, half-sister it would be. He had spoken occasionally of Lord Norcrest, his half-brother who was twelve, but usually when he remarked that he would not live at Norcrest Manor on his brother's support and sufferance much longer. Indeed, it was only the search for fortune that had induced Peter Wendham to join the army.

On this point, Thomas had been less than encouraging. Foot soldiers could make some money by looting bodies or engaging in illicit trading. Wellington would have hung them, to be sure, but they had nothing to lose but their lives, poor wretches.

But officers? An officer caught looting would put such a blot on his family's copybook as to wish he had never been born. At best, he could hope to be shot by the enemy.

But Miss Norcrest was speaking, and he should attend. "Melisande should be down shortly. Have you been offered refreshment? Was your trip here very tiring? And it is Major, Major Lord Thomas Dashley, is it not?"

This speech, delivered at double-march speed with an inquisitive tip of her head, made him blink. "Yes, ma'am. It was major."

"Was?"

"I left my rank behind. I sold my commission."

"I see." She chewed her lower lip. "You were enjoying the pictures when I entered and surprised you, Lord Thomas. I am sorry for that. I tend to be impulsive, I am told." She brightened. "But perhaps you have not seen this statuette?"

She indicated a rendering of a peregrine falcon in gray stone. The bird sat restlessly on its perch upon a simply carved pedestal in the middle of the room, the left leg forward of the right, the head peering, cruel curved beak poised, one shoulder dipped. The granite had been cleverly rendered to give an impression of individual feathers while maintaining a smooth, perfect line.

"It's Cavalcari," Thomas said. He spoke matter-of-factly, but still, something about the statuette nagged at him.

"You know the artist?"

"I visited his workshop, in Portugal. With your brother, ma'am. Cavalcari is fond of birds of prey."

"Oh," she said, looking down.

Thomas became aware that her eyes were green, a forest of green waving on a far hillside, merely because they were no longer fixed on him. It was an odd feeling.

"No wonder you and Peter were friends," Miss Norcrest said. "You share his love of art and beauty."

"His love, perhaps, but not his knowledge."

Her lithe white hands touched the falcon, stroked its back, as though soothing a real bird with the promise of a succulent morsel. "So you were a novice, too, then?" she asked. "About things artistic, I mean. You stand so straightly, you look like you were quite a capable soldier." She blushed, casting her green eyes into greater relief.

But Thomas had to turn away. In a long line of adjectives describing his military career, *capable* did not top the list.

Miss Norcrest appeared beside him. Her head barely topped his shoulder. "I have caused you pain. I am sorry. I should have known better than to dredge up unpleasant memories. I know so many people who do not want to talk about things they have seen over there."

Thomas said, "No, it is I who am sorry. You were Wendham's sister."

"Only half," she said, as though she tried to convince him that that mattered. Had the right tone been in her words, Thomas might have been convinced. "My brother, my other brother, Frederick—Norcrest, I mean—we came from our mother's second marriage and my father's old age." She paused. "Peter never spoke of us, or at least of me, did he?"

Thomas cursed himself for not hiding his surprise better. But before he could protest, she said, "That would have been like him. He knew Freddie was well provided for, and I—I shall be taken care of. Mel was the one he worried about."

"I see," Thomas said, feeling awkward. Was it her brother Norcrest she referred to, or did she consider an offer of marriage? Thomas felt oddly disappointed at the idea of her marrying some nobody.

Miss Norcrest went back to the falcon. "You must not be embarrassed by my thoughtless tongue."

She was all generosity, so he said, "Your brother and I were friends, yes, but I was often away. Likely he spoke of you then and assumed he had spoken to me as well."

"That was kind of you," she said.

Thomas joined her again by the falcon, his back to the door. He also studied the bird, wondering what it was about it that nagged at him.

"Are you sure you do not care for refreshment?" she asked.

"No, thank—" He broke off.

"What is it?" she asked, all concern.

He smiled. "The feet. It's in the feet."

She looked puzzled.

"Do you see how the left leg is poised before the right? A right-handed person sculpted this statue. A very good right-handed person, but not Cavalcari. Cavalcari is left-handed. His birds all have their right legs forward so he may work the angle in comfort. He does not like to strain his hands."

Miss Norcrest laughed, put a hand over her mouth to muffle the sound. "Do not tell Mel her Cavalcari is not genuine. She would be very put out."

"You think my Cavalcari is a fake?" said a voice behind Thomas.

The hand over Miss Norcrest's face stayed there. Her eyes widened.

Thomas turned. The woman who stood there lived up to all her brother's praise. Dark-haired, dark-eyed, classic of face, tall and willowy, she commanded attention. Her expression, the inquisitive lifting of well-formed brow, and the tilt of chin proclaimed self-confidence. "If ever there were a woman who could impress you, Tom old boy," Peter had said one night over the fire, "it would be my sister Melisande."

Thomas was impressed. And depressed. He did not

want to make his confession to this image of perfection. But then, he had known that all along. He had thought, once, so long ago in his innocent age, that he would come here for the sheer pleasure of seeing if she was as wonderful as she sounded. He would fall more deeply in love. He would propose. They would live happily ever after.

"You have an opinion of my statue, sir?" Miss Wendham asked.

Thomas bowed, pulled his mind from the mire of might-have-beens. "Yes, ma'am, but it is merely the opinion of a former soldier. Hardly compelling. I meant no offense."

"I shall have the matter looked into." She spoke with the voice of someone used to having her orders carried out to the letter, but something about the way she looked away from the statue bothered him. Had it been his, he would have pored over it a moment, trying to gauge the validity of what a critic said.

But perhaps that was the true measure of Miss Wendham. She could be true of purpose, and right now, her purpose was welcoming him, undeserving wretch that he was.

"This is Lord Thomas Dashley, Melisande," Miss Norcrest said. Her gaze flew between them, quick as any real falcon. "He was a friend of Peter's."

"Yes, I know that," Miss Wendham said, and something in her tone made Thomas wary. Had someone told her what he came to tell her? It was not an impossibility. But then she said, "Will you not sit down, Lord Thomas?" She gestured toward a grouping of red-and-cream-striped divans before the large white marbled fireplace, and glided over.

"Peter wrote often of you," Miss Wendham said when they were all seated.

"I am very sorry about your brother," Thomas said.

"Of course you are," Miss Norcrest said. "I think you too kind to come and visit us. It has been over a year, after all."

"I would have come sooner, but Lord Wellington—"

"There was a war on," Miss Wendham said smoothly, with a pointed look toward her sister.

"Yes, ma'am," Thomas replied, trying not to witness Miss Norcrest's embarrassment. Her sister's method of curbing her enthusiastic interjections worked, but it left Thomas feeling sorry for her. He also felt some surprise at Miss Wendham's interrupting him.

"Your family is from Somersetshire, as I recall," Miss Wendham said. "Your brother is the Marquess of Dash."

Thomas nodded.

"Do you plan to stay long here in Oxfordshire? Or does your brother wish you home after such an absence?"

Thomas thought of the rowdy, dissolute parties his brother had hosted when he had come home, needing nothing more than rest and quiet, time to recoup his strength and firm his mental purpose. They resembled strongly the parties Dash had thrown before Thomas bought his commission. Thomas and Dash had no sister to keep things running smoothly, no mother to curb his brother's lust for lust. The only thing that had surprised Thomas was how much older his brother had looked.

"I visited with Dash when I first sold my commission, ma'am. Since then, I have traveled about a bit."

"Melisande, while Lord Thomas is in this country, he should stay here, should he not?"

Thomas had anticipated that they might offer their hospitality, but he could not take it. Indeed, it hurt to have it offered. "You're very kind, Miss Norcrest, but I have taken a room at the King George."

"Oh, we could send someone for your things," Miss

Norcrest added. "I should so like to hear of Peter's adventures. My sister mentioned some of them to me, but I had questions . . ."

Thomas could not quite contain his grimace.

Miss Norcrest took a deep breath and said, "Oh. Maybe that is why you would prefer to stay at the George."

Miss Wendham tightened her lips.

Before Thomas could protest that Miss Norcrest did not embarrass him, a man's voice came from the door.

"No, Miss Norcrest, that is not why Lord Thomas should not stay here."

Thomas well recognized the voice. He had wondered if he would meet Jack Bowes, a captain in the 52nd, here. He knew Bowes and Peter had been neighbors. Thomas also knew Bowes had proposed to Miss Wendham before leaving for the Peninsula, and that Wendham had opposed the marriage. Thomas did not understand all the reasons, although he was grateful for them. Wendham's opposition had increased Thomas's chances of captivating her.

Bowes dressed like the gentleman he was, although civilian clothes did not wear as impressively as his bright uniform did. Still, he was a handsome man no matter what one dressed him in. The camp followers had certainly said so. But Thomas had never trusted Bowes, although he knew some of his distrust rose from Bowes reminding Thomas of his older brother Dash.

Thomas stood.

"Dashley," Bowes said with a sneer.

Thomas bowed. "Bowes."

"Oh, you know," began Miss Norcrest, "that he—"

"Mr. Bowes," Miss Wendham said, making her sister bite her lip, "what is the meaning of this? Lord Thomas has come to tell us of Peter."

Bowes stalked over to Miss Wendham, and made as though he would take her hand. She glanced sharply at him, and he put his arms behind his back. "I would not like to wager upon what he says. Or rather, what he will not say."

"Whatever do you mean, Mr. Bowes?" Miss Wendham asked.

"Captain Bowes wishes to tell you that I am directly responsible for your brother's death," Thomas said.

Chapter Two

Caroline was dumbfounded. She could not believe that this handsome man who stood so steadfastly, as if nothing could force him to move one inch from his desired stance, who spoke eloquently of art while protesting his ignorance, could be directly responsible for Peter's death. No, he could not. Caroline knew it from the sudden pain she felt, the pain she saw trying to escape Lord Thomas's face with a twitch of his jaw, a pulling back of his chin bracing for a blow, the hands clasped so tightly.

And she knew as well that Mr. Bowes took a satisfaction from Lord Thomas's confession so intense it was pleasurable. Mr. Bowes's thin mouth had curved back upon itself in a spiteful smile, and his gaze, darting between Mel and Lord Thomas, seemed to glitter like those of the villains in the novels Caroline was fond of.

Then Caroline remembered how Lord Thomas had shied away from being called capable, how he had refused her offer of lodging. Something had happened in Spain a year ago, and this matter, she felt certain, would prove itself more complicated than it now seemed. Or render itself more complicated, if that were possible.

Mel was staring hard at Lord Thomas, but Caroline

could not tell her feelings. Melisande excelled at keeping her feelings close in.

Had she admired him before she heard Mr. Bowes's accusation? It would be hard indeed not to admire such a one, especially, for Mel, someone as sandy-haired and tanned as Peter had been. How splendid they must have looked together, against the sere backdrop of northern Spain, in their regimentals. Were those the thoughts that had gone through Mel's perfect head while she had put forever wayward, erring Caroline firmly back in her place?

Caroline knew she could not ask. Mel would not appreciate her being the one to ask. But she did seem to appreciate Caroline's taking her hand. Melisande squeezed it, then said, "I beg you to explain what you have said."

"Yes, *Major*, do," Mr. Bowes said, and sat down on Mel's other side, setting one booted ankle upon his other knee as if he were in his own drawing room, in solitary comfort.

"I have sold my commission," Lord Thomas said.

"That was a charity of his beakiness," Mr. Bowes retorted. "You should have been stripped of it entirely."

"I shall ask you not to refer to Wellington by that appellation in my hearing," Lord Thomas said.

"What?" Mr. Bowes asked in mock surprise. "Do you yet harbor feelings of loyalty for him? Just because he allowed you to sell your majority instead of taking it?" He shook his head. "You astonish me, Dashley. You really do."

"Mr. Bowes," Melisande said, "do you permit Lord Thomas to tell us what he came to tell us?"

Mr. Bowes seemed surprised to remember Melisande was in the same room, he had become so fixed on exchanging insults with Lord Thomas. He recognized the firmness of her tone, however; he flushed, then subsided with a tight smile.

Doubtless, Caroline thought acidly, he thought himself showing all proper restraint and deference.

Caroline straightened her spine to dispel such thoughts. They were not like her, and she had never felt anything other than a bored acceptance of Mr. Bowes. Although his sister Lucy was her best friend, she would not have liked him as a brother-in-law, that was certain. She had rested unworried about Mel's accepting him, for Peter had been opposed to any match between them, and what Peter opposed, Melisande did not do.

But, Caroline thought, much struck, Peter was dead over a year. Buried in some Spanish place. Here still was Mr. Bowes. And Lord Thomas, whose story Caroline was not at all certain she wanted to know.

"We were told, Lord Thomas," Melisande said, a guarded note entering her voice, "that Peter had been killed by French infantry. I understand that you were an exploring officer of the 43rd Foot."

"Dashley here was freed from the drudgery of regimental life," Mr. Bowes said. "He rode ahead and scouted the territory, reporting back whenever the feeling overtook him."

Lord Thomas looked wary. "You have related my role to Miss Wendham?"

Mr. Bowes looked at Melisande, who shook her head slightly. "Oh, no," he said with a wave of his hand. "I saw no reason to stir the pot, such a shoddy business it all was. You do go on."

Caroline tried to gauge the effect of these words on Mel. She herself felt indignation at Mr. Bowes's calling their brother's death a shoddy business. But Melisande appeared at her most opaque. And what had that little shake of her head meant?

"I would return to camp, not when the feeling took me, sir," said Lord Thomas, "but when I had information to report."

Mr. Bowes smiled that thin smile again.

"One day I was captured by the French," Lord Thomas said, turning back to Melisande. "I was questioned about Wellington's plans."

His voice stuck a little over the word questioned, and Caroline shivered. She had an idea of what questioning by an enemy could mean, and admired the way he could say it with such calm. She wondered if Melisande knew what it cost him to admit such things in such a way.

Mr. Bowes snorted. Melisande tapped him on the wrist, and he subsided.

"Exploring could be a lonely proposition. One would meet Spaniards, Portuguese—Gypsies, even—and I cannot deny I enjoyed their company. But by and large, I was alone, and happy to return to camp with a report, where I could spend time with fellow countrymen."

Melisande raised her brows, and this time Caroline could guess what she was thinking. Mel hated people who made excuses.

"Wendham and I had met over another matter," he said, with a surprisingly pointed glance at Bowes, who scowled. "When I was yet attached to the regiment. Shortly after our two regiments were brigaded together when we trained as Light Infantry under Craufurd. Whenever I would return to camp, I would seek your brother out, for he was good company." Lord Thomas bowed to Melisande. Then, with a slight turn, he remembered Caroline, and bowed to her as well.

Caroline found her shoulders twitching in sympathy. She said, "Well, Peter could talk the whiskers off a cat."

Melisande glared at her, but the corners of Lord Thomas's sad mouth curved up briefly. Caroline felt

exhilarated, and could not for the life of her understand why.

"I was fortunate our regiments stayed close to Wellington's camp," Lord Thomas continued, "for I could see
him whenever I came back in. We grew to be good
friends. He would even read from your letters, ma'am."

He was talking to Melisande again, as if they were the
only people in the room. What had Peter told this man
about Mel? Caroline thought, not liking herself for her
jealousy. And why had he never mentioned herself? She
believed Lord Thomas's answer before had everything
to do with his own sense of charity and fair play, and
everything to do with Peter's continual favoritism.

"One night he and I were talking about the strategy of
the spring offensive, into Burgos and Vitoria. We discussed plan after plan, playing at being Wellington,
really, as was doubtless going on at every other campfire.
Or hearth, for those fortunate enough to be garrisoned
within Ciudad Rodrigo." He smiled slightly, and Caroline filled in the thought: *Were they not already discussing
women, drink, or gaming.*

"At the end of our discussion, and it carried on for
some hours, ma'am, Wendham said that he felt confident Wellington would advance north of the Tormes,
even north of the Douro, and that the last place Wellington would want to take advantage of seemed to be south,
by way of El Puente de la Dama Blanca, a bridge that
crossed over a tributary of the Tormes and connected to
an old Roman road that turned almost immediately up
toward the mountains. I agreed, for the road in that part
was barely four feet wide. Exposing a column of men,
who could at best march two abreast, did not seem wise.
Daring, perhaps, though."

"Why is it called the White Lady's Bridge?" Caroline
asked.

All eyes were upon her, Lord Thomas's with surprise, Mr. Bowes's with wariness, and Mel's with annoyance. Caroline blushed, was disgusted at herself for it.

"Do be silent, Caroline," Mel said. "Why it is called anything is not germane. It was at this bridge that Peter was killed."

She had turned her attention back to Lord Thomas, who clasped his hands behind his back and nodded sharply. "Yes, ma'am. I later learned from Wellington that our suppositions—your brother's and mine, ma'am—were correct. He intended to advance north of the Tormes and Douro Rivers. Over the next several months, he sent me out toward Burgos to take note of a few salient details."

You were capable, Caroline thought, *however you deny it.*

"I was captured my third trip out, at Burgos. Under questioning, I made up a story. I told the French colonel in charge of the local garrison that the bridge was an objective, that there was a supply depot there to provision troops going across the mountains to strike at Madrid." He paused, seemed to ponder the falcon statuette, then said, flatly, "I was lying, but I was persuasive. The colonel detached a company of foot and took your brother and his company by surprise." Lord Thomas bowed his head. "I am very sorry, ma'am."

Caroline shivered. She could tell how painful it was for Lord Thomas to say what he did. Until that bow of the head, his rigid posture had reminded her of a broadsword, poised at the top of its arc, just before cleaving an enemy, forcing its bearer's arms and back and legs into obedience to its demanding weight.

Mr. Bowes's lips curled in a sneer, but it faded as Mel stood up. "You came to say you are sorry?" she asked Lord Thomas.

He nodded, his expression both sad and wary. *He has*

done this before, Caroline thought, *or he has imagination enough to realize more could be coming.*

"Do you ask forgiveness from me?" Mel asked.

"No, ma'am, I—"

"Thank God you do not ask forgiveness from me," Mel said. "For I cannot give it."

Mr. Bowes's eyes gleamed, and Caroline said, "Melisande—"

"Be still," Mel said.

Caroline flushed but subsided. She had seen Mel like this before, and it never did to argue with her. She could not be talked from her course, and she was usually right in the end.

"I wanted to say, ma'am," Lord Thomas said, again broadsword-straight, "that, knowing the bond between you and your brother, I could not presume to ask your forgiveness outright. It has been my goal, not to ask forgiveness, but to have the chance to atone."

White-faced, Mel crossed the room and jerked the bellpull. "Your arrogance, Lord Thomas, disgusts me. Please leave us."

Appalled, Caroline watched Lord Thomas take the blow and put a good face upon it. He bowed, said, "Miss Wendham, Miss Norcrest, good day. Captain." Then he spun on his heel and was gone.

Melisande sank limply into her chair. Caroline sat down next to her, put her arms about Mel. Mel stiffened, although she did not shrug off Caroline's proffered sympathy, and said, "How dare he? How dare he come here? The impudence!"

Caroline admired Mel's control. Truly their brother Peter had been correct to judge Mel the most excellent and excelling of women.

But poor Lord Thomas!

"He has long had a reputation for impudence, Miss

Wendham," Mr. Bowes said, rising and stalking about the room so, it seemed to Caroline, that he might better judge the effect of his words. "It is what prompted him to become an exploring officer, I do believe. Were it not for their uniform, which they take pains to cover, they would be little better than spies. And Bedlamites all, I do declare."

Annoyed, Caroline said, "If you knew all this, sir, I wonder at your withholding it from us."

Mr. Bowes stared at her.

Mel lifted her head. "Do desist, Caroline. Mr. Bowes did not withhold it from me."

"Mel," Caroline said, hugging herself now. "You never said." That hurt, her sister's not bothering to tell her all of what had happened to Peter.

But Melisande ignored Caroline's protest. "I am more aggravated by his trying to apologize where no apology can possibly be given, and by having the nerve to show his face, hoping that should I see a well-favored man, I might forgive him. But I am not so weak. It has been over a year since Peter died. Did he truly believe no word of his perfidy would reach me?"

"Why then did you permit him even to speak to you?" Caroline asked.

Mel drew herself up and gave Caroline full benefit of her irritation. "I wanted to see how far he might go."

But Caroline could not accept this too-smooth explanation. She flung herself up, hands curled in fists at her sides. "Nonsense."

"Caroline, calm yourself," Mel said.

"I will not calm myself," Caroline snapped back. "You enjoyed his humbling himself. And I think you are as angry at him for telling you—us!—about Peter as for his calling your Cavalcari a fake."

The falcon sat proudly in its left-leg-forward position.

"He knew about the Cavalcari?" Mr. Bowes asked, alarmed.

Then Melisande gave him a stern look and said to Caroline, "You are overwrought."

"Why should he not know about the Cavalcari?" Caroline asked.

"Go lie down and rest."

Caroline realized the futility of arguing, although she dearly wanted to. She bowed her head, much as Lord Thomas had done, and said, "You are probably right. My apologies."

And she walked from that beautiful room, past the falcon in its place of honor. She paused, however, at the bottom of the long staircase, and took several deep breaths.

Mr. Bowes's voice drifted from the drawing room. "I told you he was a dangerous man," Mr. Bowes said. "He went back there. He will ask—"

"Do control yourself," Melisande said.

"I am in perfect control of myself. And you were magnificent."

A silence followed, and Caroline found herself leaning backwards as though to hear better.

Then Melisande asked, "How dare he come here and bring us such distress? He needs to be gone, and directly."

Caroline blinked. There was proper feeling, high above her rant about a carved falcon.

Gripping the banister, Caroline ran up the stairs and all the way down the hallway to her chamber, where she shut her door and leaned a heated cheek against its cool wood.

Melisande was right to be angry, but Caroline could not help feeling that she had toyed with Lord Thomas. Such thoughts, however, were disloyal, and unworthy of her. Had not her mother always told her to emulate

Melisande in everything? Had not Peter so esteemed her?

Caroline shook her head, found herself echoing Melisande's sentiment that Lord Thomas be gone and directly, although for a very different reason. Caroline did not like feeling so torn.

Chapter Three

The reedy, sixteen-year-old boy brushed the remaining dust from his gray vest and brown trousers and crumpled his felt hat over his heart. That poor hat, thought Caroline, for it must contend both with Jon Hatcher's hands and his unruly shock of tow-colored hair.

"All set back, miss," he said, smiling proudly as he always did.

"Thank you, Jon," she said, surveying the chairs at the back of the large room that served every Monday and Thursday as her village classroom. The house belonged to Mr. and Mrs. Quigley, well-intentioned members of the local gentry. "I think Mrs. Quigley will let us meet here again now."

"Yes, miss," he said. "Anything else I can do for you, miss? Can I take those books for you, miss?"

She would be disappointing him. She knew he fancied himself smitten with her. In one or two of her other students, that might have been cause for alarm. But Jon's affection resembled the songs of chivalry. He was content to worship from the relative afar of her first row, right, as she looked out. "No, thank you. And they are not heavy. Shall I see you on Monday?"

Jon touched his forehead, and said, "Yes, miss." His quick legs brought him to the door, but he had no more than crossed the high, narrow opening than Caroline

heard a voice she had been hearing in her dreams the
past two days.

"Would you by any chance happen to be Jon Hatcher?"
Lord Thomas said.

Caroline held her breath and stood quite still, wondering how he came to be in the Quigleys' house.

"I'm Jon Hatcher, sir. Yes, sir."

She pictured Lord Thomas standing as he had in her
drawing room, his hands clasped behind his back, legs
slightly apart.

"Excellent. I am in need of someone to help me with
small errands and messages and getting the lay of the
land. Bill Little, over at the King George, thought you
would be the best man for the job, and your father has
agreed that you may be so employed, if you are interested. Would you be interested?"

The lay of the land, thought Caroline in wonder, and despite all she was supposed to feel, some amusement. He
made resting a few days before heading back to Somersetshire—or wherever he might be bound—sound
romantic and adventurous. Then she realized what *the
lay of the land* meant to someone who had been in Lord
Thomas's profession. Had he enlisted Spanish natives in
just such a way, with this tone that was all ease and friend-
liness and had a compliment woven in?

"'Tisn't that I'm not grateful, sir, I mean, my lord—"
Jon paused. "That is right, isn't it, sir? That you're Lord
Thomas Dashley, that is? Only gentleman I know of stay-
ing at the George."

"You're exactly right," said Lord Thomas, and the
warmth in his voice touched Caroline.

"Well, my lord, Bill Little has two other boys who work
at the George, younger boys, although you can still
count on them to get where you need them to go, don't

misunderstand me. It's just that you could pay them less than me, sir, and only when you really needed them."

"I appreciate your honesty, and would take your recommendation except that I shall need someone with great frequency. I am thinking of leasing Bonwood House."

Caroline dropped her books. Although they were not heavy, they made a respectable thud on the uncarpeted floor.

Footsteps thumped outside, bringing him into the wide room, Jon in his wake.

"It's Miss Norcrest, my lord."

"So it is." He bowed. "Your servant, ma'am."

Caroline flushed. "I did not mean to—"

"Of course not," he replied and picked up the books scattered about her feet. Caroline stepped back without thinking.

"Miss Norcrest teaches some of us in the village, my lord. Since Miss Walters left to go marry a reverend over t'other side of the county and we were all at—" he looked at Caroline, doubtless remembering to choose his words judiciously, "—sixes and sevens. She lets me move the chairs for her."

Lord Thomas raised his brows, but said, "Indeed, one of the things Bill Little told me was that you were not afraid to work hard. What do you say?"

"He has another lesson on Monday," Caroline said, surprising herself.

"That's right," Jon said, although from his chagrined expression Caroline surmised the prospect of working for Lord Thomas had dimmed some of his eagerness for lessons. Likely he was planning to lord it over his friends, neighbors, and relations that he had earned himself such a good job and could be a first source for gossip.

Caroline smiled gently at his demonstration of one-up-manship. Such a universal human trait.

"What time is your lesson?" Lord Thomas asked.

"From nine o'clock to noon, like most days," Jon said. "You'll see some of the other children from town and around come here. But you'll not find those two from the George."

"Why not?"

"Because Bill Little doesn't want them to read, my lord. He just wants them to know where they need to go."

The two men, one young and fresh-faced, the other weathered and handsome and remarkably composed, looked at each other in such perfect understanding that Caroline felt pushed out of the way. "May I have my books back, please?" she asked.

"Indeed not, Miss Norcrest," Lord Thomas said, her books comfortably tucked under one of his broad arms. "I shall walk you home."

Mel would have a conniption should Lord Thomas walk her home. Indeed, Mel was going to have a conniption when she heard about his plan for Bonwood House. Mel had not said much in the two days since Lord Thomas had presented himself in their drawing room. She had conserved her words so that when she did speak, her clipped, icy condemnations hammered with extra force.

But Caroline did not want to argue the point before Jon. She said instead, "May Jon attend his lessons that day?"

"I shall plan other business for that time."

Caroline replied, more tartly than she intended, "Thank you."

"So, lad, what do you say?"

"I accept, sir, I mean, my lord."

"Good. And 'sir' is fine. Truth is, I'm more used to it."

"Yes, sir."

"Get yourself where you need to be, now," Lord Thomas said to Jon. "I shall make sure Miss Norcrest is safe."

With a cheery doffing of his hat, Jon quit the room with a stride barely short of a run. From her position near the window, Caroline saw him run in earnest down the village's main street. Caroline imagined the excited tales he would soon be telling.

"Is there anything else you need, Miss Norcrest?"

There were many things she needed, but nothing Lord Thomas could provide her with. Oh, she did not doubt that he could protect her from highwaymen, or rescue her from the vile clutches of any other would-be dragon or villain. For all his denials of capability, she knew something of what it took to be an exploring officer. She had tried to tell Melisande, although to no avail. Mel informed her she already knew everything she needed to know about exploring officers.

Caroline wished she could protect Melisande from his presence in the village. "No," she said.

"Then shall we?"

"No."

He folded his arms around her books and began pacing. "No?"

"No."

He walked all the way around her in a broad circle. Caroline felt like she was on display. She sat down on the chair she had used during her class, determined not to feel intimidated. A small smile dusted Lord Thomas's mouth.

Caroline was struck by the warmth that smile conveyed, and the intelligence behind it. Presented with the same situation, Mr. Bowes would have sneered. Even Peter, wonderful Peter, would have issued an order to her, the ever-unruly child. Lord Thomas resembled them as a rainbow resembled a storm cloud.

But such thoughts would not profit her. Such thoughts would upset Melisande.

"You sit very straight, Miss Norcrest."

It was such an unexpected thing for him to say that Caroline's lips twitched. She could not help it. Fortunately she had time, before he came back in front, to control her unruly lips. She thanked God, however, that she had worn her hair in a sensible chignon for her normal days at school, rather than loose curls, which might have betrayed her expression from behind by bobbing.

"Thank you, Lord Thomas."

From the front, "Do you sit so straightly while you give your lessons?"

"When I sit."

"You are required to be on your feet mostly?"

"I find it easier."

From the back, "Why?"

"I have not great stature, my lord. Even when my pupils sit, I cannot see much beyond the front ranks to the back."

"So you adjust yourself, rather than them."

Caroline blinked. That was a novel thought. "It appears so," she said slowly, and was disgusted at herself for not thinking it before. There were many ways she could have arranged the chairs and settees and hassocks. Four broad, shallower arcs sprang to mind. Had she been able to sit more during her lessons, she might have been less tired after them. Why had she never thought of it before?

From the front, "Do you know how long you can continue sitting so straight, then?"

"I have never put it to the test, my lord. That is, until now."

"Now, hm?"

"I shall continue sitting very straight until you have put my books down and left me to walk home."

He stopped in front of her. "I cannot do that."

She did not want to ask him why, although she did not fully understand her reluctance to do so. Then she realized he also had not asked her why, although that would have been the most efficient way of getting a direct answer. She said, "You must."

"For all my other faults, I have never laid down the title of gentleman, and a gentleman walks a lady home. A gentleman does not leave a lady to fend for herself, whatever the lady's feelings for the gentleman."

She tipped her head. "You begin to sound like Peter." The moment the words came forth, Caroline wished she could recall them.

His expression shuttered.

He had misunderstood her. She had wished he would not sound like her older brother when he had disparaged her, but Lord Thomas had read her dislike as directed solely at him, not at all at Peter. How could he think otherwise? He must either think she had not loved Peter, or that he had, up to that point, compared unfavorably to Peter. With regret, Caroline knew she should not correct the impression.

"Your brother would have been the first person to have wanted me to walk you home."

"My brother would have been the last person to have wanted to make Melisande unhappy."

He nodded once, slowly, his lips pursed. He still looked shuttered and composed, although Caroline suspected he was anything but.

"She remained angry with me, I take it?" he asked.

"Furious," Caroline replied.

"Would not see me again if her life depended on it?"

"Do you jest, Lord Thomas?" she asked indignantly.

"Apparently not anymore," he replied.

Caroline's lips twisted—not a smile, but an acknowledgement. They studied each other, and Caroline felt herself softening toward him as she had upon first meeting him. Something about him made her want to help him, to prolong their conversation and time together.

Was she so shallow, as Melisande professed not to be, that she could be swayed by his handsome face? Was she so naïve that she believed no one with his keen mind and manners could ever do anyone harm? Or did she dress him in a beautiful, romantic cloak of her own imagination about the daring exploits she surmised he had performed?

No explanation satisfied. All she knew was that looking on him, talking to him, made her feel warmed and accomplished, as close to perfect as she could get.

The radical thought amazed her, and she found herself saying, "Did you know that Peter and Melisande were twins? Peter was a bare quarter-hour older than Melisande, but to them, that fifteen minutes made all the difference in the world, especially since their father died before they were born. Melisande grew up looking to Peter for everything. She read books that he recommended. She learned what he thought she should learn. She comported herself according to his taste of what was most attractive in a woman. When he went into the army, his letters became her lifeline. When he died . . ." Caroline swallowed.

"Your sister was cast adrift," Lord Thomas said.

Caroline nodded. "But your coming here has tossed her another rope. She has you to despise."

He raised his brows.

"Do not think it. Not for one moment," Caroline said severely. "I do not think I shall like the person Melisande may become. That does a disservice to Peter. It is not the way you may atone for your mistake. So put my books down and let us be."

"You misunderstand me. I have no desire to make your sister feel better by letting her despise me."

"What do you intend to do, then?" Caroline asked, both curious and frustrated and trying hard not to reveal too great a degree of either.

"Eventually I intend to persuade her to marry me."

Caroline could not hide her shock. "I thought you had put aside your jesting, Lord Thomas."

"I am not jesting, Miss Norcrest. I know your brother looked at his commission as an investment in his future, and your sister's. With respect, although he performed his duties conscientiously, he had no love for soldiering."

But you did, Caroline thought before she said, "Freddy— my brother Norcrest, I mean—will always take care of Melisande. You may depend on it."

"Financially, perhaps. But your family's current situation is not conducive to her marrying and having a family of her own. Wendham was in a better position to provide that for her."

Caroline could not identify the mix of feelings roiling within her, but she knew Lord Thomas's marrying Mel was wrong. "You assume Melisande must marry."

"It would relieve my mind to know that she would always be free to continue those pursuits she enjoys."

Caroline wondered how much of Melisande's pursuits Lord Thomas knew of, and how she and Peter had wanted them used. Again it rankled her that Peter had never once mentioned her to his friend. She said, archly, "There is Mr. Bowes. He has desired to marry Melisande for some years."

A hardness entered Lord Thomas's face. "Your brother objected to Mr. Bowes."

Caroline sighed. "Well, I do not much like him, either."

His expression softened. "So how would you suggest I go about it?"

That question caught her aback. Few people asked her opinion about things that truly mattered. Her friends Lucy Bowes and Peg Denbigh sought her advice on fashion and how to treat some local ladies gently. Peter and Melisande had been so convinced of their own superiority in all things requiring taste and discretion that they had never bothered. Their attitude had colored their brother Frederick's view of her, although he treated her with great affection.

The servants knew who ran the house, and it was not Caroline. Even her village students asked questions of fact—how many times three went into twenty-seven, for example, or what year had the Black Prince fought the Battle of Agincourt—not opinion. At least in their case it was likely because they did not want to embarrass her with their problems.

Yet here was Lord Thomas, treating her as if she were a reasonable creature capable of rational thought about such a delicate, important subject. All she could think to say was, "I do not know, but you may start by not walking me home."

He smiled. "You are positively tenacious."

"There are other words for it, too, all considerably less flattering." Caroline said. "It is one of my worst traits. At least, according to Mel and Peter, that is." She took a breath, blazed ahead, "So? What will it be?"

"I remain reluctant." He bowed, hand over his heart. "Regretfully."

Caroline thought about for another reason to give him, or at least some other way to reason with him. But she became distracted by the sheer interest she found in looking at him. For all he had relaxed during their conversation, nothing could diminish the breadth of muscle hinted at by his impeccable dark green coat and brown inexpressibles. Nor could he move, not even that brief bow, without the grace of someone who had stalked his prey far from the assistance of other men.

A chill ran down her spine, as though she were the hunted. She thrust it away. She was not his quarry. She was safe.

Then the thought struck her that for so cautious and controlled a man as he appeared, he was trying to do something very risky. Wading into the complex emotions of someone like Melisande and trying to change them would be no easy feat. More, he was enlisting the help of his quarry's sister, who could as easily betray his aims as assist him. Her illusion of safety faded rapidly. Either way, as his ready assistant or her sister's line of defense, she could not count herself safe.

And could she imagine this man as her brother-in-law? Caroline tried again. He looked as though he could hold his own next to Melisande, but still she felt she could not like him as her brother-in-law. It went beyond his professed responsibility for Peter's death to something deep within her. But to where, she could not determine. She was, she decided, a decided ninny for being so indecisive.

A little strangled laugh escaped her, and she put her hand over her mouth.

"Would you share *your* jest?" Lord Thomas asked.

"There is no jest but myself," Caroline replied, "and the strange position I am finding myself in."

It was as near a complaint as she could muster, but she knew he had registered it. He raised his chin slightly, an echo of his manner when taking a more severe blow.

"I cannot help you, Lord Thomas. All I can tell you is that like any fine carving, you should work on Melisande chip by chip. Wear her down. Over a long time. And do not start by shocking her again."

"Sound advice. Thank you."

"It is as well, then, that you are taking a lease on Bonwood House. You will need it."

"I cannot say too much about your encouragement."

He was teasing her, she decided. "You may thank me by letting me walk home alone."

He bowed his head graciously. "Very well, Miss Norcrest."

Caroline breathed a sigh of relief that turned into a little yelp of surprise and pain as she stood and fell off something, twisting her ankle.

Instantly Lord Thomas was at her side, one arm around her waist, the other under her elbow, steadying her. Caroline stiffened as some indefinable feeling shot through her like a dosing of water so hot it first felt cold.

"What is wrong? Have you hurt yourself?"

"No," she said, glancing down, "it's nothing. One of my books fell behind me, and I have stupidly tripped upon it." She looked over her shoulder, and caught her breath at the expression on his face. There was concern, to be sure, and something else—a confusion, perhaps— and who could blame him, with her being such a ninny. She blushed and looked away. "Please do let me go."

"It is not nothing," he said. "You have deliberately not put weight on it yet. Put your foot down and walk and we shall see what nothing it is." He took his arm from around her waist, but kept hold of her elbow.

As the warmth of his arm left, Caroline contrarily missed it with a yearning that frightened her. "Whatever I feel will go away in a few minutes."

"Your sister is correct about this stubbornness being an unfortunate trait."

Thus goaded, Caroline tried to take a step. Only Lord Thomas's hand on her elbow kept her from crashing forward. Instead he caught her by the other arm and she fell against his chest. *I will not cry*, she told herself.

"Brave creature," Lord Thomas said, bemused. "Foolhardy, but brave." Without seeming to exert any effort, he picked her up and carried her into the next room.

It took her a moment to recover her voice. "What are you doing?" she asked, one part of her reveling in the feel of strong arms protecting her, and another writhing in embarrassment.

"I have a phaeton at the George. I will drive you home."

She could feel his baritone voice rumbling through him as well as hear it, and it made her shiver. "But your plans! Melisande, remember Melisande?"

He nodded to a maid who had appeared in a doorway as he strode through a hall. "Would you open the door for us?"

The maid curtsied, wide-eyed, and jumped to do what he asked. Caroline knew this incident would shortly become the talk of the village. The village stretched before them, the King George Inn at, thank God, the closest of its tips.

"Will she come to think better or worse of me if I abandoned Peter's other sister?"

Caroline did not know if Mel would care, and the stark truth of that rendered her speechless. That and the heady feeling of being held so securely in Lord Thomas's arms.

They passed a couple of villagers, who doffed their hats at Lord Thomas. He nodded politely back but did not stop for greetings. Caroline blushed anew.

Presently they were surrounded by those boys at the George whose skills Jon Hatcher had so lamented. Lord Thomas issued them orders, and they scattered about their business with grins and tugs at their caps. Grooms and ostlers paused from their work and raised their caps as Lord Thomas swept Caroline into the George itself and set her down gently in a private room.

She brushed off, politely, the concern of Mr. Little and his wife, while she waited for Lord Thomas to return from organizing her conveyance. That accomplished, he waved aside her protests that she could likely go to the phaeton unassisted, swept her up again, and drove her smartly home.

Caroline hoped that Mel would not be home when they pulled up, or, if home, oblivious to the workings of her house. Such was not to be the case. As Lord Thomas refused to hand her off to a footman, he carried her straight into the red drawing room.

"What on earth!" Melisande exclaimed, standing in awesome indignation, the image of perfection. Not a hair was out of place. Her light blue dress reminded one of the free sky outside, and her haughty, aristocratic aspect inspired respect.

"My apologies, Miss Wendham," Lord Thomas said, setting Caroline down and giving a little tug to his jacket to straighten it. "But your sister injured herself and could not get home another way."

"But you—"

"I was thankful to render this small assistance to your family."

The look Melisande gave him could have boiled lobsters. Then Caroline remembered what Lord Thomas had been, and she could not contain her smile.

Melisande rounded on her. "And you, Caroline, what has happened to you?"

"I twisted my ankle. It will soon be nothing."

Mel's eyes flickered, but she was still angry. "And how did you come to twist your ankle where that gentleman could render you assistance?"

Lord Thomas said smoothly, "The important thing,

surely, is that Miss Norcrest is returned where she may be seen to."

"Were you at your village school this morning?"

"It is Thursday," Caroline replied.

That should have explained everything, but Caroline could tell from the narrowing of Mel's brilliant, dark eyes that Mel had added another objection to Caroline's teaching the village school, and that she would not long remain silent on the issue. Caroline also knew that the longer Lord Thomas stayed, the more unpleasant the tongue-lashing would be.

But Lord Thomas *had* helped her, and her reputation would survive being carried through the village. *Well,* Caroline thought, *in for a penny, in for a pound.* She held out her hand to Lord Thomas. "Thank you very much for helping me."

He bowed over her hand. "My pleasure, ma'am. But you are certain you shall be fine?"

"It is nothing serious," Caroline said, trying not to blush from the firm but gentle pressure of his hand. "I assure you. You shall see me walking about at church on Sunday without a care in the world." She knew he understood the not-so-subtle hint, for he squeezed her hand before he let it go. Caroline did not think Mel had seen him, and she felt warmed through. "Thank you again, Lord Thomas."

He bowed again, looked searchingly at Melisande, and left. Caroline watched him walk, for the first time noticing that he slightly favored his right leg. The limp was very slight, but she bit her lip to think that his exerting himself on her behalf had given him any strain or pause.

"Well you should be regretting that last remark," said Melisande tartly. "It was a thoughtless thing to say. It sounded like an invitation. He might have been gone by Sunday. Now he may use that as an excuse to linger."

Caroline sighed, although she supposed she should be happy Mel had misinterpreted her biting her lip. "He needs no such excuse. I found out in the village that he intends to take Bonwood House."

"How dare he," Melisande said between clenched teeth.

"I suppose he intends what he meant," Caroline replied, fingering her skirt to give her nervous hands something to do.

"That ridiculous notion that he could pay us back for Peter's death?"

"I do not know how ridiculous it is, Mel, but I know he wants to apologize as best and as fully as he is able."

"By sitting in the village like a wart on a pretty woman's face?"

Caroline winced.

Melisande shook her head, stalked across the room, rang the bell, and picked up some embroidery. She sat down near Caroline and began stitching. Anyone else might have expected Melisande's stitching to be rough and uneven, given her present agitation. But Caroline knew better. Melisande's stitching, even on the back, which was the side Caroline could see, proceeded with the precise regularity Caroline expected. Caroline admired her for it. She herself could not have done it.

"I never liked your taking over that school. You let people impose on you far too readily. Now it has done you an injury, and before such a one as him."

"It was not the school," Caroline replied, more hotly than she had intended. To have both Melisande and Lord Thomas criticizing her on the same point within a half hour unsettled her. "I tripped on a book I had dropped. All I need is a day of cold compresses, and I shall be right as rain."

Melisande pursed her lips, but her needle kept its regular in-and-out from the fabric. Melisande was stitching a rosebud design in pale pinks for pillowcase borders.

"How did you come to trip?" Mel's voice had softened. She was more the big sister Caroline had so long looked up to. The stitching had calmed her. So few things could since Peter's death, and Caroline pitied Mel for it.

"Lord Thomas came."

"To speak to you?" Melisande asked, astounded.

"No, to find young Jon Hatcher. Then he spoke to me. Mel, I know how little you like his being here, but maybe he does mean well."

"It is an affront to all proper feeling."

Caroline considered the implication, sighed, and let the subject drop.

Griggs, their butler, appeared.

"Summon a footman to take Miss Norcrest upstairs," Melisande said, "and arrange for her maid to apply cold compresses."

"Very good, Miss Wendham," Griggs replied. His mouth stretched a little in a sympathetic grimace at Caroline before he bowed himself out.

"What did he speak to you about, anyway, Caroline?"

But Caroline found herself unable to give a wholly truthful answer. "The future," she said, but instead of seeing Lord Thomas and Melisande in their own home, happily married, she recalled Lord Thomas's strong body hip to hip with hers, his arm about her waist, then his arms about her, holding her effortlessly.

Such a waste, she thought, and surprised herself by having to hold back tears.

Chapter Four

The French had made no distinction for his rank, but thrown him in a high-ceilinged cellar deep within the large, hillside mansion that held the local French command. The room smelled of putrid fear and sour desperation. Although there was a slit window fourteen or so feet above, the window allowed too little light to make out the source of the smell. Thomas assumed it rose from the floor, which squelched under his boots. There was no chair or pallet. The stone walls likewise felt damp and unhealthy.

He would stand until called for questioning. He would not lower himself into the filth. Then he remembered the ball that had passed through his leg, which derided him for any such foolhardy boast.

Thomas woke up, clapping his hand over the spot on his right thigh that burned as though freshly injured.

He pushed himself from his bed as the pain peeled back and fell away. It had been over a year since he had been shot, and his much-loved horse Aragon shot from under him, and still he dreamed about that prison cell four nights out of five.

Thomas staggered toward the washbasin, poured some water into it, and sluiced his face. He looked haggard, as haggard as his brother Dash after a night of dissipation. Thomas almost wished there was true dissipation to be had. Almost. If he had been dissolute, then he might say he came across such a face honestly.

He had had his opportunity to be dissolute, when he had come home to Dashwood, but it had not been the time for him. Thomas's lips twisted. Getting the time right seemed to be a recurring theme.

Like the dreams. He had not been questioned in that cellar. For that, four soldiers had dragged him up an interminable flight of stairs and thrown him onto a canvas tarp before an ornately carved desk.

Behind the desk sat a French colonel in equally ornate regalia with a waxed mustache and goatee. In his hazy state, Thomas had watched the ends of his mustache move up and down as the colonel spoke, and tried to discover if there were some kind of semaphore message being sent that said, *Relax, we are only pretending to be French. Really we are English and you are dreaming all this.*

Of course he had been delirious from loss of blood, thus the tarp to protect the colonel's fine, appropriated carpet. But Thomas had had enough sense to point to his uniform and say the obvious in French in response to every question so there would be no misunderstanding, "My name is Major Lord Thomas Dashley. I am an English officer. I am no spy."

Enraged at Thomas's lack of cooperation, the colonel had ordered him thrown back into the stinking cellar room. There Thomas had remained some time, finally passing out onto the filth. At some point he had contracted a fever, and the furious French colonel had taken it as a delaying tactic.

The torture, when it came, felt natural, inevitable. Thomas thought he remembered himself thinking that if he gave some plausible answer to their questions about Wellington's plans, they would take the time to check it out, and he could go back to that horrible cellar, recover his strength, plan an escape.

Escaping had been an imperative. He had important information he needed to get to Wellington. Bad luck all around that his host's damned *afrancesado* brother had given him up. Bad judgment on Thomas's part that he had stayed there despite the brother.

So Thomas had given the French colonel a plausible answer, and that answer was why, when he did not dream of his cell, he dreamed of Peter Wendham, surprised as he was set upon by the French.

After Thomas had broken himself free and returned to Wellington's headquarters at Ciudad Rodrigo, Thomas had learned that Peter had taken several blows during the course of the hot, hand-to-hand fighting around El Puente de la Dama Blanca, had kept staggering to his feet and encouraging his men, before the last thrust of a French lieutenant's sword had laid him in the mud, never to rise again.

El Puente de la Dama Blanca had been a plausible answer, but it had not been the real answer. Thomas had been told the real answer, and sent to make sure the way was clear. Wellington had always trusted him, had always been truthful with him.

El Puente de la Dama Blanca, though, had made Thomas doubt. But Wellington continued to insist, his back straight against his chair, chin outthrust, that he had told Thomas the truth, and *Damn your eyes if you refuse to believe me, sir.*

So why had Peter Wendham and his company been at El Puente de la Dama Blanca? No one in the command structure knew.

Thomas had observed how everyone dwelt on why Wendham had been there, how he had taken his company and departed at night, whose orders he might have carried. To Thomas, the reason no longer mattered. Wendham had been killed there because Thomas had spoken of the bridge, and Thomas could not forgive himself either for giving an answer to save himself pain he could have withstood, or for not thinking he could withstand the pain he had endured.

He could acquit himself of cowardice, but he could not boast of his strength.

The truth was, he could no longer trust his memory to be accurate on the details of his capture and interrogation. He only remembered the whole business without haze in his dreams.

Thomas went to the half-opened mullioned window, pulled back the light curtain, felt the cool morning breeze, and looked down on the commotion in the inn's courtyard. Grooms and handlers bustled around a mail carriage, loading and unloading. Passengers stretched their legs. A maid yawned as she crossed the yard, bound for the inn proper. One of Bill Little's boys slipped something into his brown coat pocket and knuckled a smudged forehead before running off down the street toward the village square. Bill Little himself watched the boy go, then rubbed his hands together and greeted someone coming off the coach.

So many lives, so many concerns. Thomas refused to believe that his was any more pressing to anyone but him. He had seen too much of life and death, and caused too much death, to believe that.

But he could not deny his feeling of urgency. He needed to settle the question of Melisande Wendham, dearest sister to Peter.

It had long been his intention of asking her to marry him. Thomas thought he had fallen in love with her over Wendham's letters. Now that he had seen her, he knew he had not fallen in love with an illusion. Of course she was angry. Such a person as Miss Wendham, with her high ideals, could not help but be angry. Thomas understood it perfectly, had expected it. But he would prevail. He had learned how to be patient, even if he had never learned to like it.

At least he now had a position on a hill near the fort. Miss Norcrest's assistance would prove invaluable.

But why had Wendham never mentioned his younger sister?

Recalling Miss Norcrest's brilliant golden hair and straight spine, Thomas thought her every bit as dauntingly beautiful as Miss Wendham, although in such a different way. Blonde to brunette, petite to tall, rounded to willowy, impulsive to controlled, touchable to remote.

Something about Miss Wendham made him want to kneel before her from a few feet away, perhaps touch the hem of her dress like a knight of old to his queen. Thomas did not think he could have picked Miss Wendham up and carried her down to the village, not initially, and certainly not after her first protest.

Something about Miss Norcrest, on the other hand, made him feel as if picking her up was the most natural thing in the world.

As though she were his sister already?

Thomas turned away from the window and thrust his legs into the trousers he had prepared last night. Since the army, he rarely bedded down for the night before tending to his clothes. He never knew when he might be wakened or what might waken him. Thomas had also had to eschew the services of a batman for weeks on end when he went out behind the French lines. His batman within Wellington's camp had been killed on a forced march. Poor Johnson had been carrying Thomas's dress coat while Thomas had been out on his last patrol, and likely mistaken for an officer by a French sniper. Thomas had not had the heart to re-place him, nor, indeed, felt any pressing need. He knew he would resign his commission.

As for a valet once he had returned to England, what valet in his right mind would want to traipse around England helping his master apologize? Thomas imag-ined an efficient valet such as the dour-faced man who worked for his brother Dash trying hard not to shud-der at the primitive conditions. Even this inn, with its well-proportioned rooms, clean sheets, and tasteful though rustic furnishings, would likely have given any respectable valet a rash.

So Thomas noted how many more crisp cravats his brother's valet had provided him with—seven left—and thought it a good thing he would move into Bonwood House on Tuesday. Then he could hire a valet.

As he buttoned his shirt, however, he knew he could no longer avoid answering his question about Miss Norcrest. Did he think of her like the sister she would become?

The truth was, he could not tell. He felt again her slender weight, how neatly she had fit against him, and the smell of sweet spice. He remembered having the sud-den thought that he had been picking up Miss Norcrest all his life.

Would he feel that way if she had been his sister?

Thomas pulled out one of the seven cravats and, look-ing at it in the mirror above the washbasin, began tying it in his own simple pattern of a weave ending in a smart knot.

He felt responsible for Miss Norcrest as well as Miss Wendham. Whatever Peter Wendham had said or not said to him, she was his sister, too. He wanted to make sure of her future as much as Miss Wendham's. But a small niggle inside him told him there was more to it than that, although he could not put his finger on why he felt that way. Perhaps he would figure out what bothered him while he conversed with Miss Norcrest later this morning after church.

He glanced up from his cravat in the mirror and saw himself smiling. The expression startled him. He had not thought of himself smiling this last half-year or more. Apparently Miss Norcrest raised his spirits.

He shook his head at himself. He should not be indulging in smiles and happy thoughts. He had a fortress to take in Miss Wendham. He should be keeping to his task.

Thomas shrugged his coat on and went downstairs for breakfast. Bill Little met him around the corner of the stairs, bowing. "My lord, good morning. Will you be wanting a private parlor this morning?"

Thomas believed Bill Little asked the question for form's sake, bowing to the "Quality"'s known desire for privacy, but was secretly as happy as a dragoon with a well-balanced pack to have the second son of a marquess gracing his public room.

"No, thank you."

"Very good, then, my lord," the estimable Mr. Little said and rubbed his hands together.

Thomas sat down in a corner by the front windows, looked beyond the flower boxes to the still-busy courtyard. The inn's front room was filling up with some locals Thomas was beginning to recognize, and people off the mail carriage passing through.

The serving girl brought him tea, toast, eggs, and bacon, as she had every other morning he had been at the George. He thanked her, then stirred milk into his tea. He sat back to sip, then immediately straightened and put down his cup.

He recognized the tall, sturdy man about to come in

the door, although he wore the brown of a prosperous farmer, rather than the scarlet Thomas had never seen him out of.

Regimental Sergeant-Major John Rowan had been Thomas's company sergeant before Thomas had been promoted and gone exploring. Thomas had long respected Rowan's temper for its steadiness and impartiality. He would mete out punishment without favoritism to anyone who deserved it, was not above giving some stringent advice to green officers, and could be counted on to push spooked troops back into formation, no matter how furiously the cannons roared and the muskets sang.

Rowan did not see him upon entering, but waved to a couple of the locals before heading toward the counter and Bill Little, with whom he exchanged a hearty and familiar hello.

"You're back, then, Mr. Rowan?" Bill Little said.

Rowan shrugged. "I'm still swaying on the top of the mail. Pint of bitters?"

Bill Little pulled the pint and slid it across the counter. Rowan took a deep draught and sighed. "Better. So, what's been going on since I've been gone?"

Bill Little leaned close toward Rowan, and Thomas looked out the window, but not before he saw Bill Little's chin jut in his direction. Thomas heard Rowan's boots clump onto the floor, Bill Little's "Hey, there, Rowan," then Rowan stood before Thomas's table, pint in hand.

"Well, damn my eyes, sir, if it isn't good to see you hale and hearty." He doffed his hat to a heavyset matron sitting at a table left of Thomas and said, "Your pardon, ma'am."

She raised her brows and sniffed.

Thomas stood and spread his arm. "Sergeant-Major, do you sit and join me?"

Thomas was not unaware that the locals had gone

painfully quiet. Nor, apparently, was Rowan, for his gaze flickered sideways in a gesture Thomas recognized from regimental days. The troops claimed that when Rowan merely glanced to one side, he could see behind him, too.

"Don't mind if I do, sir. Thank you, sir." And like that, Rowan pulled out a chair opposite Thomas, drew off his hat, and sat down.

"I did not know you were from these parts, Sergeant-Major."

"Wasn't what we talked about there, was it, sir?"

"No. No, it was not."

"I was born here, sir, then went north with my mum when I was nine or so. I'd come back to visit some family, as are gone now, and married a nice lass. Annie, her name is. We have a farm about a mile that-a-ways." He gestured northwest. "She's been keeping it together for us."

"She sounds a fine woman."

"Well, sir, she puts up a mean fight, my Annie, but I must say she is a lot nicer to fight with than the French." Then Rowan leaned forward, lowered his voice, and said, "So, you've done it, then, that notion you had of apologizing to her? I heard talk about your approaching Lieutenant Gershwood's family, sir, but I didn't think you'd get this far."

"Who told you about the lieutenant's family?"

"Sir," Rowan protested.

"My apologies."

"And I understand you're taking Bonwood House?"

"Mr. Little speaks very quickly," Thomas said.

John Rowan laughed, making heads that had not been turned toward them swivel in their direction. Then he again lowered his voice. "I'm told you've already been up to the manor."

"And met with a stern rebuff," Thomas said.

"Well, we never knew you were short of daring, sir."

They gazed on each other in perfect amicability and the understanding of one true soldier to another. There had been no such understanding with Jack Bowes. But with John Rowan, Thomas relaxed as he had not relaxed in some time.

"Your stern rebuff is current knowledge, sir, if you take my meaning, although no one knows why she decided to take you into dislike."

"I do take your meaning. Thank you for telling me. I am surprised. I did not expect Mr. Bowes to remain quiet about the subject."

"Never understood Captain Bowes, sir, and never wanted to."

"I am forgetting my manners. Won't you join me for some breakfast? Or do you need to hurry home to your Annie? You've been gone some time, I gather."

"Ten days, up north, to my mother. I go whenever I can manage. She can't travel much. And Annie, she told me that if I were on time, to clean myself up and make myself presentable, and she would meet me at church."

"I was planning to attend myself this morning," Thomas said, then snapped his fingers for the serving maid. "Some breakfast for the sergeant-major, if you please."

The girl bobbed a curtsy, and while they ate their breakfasts, the two men exchanged reminiscences of their old regiment and related stories of what had happened to certain people in the last year.

Thomas noted the disapproving glances of the estimable Mr. Little at his lordship breakfasting with a farmer, but could not work himself into any sort of noble indignation. Likely enough Mr. Little and everyone in the area would soon think meanly of him. It was a surprise Mr. Bowes and Miss Wendham had kept his reason for visiting the neighborhood to themselves.

After breakfast, Rowan cleaned his travel dirt off, and asked if he could show Thomas the village, by which Thomas properly took to mean the time for serious conversation would begin.

They walked along a narrow track running beside the small river that had once induced settlement. The occasional side street off the village's main reached toward the river. Well-tended vegetable gardens ranged in between, but the river banks themselves remained wild, overgrown with shrubs, grasses, and the odd cottonwood or willow.

The morning air, crisp yet promising later warmth, sparkled as the sun rose higher over the prosperous village. The river gurgled, as rivers seemed to do no matter where they were, England or Spain. The sound comforted Thomas as he knew it had comforted many people before him, and would likely comfort many after. That, in itself, was a comfort.

"It will be entirely natural," Thomas said, "and you know it, if your neighbors begin to positively distrust me, and everyone about me. I would like to thank you for your loyalty to your regiment back there."

"A regiment, sir, is only as good as the men commanding it, and my loyalty to it works in what my father-in-law calls a direct proportion. Last year was more of a slog. Before that, we could count on your coming in every now and again and putting some cheer into us."

Thomas was touched. "What does your father-in-law do?"

"He's the chemist here in the village." Rowan broke off a twig from a tree that would have caught at his clothing. "So you are going to church this morning, Major?"

Thomas did not correct Rowan about the title. If

Rowan knew about the apologizing, he knew Thomas had managed to resign his commission after Wellington had entered Paris.

Rowan had also been present the year before when Thomas had first tried to resign, had heard the whole showy affair, with raised voices from Wellington's tent. Thomas had quickly realized that he had compounded his notoriety when he had wanted only to fade into distant memory. A man's embarrassment, he had thought bitterly, traveled more quickly than a flying column.

So Thomas again was touched by Rowan's loyalty, especially since Rowan had never possessed the simple loyalty of so many of the troops. The son of a country doctor, Rowan had letters but little money for a commission. He had enlisted instead and refused Thomas's later offer of a brevet ensigncy, saying, *I can do more service to King and Country keeping the ranks together than swanning about the officers' mess, beggin' your pardon, sir.*

"I had not planned to attend church," Thomas said, "but then Miss Norcrest issued me a backhand invitation."

That comment prompted Thomas to tell what else had happened during his short time in the village, although he did not mention his less than clear feelings toward Miss Norcrest.

"In this area, sir, you can think of Miss Wendham as that major Colonel Crowley replaced you with. He looked mighty smart, never a spot on him, and we thought well enough of him to follow his orders. He was a sensible bloke. But nobody I know would have stood with him inside a closing ring of French Lights."

"I intend to marry Miss Wendham," Thomas said mildly.

Rowan gave him a look that Thomas suspected saw more than it should. Rowan said, "I can see how you'd feel that way, sir."

They came to a stop at a small bridge whose entrance overflowed with a profusion of fall rose bushes. Thomas absently pulled a white flower off a bush, remembered some of the times Peter Wendham had greeted him upon his return. Wendham had been one of the few who had ready smiles for him. He would come out to the area where Thomas staked out Aragon, his sergeant carrying a mug of coffee well-laced with brandy, and invite Thomas back to his fire.

"And if that's what you want to do," Rowan continued, "you're a fortunate man to have Miss Norcrest's help. There are not a few men in these parts who would not do whatever they could for her. Not just because she's comely, although she is comely. She's kind." Rowan picked a flower as Thomas had done. "If you think you owe something to Captain Wendham's sisters, Major, you would do as well to look out for Miss Norcrest."

"I have thought of that, and am glad your opinion runs with mine. I shall be glad of a friend here."

"That I shall be, sir. Never questioned it."

Thomas reflected that were he many other officers he knew, he should be feeling an acute embarrassment that a man who had been enlisted should know so much of his business, and self-confessed. But Thomas felt not a trace of embarrassment. Embarrassment had been scoured away from him, first by the French colonel, then by the men of what was left of the 52nd, who had spat at his feet the moment his back had turned.

Thomas put out his hand. Rowan pumped it, and they smiled, both pleased with the other.

A church bell rang out.

"It's the quarter-to bell, sir," Rowan said, an eagerness entering his face that made Thomas happy for Rowan's being snug and secure in his marriage, but sorry for himself. He still had so far to go. Nor could he convince himself that should he marry Miss Wendham, he would be able to be happy. He felt sometimes that happiness, like embarrassment, had been removed by the French.

They began walking up a side street and onto the village's main. "When do you move into Bonwood House, sir?"

"The plan is Tuesday. I have what feels like half a company cleaning it out, for it was thick all over dust, and I do not think they will be done by Tuesday, either."

"It's been vacant some time. Old Widow Barnes lived there, and her family could not sell the house after she finally died. I think they gave up after a while. It's good you've taken it. It's not good for places to sit empty and forgotten."

They heard voices ahead of them as they passed between a milliner's shop and a haberdasher's. Other sturdy village folk in their Sunday best began a small parade that turned into a regular crowd before the ancient stone church, a remnant of early Norman occupation, nestled beneath tall oak trees at the other end of the village.

Thomas did not miss Rowan's scouting for his wife, and knew the moment he saw her, for he took a larger step forward, and Thomas had to jump lest he walk into a buxom matron while keeping up.

Then Rowan took a young woman's hand, led her forward to Thomas. "This is my Annie," he said with pride.

Although Annie Rowan's head reached Rowan's shoulder and no farther, Thomas did not judge her by her size, for she had a face that managed to look both sweet and shrewd. The shrewd came from the rather determined, pointed chin, the sweet from the brown curls that peeked out from under her straw hat.

"And this is Lord Thomas Dashley, Annie, who was my captain for my first three years over there in Spain."

Thomas bowed. "Your servant, Mrs. Rowan."

Annie Rowan sized him up as thoroughly as her husband had done. "I've heard of your visiting, Lord Thomas, and your plans for Bonwood House."

Thomas's heart sank.

"And I heard you helped Miss Norcrest t'other day. I would take it kindly if you would have supper with us after church."

Thomas bowed again, relieved and warmed by her generously opening her home to him. Leasing Bonwood House he might be, but from the look of her, her position in the village was well enough established not to require anything more than lip service to the aristocracy. "Mrs. Rowan, it would be my pleasure."

Annie Rowan tossed her curled head, and surveyed some of her neighbors, who had been watching the interchange, with a smile that might also be considered a challenge. "And did my husband here find you at the George, Lord Thomas?"

"Coming off the mail, Annie," Rowan said. "Right on time."

No doubt about it, Thomas thought with amusement, but his sergeant had met someone who could out-sergeant him.

"There's my da. He shall be at supper with us, so let us introduce you now, Lord Thomas." She appeared to pluck a trim man in his forties with gray-and-red whiskers and a mild eye from the crowd and accepted a kiss. "Da, here is Lord Thomas Dashley. He shall be having supper with us."

Thomas had time to bow before Annie Rowan said, "I should very much like to sit down, John. Do let us go inside."

"Of course. At once." Rowan was all solicitude, but after he took his wife's arm and started toward the church door, he winked at Thomas.

Firmly armored on one side by Annie Rowan and the other by her father, who murmured his name as William Winthrop, Thomas felt he could withstand the disapproval of the entire congregation. The church's cool, dim interior augmented his feeling of security. He nodded in response to a smile from Jon Hatcher, who had come in with his family, and let the villagers' voices wash over him.

Then everything grew silent, from the back of the church forward. Thomas surmised that Miss Wendham, at the very least, had come into the church. The villagers would be watching her avidly to judge her reaction to being near someone who had displeased her.

But Thomas found the thought did not press upon him for wondering if Miss Norcrest had been able to come, too. Thomas hoped so. He did not like the idea of her being in pain, and her smile had already brightened one day for him.

Miss Wendham was indeed walking up the center aisle, her posture as upright as ever, and impeccably dressed in rose-and-cream muslin. Thomas thought he stopped breathing at the sight of her magnificence. She swept past him without a reaction, although Thomas knew she had seen him. He sighed, disheartened by how much further he had yet to go.

Then he brightened, for Miss Norcrest did follow. Thomas could not tell if she limped, for her arm was comfortably linked with a boy about twelve years of age who resembled her blond looks to a great degree. That would be Viscount Norcrest, Thomas thought, home from school for some reason. Norcrest did not know who he was, of course, nor did Miss Norcrest so embarrass everyone by pointing him out to her brother, so Norcrest's gaze passed over Thomas without undue interest.

But Miss Norcrest tipped her head underneath her

fetching bonnet and nodded at him with a slight smile
that promised more would come from her later.

Thomas felt rather than heard the exhalation of
pent-up breath around him.

The ranking local aristocracy seated in their box,
the vicar began the service. Thomas wondered with a
decided tightening of his stomach if the vicar were the
only one who regarded it as the preliminary to far more
interesting, but less heavenly, events.

Chapter Five

Two days of thinking and wondering how she would feel when she next saw Lord Thomas did nothing to prepare Caroline for the actual seeing of him. She felt lightheaded with relief that he had not given up. Not so much because she thought he should marry Melisande, but because seeing him made her happy.

At first she had told herself that her happiness came from thinking of a time when he and Peter had been whole and vigorously fighting the French.

But as Friday had passed into Saturday, Caroline had decided she just liked looking at him. She admired him, whatever he said about himself, or Mel said about him. It had taken courage to do what he had done, and more courage to come here.

Of course he would not admit that. She knew him well enough instinctively to know that. It was that feeling of knowing him, too, that had made her so eager to see him again. Caroline could predict when Melisande would do certain things, but she had never really understood why. With Lord Thomas, Caroline readily perceived the why of things. She did not understand the what, yet, however.

She had thought long on Lord Thomas's desire to marry Melisande, and the longer she had thought, the littler sense she could find in the idea.

Perhaps her greater knowledge of Mel informed her. When Peter was alive, Mel would never marry someone she thought Peter would not have approved, Jack Bowes's hopes to the contrary. With Peter dead, Caroline could not conceive of Mel's marrying someone she thought responsible for it. At best she might develop a grudging nodding acquaintance.

Both outcomes lay on the same path now, though, so Caroline had no scruples about helping him. Should those paths diverge . . . well, Caroline would have to see.

"Whom did you just nod to, Caro?" Freddy whispered when they were seated.

"That was Lord Thomas Dashley," she whispered back, then gripped his arm. "Do not turn around, Frederick William. I shall introduce you after church, if you like."

"He is standing with Farmer Rowan and his wife."

"Yes. Perhaps he has found a friend." The thought gave Caroline an absurd happiness. Then she discerned Melisande's irritation. She squeezed Freddy's arm, pointing subtly with her thumb toward Melisande. "Pay attention to vicar."

Caroline tried to as well, but although she sang hymns and made the correct responses at the correct times, her thoughts raced ahead to the churchyard, picturing where she might speak to Lord Thomas again, by the long boxwoods or under the sheltering oak.

It turned out to be the sheltering oak. Lord Thomas stood with the Rowans. Mr. Rowan was introducing him to Dr. Bushnell and his wife.

"Where are his regimentals?" Freddy asked.

Caroline looked about for Melisande.

"Mel's still in church with the vicar," Freddy said. "You can talk for a minute without her losing her hair. So, where are his regimentals?"

"He sold his commission."

"I would have liked to see his saber." Freddy made a cutting movement with his arm. "Whoosh."

"You will have to survive your disappointment," Caroline told him, nodding politely to Mrs. Westerby, one of the local gentry. "And did I not tell you Lord Thomas dislikes references to his soldiering days?"

"Then why's he standing next to Farmer Rowan? Farmer Rowan was a sergeant-major. He told me so."

"You are right, of course," Caroline said slowly, putting it together.

"Of course I am."

"Of course you are," she said, trying to turn his indignation into a joke. "Are you not always right?"

"Only with you, Caro," her brother said. He wriggled his shoulders, then set them, no doubt remembering the dressing-down Melisande had given him the night before for not having the highest, or even next-highest, marks in his class.

How well Caroline remembered feeling that way around Melisande and Peter. Yet she had loved Peter dearly, as dearly as she still loved Melisande. But it hurt to watch dear Freddy experience the same self-doubt and unhappiness. "Mel is on edge now. Do not be bothered by what she says."

Freddy scowled. "Seems to me Mel's been on edge since I was born." He brightened. "So come, please introduce me to Lord Thomas before Mel comes out, or I decide to make an exhibition of myself and do it man-to-man."

Caroline smiled gently at her brother. At twelve he stood as tall as she, but since she did not count herself as more than short, that did not say much. Freddy's arms and legs looked long for his body, though, which in her experience meant he had quite a few more inches to grow. Soon her baby brother would tower over her. She was not sure she would like that, although Lord Thomas's towering over her bothered her not the least.

"Do you resent him for what happened to Peter?" Caroline asked.

"I don't know that anyone knows who is responsible for Peter. My history tutor says war's an unpredictable business."

"Freddy, you may grow into a sensible gentleman."

Her brother flushed to the roots of his blond hair. "Well, I can say so because I'm not Mel. I was not his twin."

The echo of her own thoughts reinforced them, and made her feel sorrier than ever for Lord Thomas. She looked across the churchyard, and her gaze tangled in his. She realized she had forgotten to breathe for a moment when Freddy tugged her arm and said, "Well?"

Caroline was aware of how many people watched her, on Freddy's arm, walk over to Lord Thomas. She curtsied on legs remarkably steady as he bowed. Then she greeted Farmer Rowan and Mrs. Rowan, who nodded and fell back a few steps. Caroline appreciated their tact and said, "Lord Thomas, may I introduce my brother, Lord Norcrest. Freddy, Lord Thomas Dashley."

"I am happy to make your acquaintance, Norcrest," said Lord Thomas. "I came here intending to make an apology to your entire family, but—"

Freddy shook his head, starting to flush again. "I was yet at school. Please consider it given through my sisters."

Lord Thomas bowed again before turning to Caroline. "I am happy to see you well."

"Without a care in the world," she replied.

His face took on that closed expression she had come to associate with his having a painful memory, and she cursed herself for her hapless tongue. She hurried on,

"I did not know Mr. Rowan had returned from visiting his mother."

Lord Thomas's face relaxed. "I saw him coming off the mail this morning."

"Did you know each other in Spain, sir?" Freddy asked.

"I did. He was my sergeant when I was a captain."

Happier times, Caroline thought, suddenly wishing she could be in a place and a time where she could talk to him freely, ask him the questions she really wanted answered. This conversation felt awkward to her, and frustrating. Their conversation at Mrs. Quigley's, although she had not known how to treat him, had been honest. Or at least, as honest as Caroline could be with him. She carried too many of Melisande's secrets to be as forthright as she wanted to. It would be better if she kept away from him in the future. She wished she did not feel so stabbed by disappointment.

"What school do you attend, Norcrest?" asked Lord Thomas.

"Eton." Freddy made a face.

"First year? The first year is the most difficult. I well remember."

"I am on a long leave. I intend to eat enough this week to last me the term."

"But Freddy," Caroline said, "I have sent you a package every week."

Freddy looked guilty, and he hunched his shoulders.

"Sometimes a growing man needs more than one thinks," Lord Thomas said, meeting Freddy's gaze.

Freddy tipped up his chin, much like Lord Thomas was wont to do, and Caroline marveled at the ways men could come into complete accord with each other.

"How go your plans for Bonwood House?" Caroline asked.

"Very well, thank you. I should be able to move in on Tuesday."

"That is good news," Caroline said, feeling like a traitor to her sister for being encouraging, and to herself for not expressing more happiness.

"How is your sister?" Lord Thomas asked.

"Well enough," Caroline said.

"Growly as a bear," Freddy said over her.

Caroline glared at Freddy, who did his best to look chagrined, and so missed Melisande coming up with Mr. Bowes behind her.

Lord Thomas bowed. Caroline turned around with a sick feeling in her stomach that had as much to do with her own dissatisfaction as anticipation of Mel's displeasure.

Melisande's expression did not disappoint. Her chin lifted haughtily, her gaze could have frosted glasses in the summer, and her talented hands looked as rigid as the Cavalcari falcon's talons. "Come, Caroline, Norcrest."

The Rowans had moved up, Farmer Rowan on one side of Lord Thomas, his wife on the other. Caroline marveled at the former sergeant's loyalty, which had rubbed off so quickly on his wife.

Melisande inclined her head to the Rowans. "It is good to see you all well this morning."

Mrs. Rowan bobbed a curtsy, her husband and father doffed their hats.

"You are very kind, Miss Wendham," Lord Thomas said.

"Unlike some," Mr. Bowes said, "it is Miss Wendham's pleasure to do her duty and do it well."

The color drained from Lord Thomas's face, as color entered Farmer and Mrs. Rowan's. Caroline gasped her shock, heard hers echoed by some of the villagers nearby. Freddy went blank. Melisande turned back, her mouth fixed in an unpleasant smile. Caroline had the odd thought that it was the kind of smile a frog would make when it caught a fly.

"Have a care," Farmer Rowan said to Mr. Bowes.

"Have a care, *sir*, Sergeant," Mr. Bowes said.

"You may well remember that I never saluted you. *Sir*. I made it a point not to get into a bad place where I would have to salute someone who wasn't considered a proper officer."

Mr. Bowes's face darkened, and he darted a glance at Lord Thomas, breathing quickly.

Lord Thomas stepped forward. "Enough, Rowan," he said.

A step behind him, Rowan said, "Yes, sir."

The point could not have been better made, nor the lines so defiantly drawn.

"You may come to regret your quick words," Mr. Bowes said.

"Not likely," Rowan answered in a clipped tone. "Annie, it's time we went home to dinner. Is there room for Lord Thomas?"

Oh, Caroline thought, Lord Thomas had been invited for dinner. The lines were not only drawn, they were drawn thickly.

"No. I brought the wagon," Annie said, apologetically. "For your trunk."

"I shall pick up my horse at the George, ma'am, so I do not have to trouble you to get back to the village."

Melisande sniffed loudly, said, "Come, Caroline, Norcrest. Now."

Caroline's gaze slid back to Lord Thomas. He had been watching Melisande, to determine what effect this interchange had on her.

Caroline judged that although he had not expected Melisande to come to his rescue, he may have hoped for some mild word of protest at Jack Bowes's treatment.

Caroline felt equal measures of pity and exasperation, and wondered with trepidation what she herself could say. That is, if she should say anything at all. What part of that line should she tread?

She put her arm on Freddy's, found it and his expression taut. He was, she felt certain, about to blurt out something impolitic, and she spoke before she thought. "Come, Frederick, we should not keep Lord Thomas and his good hosts from their dinner."

Lord Thomas smiled faintly at her, but it was enough to warm Caroline through. She tugged Freddy's arm.

"Your servant, Dashley," Freddy said, before he allowed himself to be pulled away.

"Your servant, Norcrest," Lord Thomas said, bowing. He tipped his head, and although his lips formed the correct bend for what could have been a smile, his eyes worried them.

Caroline forced herself to turn around and accept that that would be her last look at him before she walked through the churchyard to their carriage. Melisande and Mr. Bowes followed behind her and Freddy.

"The presumption," Mr. Bowes said hotly. "I have told you he would—"

"Do not trouble yourself, sir," Melisande said, and there was a gentle but unmistakable warning in her tone. Mr. Bowes pressed his lips together.

It all puzzled Caroline excessively.

Chapter Six

Annie Rowan's father excused himself shortly after dinner, pleading work at his shop, but Rowan and his wife kept Thomas long past nightfall. Indeed, Thomas had not noticed night had fallen until Annie moved a few candles nearer to her seat by the fire so she could better see her stitching of an infant dress. She had joined them a half-hour after leaving them over some pipes, her nod to what many of Thomas's class would have termed "aping her betters."

Thomas found Annie's nod to fashionable manners the more refreshing for the ending of it. She had, however, hovered in the doorway before Rowan, with a look to Thomas, had told her to come in. Thomas, too, was quick to make the offhand remark that one of the few compensations of being an exploring officer was the break from high correctness of uniforms and stultifying conversation.

Annie Rowan was far from stultifying. Thomas appreciated her frank interest in hearing him and Rowan continue their talk of the old company times, and her franker assessment of his current situation.

"Of course we have to heed Miss Wendham," she said, and snapped off a thread with her front teeth. "Norcrest Manor has been the major estate around here these twenty years, since old Mr. Barnes died and his son moved away, and young Lord Norcrest is, well—"

"A mere scrap of a boy yet," Rowan interrupted. "Away most of the time at school now, too."

Annie clucked. "He looked half-starved, poor thing."

"Aw," said Rowan, "likely he's just growing."

"Your wife's right," Thomas said. "I well remember my school days. I was never full."

"Then why'd he look so guilty over that food Miss Norcrest said she sent? Sounded to me like he was ashamed of himself for eating too much."

"It's as likely he's using it to bribe whatever upper-classman is having him fag for him into making his life less of a misery. We were all beaten, you understand, by the upper-classmen at one time or another."

Rowan frowned. "Not unlike a few sergeants I knew."

"Officers, too," Thomas said, "although sometimes they could be a little more subtle."

Rowan took a deep draught of his pipe. The stem of Thomas's lay against his hand, stretched out on the chair's arm.

Annie sewed a tight inch while the clock ticked. Thomas reveled in the feeling of comfort he had so seldom enjoyed recently.

Then Annie said, "I wish Miss Norcrest had married that handsome young man who was up last summer visiting Miss Bowes. One could sit at one end of the village and see from the other side of it that he admired her. What was his name?"

"*Miss* Bowes?" Thomas asked.

"Captain Bowes's younger sister," said Rowan around his pipe. "A plain young lady, although exceedingly pleasant."

"She and Miss Norcrest are fast friends," said Annie.

"She is away visiting just now. Ah yes, his name was Sudbury."

"Like I've said, Annie, she must have some good reason not to marry this Sudbury."

Annie's plump, pretty face screwed up in an expression of distaste. "Like as not, Miss Wendham wrote her brother, and her brother said Mr. Sudbury was insufficiently grand. He is a fine gentleman, my lord, heir to a baronetcy, but not a man of extensive circumstances."

"Wendham wanted a rich husband for her, then?" Thomas asked, wondering why he felt so thankful Miss Norcrest had passed on the handsome Mr. Sudbury.

Annie glanced pointedly at her husband. "It is fairly common opinion, Lord Thomas, *or I should not repeat gossip*, that Mr. Wendham would have done anything he could to find some measure of security."

"Opinion, woman," Rowan said. "Just opinion."

"He was overheard saying he could not stand to live on his brother's property once his brother was of age," Annie retorted, and cut another thread with her teeth.

Rowan drew heavily on his pipe. The bands of smoke above his head writhed and resettled.

"You think he would have been happier living off Miss Norcrest's husband?" Thomas asked.

"I think Miss Norcrest is entirely too nice," Annie said. "I hate the very idea of her going up to London next spring."

"It is what ladies do, so I'm told," Rowan said with a sidelong glance at Thomas, sharing the joke.

"Putting herself on display," Annie said as though her husband had not spoken.

"It's likely she'll find herself a fine husband," Rowan said.

"Fine, John Rowan? Fine? Fine feathers, maybe. But

fine feathers have fooled women before, just as they do men. Men are forever fooling women, anyway."

Rowan clapped a hand over his heart. "Ah, Annie, you pierce me to the marrow."

She giggled. "Not you, you great—" She cast about for an adjective she could use to describe her husband in front of Thomas and came up with nothing. She spluttered instead.

Rowan and Thomas grinned.

Then Rowan said, "But I'll agree with you, wife. I wish Miss Norcrest will find someone truly good and kind."

"I may die with a smile on my face now," Annie said. "My husband has agreed with me. Before a witness, no less."

"Who would ever doubt your word, ma'am?" Thomas asked.

"No one in their right mind," Rowan said.

"You will be thinking that you have appeased me, husband, but you have not. There is still no one to say 'nay' if the wrong sort makes up to her."

"What about Miss Wendham?" Thomas asked.

"It is as likely Miss Wendham will carry out any plan her brother had. Lord Thomas, I wish you had come here a month ago—more, maybe. By next spring you would have broken through Miss Wendham's ire and could have been persuading her she shouldn't be marrying Miss Norcrest off to some great pudding-faced lummox."

Rowan went still, but Thomas shook his head at him, saying, "Miss Norcrest estimated it would take longer for Miss Wendham to feel so disposed toward me."

"Well, Miss Norcrest probably knows her sister better than I, but from what I saw of Miss Wendham and her brother, I'd give equal odds she would soon turn to someone he respected." Annie frowned. "From what I heard, she's been up there lost and flopping around like a fish upon the shore. Likely the only thing she will be certain about is marrying Miss Norcrest to someone rich."

Thomas thought again of lovely, vibrant Miss Norcrest marrying some pudding-face lummox and wished, like Annie Rowan, that he had more standing with the family.

It would be a tragedy.

He tried to tell himself that tragedies happened every day. He had seen thousands. But he felt his own tragedies too keenly to so quickly dismiss anyone else's.

"Of course, we know you can't do anything, sir," Rowan said.

"You have the same tone, Sergeant-Major, as when you told me I could not do anything about getting the men extra blankets and an additional ration of spirits one cold January day."

"You did it, didn't you?"

"Do not ever ask me what I had to do to get them, either." Thomas shook his head. "Here I have nothing to trade upon."

"Not yet, sir. But you will."

"You're a damned optimist, Rowan. Your pardon, ma'am."

Annie smiled.

"There's your optimism, sir, and then there's knowing people and what they do."

Soon after that, Thomas bade his good-nights to his hosts and saddled his black mare Surrey for the trip back to the George. A gibbous moon helped him make out the road, although he kept Surrey to a walk, and Thomas felt all the satisfaction attendant upon a hearty meal and good company.

But the question of Miss Norcrest did trouble him. He hated the idea of her sister selling her to the highest bidder, but he did not know what he could do for her except to say, *If you should find yourself in some dire situa-*

tion, and you do not think you could go to your brother, come to me. I beg you.

The *I beg you* resounded in his heart. He meant it more than anything else.

Surrey danced a little to one side, wrenching his thoughts away from Miss Norcrest to instant awareness of the road. "Easy, girl," he said softly, stopping her and patting her neck. She responded with the stillness he had trained into her. He had lived as long as he had in Spain because he had bought only those horses which were exceptionally fleet and trainable to his slightest command. He also had padded their bridles with fine leather straps to reduce the jingling that so often gave a man on horseback away.

Back in England, he had left off the bridle padding, but habit had forced him to train any horse he bought to respond to a touch with his knees here or his hands there.

Now Thomas saw what had made Surrey give the alarm. The road here passed through fields and wooded tracts, some extensive. Field surrounded Thomas now, but he could make out a dim lantern from a wagon somewhere in the wooded section ahead. It was out of the ordinary but not unheard of for wagons to travel at night. With the memory for detail Wellington had so praised, he recalled the way the road through that section ran. It had a few initial bends, which was probably why he had not run over the wagon yet.

Thomas urged Surrey forward slowly, then stopped before entering the wooded tract. He listened as best he could, but heard only the clumping of hooves. The wagon had two horses, he decided.

Thomas dismounted and walked Surrey off the road and into the woods to its left side, stopping every ten yards or so to listen. He did not know why he felt such distrust of what was surely a normal occurrence, and he mocked himself for taking the war home. He had seen others do it. He had not thought himself one of them, beyond his desire to apologize.

About fifty yards along, Thomas heard a muttered snarl and someone cursed in a rough dialect, although Thomas could not yet place it. Immediately another man shushed the curser. That brought up all the hairs on Thomas's neck. He well knew the rhythm of men attempting to be sneaky at night.

Without hesitating, Thomas led Surrey farther away from the road and looped the mare's reins around a tree branch. The mare tossed her head. Thomas spoke softly but emphatically to her, and she stilled, although she rolled her eyes at him.

The wagon's lantern gleamed dimly through the trees to the right. Thomas skirted ahead on his left side of the road, going some distance so he could angle back and approach the wagon from the side, which, he judged, the wagon's team would be less likely to watch.

He slipped through the forest, and thanked God for his stout boots, dark coat, and his body's ability to re-member how to move rapidly and noiselessly while crouching and pressing up against trees to check his cover.

As he came closer to the lantern light, the night's air soft on his face, he surprised himself by thinking that he was enjoying himself. He had for so long now associated exploring with his capture, interrogation, and betrayal of his fellow Englishmen that he had forgotten some of the true joys of the job.

A noise in some bushes ahead brought him up short. Then a fox poked its head out, almost black in the night but for its sparkling, wild eyes, and fled away from him. An appreciative smile for a fellow hunter creased

Thomas's lips, and he kept going forward, realizing that he had entered a dale, and the way to the road was a fairly steep inclination. Luckily, although he could see the lantern light, it did not shine directly down on him. He carefully began to climb the inclination, but ducked down behind a tree almost immediately.

"You could get orf yer arse and he'p me."

"I tol' you. Yon's a pothole. Go lef' 'round it. But did you listen? No-o."

Thomas imagined he could hear the second man shaking his head. The breeze brought him the smell of cheap tobacco. Doubtless the second man was sitting smoking and watching his associate perform some repair.

"You said right. Go right 'round it, you said."

"Tha's right. Go lef' right 'round it."

The man Thomas dubbed "Righty" growled, then grunted.

Thomas grinned.

Then "Lefty" said, "Can I he'p it you can' hear?"

Wood spanked down on wood, and Righty grunted again.

Lefty said, "And don' you looka me like tha'. You know I threwed my shoulder loading this stuff up back Bristol way. Wha's you wan'? We break any of these damned crates, his highness Mr. Bowes will up and refuse ta pay us. Mayhap sic the local on us. You wan' tha'?"

"Ah, button it."

And what was Jack Bowes having transported in the night by these two tender ruffians? Thomas wondered as he crept farther up the hill, pulling gently at underbrush for support. It had rained steadily in the area, he noted, for the underbrush was lush and well-rooted, the best kind for quiet support.

War-honed instinct brought him to a spot, only a little

precarious, where he could see Lefty and Righty through a thicket. The vantage might not have worked during the day, but at night only he would be responsible for betraying his position.

Lefty was indeed sitting on the ground smoking. Better, he was practicing blowing smoke rings that floated, shivering, in the moist night air. Tender ruffians had not been far from the mark, Thomas reflected, for neither of them could be described as some straw soldier. They looked to be competing for the sobriquet of bulkiest man ever, and much of that muscle, for Righty was heaving a large wooden crate off the wagon.

Thomas wished for Fernando and Miguel, two guerillas he had often worked with in Spain. Although neither had approached Lefty and Righty for size, they had made up for it in determination, good humor, and, sometimes, sheer insanity.

They also knew how to treat a musket. The one Lefty had lying on the ground beside him would absorb some of the ground's moisture. If it absorbed into the charge, it would be useless. It was likely neither Righty nor Lefty had served, or, if they had, under a bad officer.

As Righty put the crate down, Thomas could see that the wagon tilted away to the other side. They had damaged a wheel in "yon pothole," Thomas surmised, and needed to unload the wagon before they could address the repair. It was their bad luck the road ran steeply away on either side, and they were forced to repair it where anyone might trot along.

Thomas figured he had been watching for about an hour, occasionally adjusting cramped muscles, while Righty unloaded eight other large crates, the time between each crate growing while Righty took time to rest, wipe his streaming forehead with a dirty kerchief, and swear at Lefty for recreation. When he unloaded the ninth crate, however, the wagon tilted alarmingly. The crate's bulk got away from Righty, and it thudded into the ground so hard Thomas felt the vibrations.

Righty swore with ferocity and thoroughness. Lefty stood up and came over to take a look, wisely not asking any questions or making unwelcome comments. The crate had broken in one corner, and spilled out sawdust.

"Aw, Ker-riste," Righty said. He moved around it, and Thomas saw a square, gold corner of an intricate picture frame.

Bowes was transporting artwork in the middle of the night.

Nothing could have persuaded Thomas to leave now. He wrapped his cloak tightly around him, huddled against the bank for protection from the night air. His future valet would have his work cut out for him.

Then he watched them fix the wagon wheel and attempt to repair the crate. The crate, however, had been made of rough wood that had splintered badly. Righty and Lefty compromised, after vigorous and heated debate, by nailing a piece crosswise over the opening and loading that crate last so it would be on top, directly below the covering tarp.

From watching the gibbous moon make its steady, winking progression through the trees overhead, Thomas figured it took them a couple hours. When they finally climbed on the wagon again and whipped up their tired horses, Thomas eased himself away from the embankment.

It had grown quite cold, but he knew he would be warm presently. He waited until they had passed the next bend, their lantern lighting their way; then he scrambled up onto the road and went directly back to Surrey.

She whickered softly at him as he neared, making it

easier to find her. In a trice Thomas was following Lefty and Righty on the road, carefully approaching any bends or entrances onto fields to make sure he remained undetected. He followed them for what felt like two miles until he identified their destination: a largish house northwest of the village.

Someone had told him it belonged to Jack Bowes.

They would be there some time, Thomas thought. Mayhap they would wake the household, and likely increase Bowes's ire. Or, if they showed some sense, they would bunk down in the stables and wait until morning. Either way, Thomas estimated he had until morning before they poked their heads back out of their hole.

He went back to the George and caught a few hours of sleep. The first sunlight warming the horizon woke him. That had been one of his skills as a soldier, too, to be able to wake himself up. He rose and dressed quickly, then sent one of Bill Little's boys, his eyes still gummy from sleep, to find Jon Hatcher.

Jon Hatcher's family had like been up well before dawn, for he was brightly awake. "Yes, sir?" he asked, finding Thomas in the common room over his breakfast.

Thomas had him sit down so he could give Jon his instructions quietly. Jon's eyes widened, but he seemed eager.

"Now I know you have your school this morning at nine o'clock. I will come relieve you at that point. If they leave before that, I want to know what road they use, and what their wagon looks like."

"Sir?"

"Is it empty, or full; and if full, with what, if you can see."

Jon nodded eagerly. This was an adventure for any young man. Then doubt clouded his face. "But the, er, gentleman, sir?"

"That is my worry," Thomas said in his best officer's voice.

"Yes, sir." And Jon hared off.

"Very good," Thomas said to himself, and smiled.

Chapter Seven

Monday morning before school Caroline spied Farmer Rowan going into his father-in-law's chemist's shop. Without giving the situation much thought, she hurried inside.

". . . and she'll feel easier," said Mr. Winthrop, handing a packet to Farmer Rowan.

After the bright morning sunshine, the dim shop felt close and foreign with its long counters and shelves upon shelves of bottles and boxes. Farmer Rowan turned to look at her, as impassive as his former major could be. Caroline bit her lip.

Mr. Winthrop greeted her from behind a long counter, wiping his hands on his long white apron. "Miss Norcrest, good morning. What may I do for you?"

"I . . ." She swallowed and clasped her books more tightly against herself. "I thank you, sir, but it is your son-in-law to whom I wished to speak."

"Of course," Mr. Winthrop said after a moment's hesitation. "If you will excuse me, there are some things I yet need to prepare in the back."

"Thank you, sir," Farmer Rowan said.

"Miss Norcrest," Mr. Winthrop said, inclining his head politely as he left toward the rear of the shop.

Farmer Rowan leaned against the counter behind him. "You want to ask me about the major, ma'am?"

His forthrightness made her smile, although not without some remaining nervousness. "Yes. The whole situation is so very distressing. May I?"

"You may ask anything you want, ma'am, but know that I never thought the major responsible for what happened to your brother. I was nary shy about my opinion, either, ma'am."

Caroline was amazed at how quick to the point Rowan was. So many people she knew would give some roundaboutation. "I am glad he has your loyalty."

Rowan folded his arms and said, "There were officers and officers in the Peninsula, ma'am, if you get my meaning. Some of them, well, we rank and file would not have sold them a crust of bread if one were begging at our tents for not having eaten for a fortnight. Some of them, we would gladly give up our own bread or meat or whatever we had to keep them going.

"The major, ma'am, he once led a couple men into a camp of guerillas and bargained with them through the night to get the lot of us decent blankets. It had snowed the night before, then the sun had seen fit to come out and melt everything so it felt even colder. Imagine what it did for us to have the major—captain he was, then, ma'am—come back in the morning, not having slept the night at all, walking, his horse loaded with blankets, with just enough time for us to pull those blankets around us before we received the order to march. Old Williams, he kept his fire going long enough to brew the major a cup of tea, and added his last sugar to it.

"That's just one example. He took care of us in battle, too, ma'am. He would talk to us before we went in, encourage us, and he always promised no one would get left behind. Once I saw him kill four Frenchies while he stood over poor Teddy Smith, and yelled at us to pull him out. A French officer saw the whole and ordered the rest of them away, even touched his hat to the major. The major bowed like we were all in some drawing room, not surrounded by gore and blood."

Rowan half bowed, as if demonstrating. A shaft of sunlight suddenly entered through a front window, making dust motes gleam and bottles sparkle. Caroline stared at them, mesmerized, then asked, "Could you tell me what led to his being captured?"

"What I know I know through others," said Rowan carefully. "His lordship had such luck with Captain Grant—you have heard of Captain Colquhoun Grant, ma'am?"

Caroline shook her head.

Rowan shook his head, too. "Everyone should know about what Captain Grant and the others did, in my opinion. Grant was of the 11th Foot, ma'am. He was one of the first his lordship sent out to explore and observe behind the lines. His lordship considered him worth a battalion, for three-quarters of the time the officers thought we had no idea where we were going, and it was dead truth, ma'am.

"Because of Captain Grant's successes, his lordship thought to put more exploring officers out. When our major died of the fever, our colonel decided to promote Lord Thomas, and he came to his lordship's eye. He was detached from the regiment, and went out for days at a time, sometimes weeks."

"Why Lord Thomas?"

"He'd taught himself to speak Spanish like a native, had the best sense of where he was going of any man I ever knew. He could draw wonderful maps, ma'am, that made you think you were out there upon a hill gazing all around you. But I think his lordship realized the most important thing about the major: people liked him. You would find yourself doing something for him you would not have done for anybody else.

"To survive out there," Rowan grandly gestured to all of outdoors, "you needed to make people like you enough to risk their lives helping you. For let me tell you, although we English and French treated each other as proper, civilized people will—even trading tea for brandy and washing our clothes together—there was nothing like that between the French and the Spanish. A Spaniard caught helping us might be killed on the spot, his house burned, his wife and children murdered right with him before his whole village."

Caroline felt sick to her stomach. She imagined how someone with Lord Thomas's conscience would have suffered, knowing that every person he talked to could meet such a fate. Nor would he have thought it merely for his cause. He would have considered they also died for him.

She swallowed, asked, "How long did Lord Thomas do this?"

"Almost two years. I often wondered if his lordship made a mistake putting him out there all the time. He always seemed so happy when he was back with us at the regiment. I was no longer his sergeant, you understand, since he was detached, but I made sure people knew he was there and took care of him."

"He said he spent a lot of time with my brother."

"Yes, ma'am. We were brigaded together, you know, us of the 43rd and them of the 52nd. Lord Thomas told me Captain Wendham helped him learn how to sketch his maps better. The captain had something else the major needed—letters from home.

"You'll understand, ma'am, that there was little for us to do out there. Oh, sometimes we could get up a play, or teach each other pass-the-times, but it left a lot of time for idle chat. So we all knew that Lord Thomas had gone into the army because he thought someone with the

Dashley name should do more than drink England's lifeblood."

"I did not know that of Lord Dash," Caroline said. But she thought she understood. A lonely man who would consider himself without family, read letters by her brother, who Caroline knew well could charm practically anyone when he so chose, could be drawn into his and Melisande's close world.

Might Lord Thomas have even fancied himself in love with Melisande back then?

But why would Peter have wanted to draw in Lord Thomas? That question had plagued Caroline. The more she thought about it, she could not imagine Peter having use for men being interested in Melisande. Did Melisande marry, Peter would have had to share his say in her work and accomplishments.

Peter had never liked to share.

Rowan studied her, seemed to come to some conclusion, and went on, "Well, the reason I mentioned Captain Grant, you'll understand, is that he was captured in the spring of '12 scouting out Salamanca. He escaped into France, of all places, and was still sending back reports, God bless him, long after. But the French knew as much, and they'd lost Salamanca, and when the major was captured a year later outside Burgos, let me tell you, they took whatever anger they had at Grant out on him."

"But how, precisely, was he captured?"

Rowan's face darkened. "He was betrayed by an *afrancesado*, a Spaniard who allied himself with France, and he must have been one desperate—ahem!—to yet be with the French at that time, ma'am. Lord Thomas managed to get from Burgos, but he was shot by some d— blasted coward. I understand the shot passed through his leg and into his horse, which threw him."

Yes, Caroline thought, that would explain the slight

limp. She hoped it never affected him other than when he was carrying the weight of a young woman quarter miles at a time.

"He was wearing his uniform, but they tossed him into a very nasty place, officer or not. That's why none of us blamed him for saying something that was not true."

Caroline frowned. "I do not understand."

"He told the French there was a Spanish guerilla supply depot at El Puente de la Dama Blanca."

"The White Lady's Bridge," said Caroline. "Yes, he mentioned that."

"Yes, ma'am. There was no clear ownership of that area, but all bridges could be seen as having their advantages—Spanish rivers being right tricky buggers."

"He said he lied but the French believed him."

"Well, no one was surprised people would believe the major, ma'am. Where it got tricky, though, was when your brother's company left the rest of the regiment in the middle of the blooming night, four nights after we had all heard the major'd been captured. Old—the colonel—was furious that no one on the general staff had told him one of his companies would be used in such a way, and then no one could figure out who had ordered your brother to go. What a hornet's nest that was!

"The colonel ordered a group of us from the 43rd out to investigate. They found five men barely alive, your brother, his two lieutenants, and upwards of thirty others dead, including some French, and a whispered story from poor Thatcher about a French group surrounding them and attacking in the dark, within a few minutes of their getting there." Rowan shook his head. "Thatcher and the other injured didn't make it back, although they had hopes of him, poor lad."

Caroline swallowed again, picturing the scene.

"Some guerillas came out and filled in some more details about the fighting. They gave no aid, though—just listened and waited, like good little Spaniards, until everything died down."

Rowan hung his head a bit, then said, "I suppose I shouldn't have said that. Why should they get involved in a battle that had no purpose anyone could see? They were spread thin, those guerillas, and it was rocky country just up from the river, with a Roman road barely wide enough to allow two men to pass abreast. Even a pleasant enough place, peaceful, you understand, if one wasn't fighting a war."

"The French were waiting for them?"

"It certainly seemed that way. But no one really understood why the French had been there, ma'am, until the major came back into camp. He had escaped during one of his questionings, found himself a right pleasant little offal cart to ride out of the castle they were holding him in, and made it back, half alive."

Caroline winced, shuddered.

"I'm sorry, ma'am."

"No, please, do continue."

Rowan shook his head. "When he found out what had happened at El Puente de la Dama Blanca, and told his lordship what he had told the French, well, ma'am, there was a lot of grumbling. The rank and file, ma'am, we could take a lot, swallow it whole, and spit it back out again. Why, I can barely look around me and think of all the comforts I didn't have in the army. But we didn't mind, when we could see what we were fighting for.

"In this case, though, no one knew what the point to it all was. There was a mort of grumbling over it. A mort. What saved the major was that no one knew why your brother had ordered his company there—and that the uproar over it began before the major came into camp with his story. Otherwise, there would have been a hue and cry about the officers covering for each other."

Caroline thought about this while Rowan drew on his pipe. "Would my brother not have had orders with him?"

"That was usually the way of things. The only paper he had on him, though, ma'am, was a map drawn of the area. It was in his hand, and sent on to your sister with the rest of his effects. He may have lost his orders, to the betterment of some high-ranked officer who ordered him there.

"And let me tell you, Wellington was furious there had been such a muddle. One company wiped out, the better part of two regiments bickering about whether the major had betrayed Captain Wendham. It tore the heart out of the 52nd, ma'am."

"It seems amazing to me that Lord Wellington did not know what had happened."

Rowan shrugged. "Not everything's cream, ma'am. The major knew that, too, better than most, but it didn't stop him from questioning his lordship about your brother's being there at the bridge. I had come with the major to his tent as, well, as part of a detail."

He had been under arrest, Caroline thought indignantly. They had arrested a hurt and wounded man.

"The major explained that he had given the French false information, to give himself time to recover and make it back with the rest of his report. He had known the White Lady's Bridge figured in none of his lordship's plans, because his lordship had told him that."

Caroline was taken aback. "He called Wellington a liar?"

"As much as. Wellington roared a bit in that cold way of his, and then refused the major's resignation. So the inquiry ended. It was labeled an accident, and his lordship kept the major attached to his staff, and the major stayed there while we pushed into France. His report had been important, ma'am. We'd have lost more at Vitoria than we did, I can tell you that."

"Still, it all sounds like it was less than satisfactory," Caroline said carefully.

"He's still bitter about it, sure. He doesn't care a whit why your brother was there, will only say he should've found another way to escape. That's why he's been apologizing. He's also been to the two lieutenants' families in your brother's company before coming here."

"Dear God," Caroline said.

"I do not know if it helped, ma'am. He's not the same major I knew, before. He's angrier. Oh, I won't say he never had a temper. We'd pity any poor sod who got him going, but it took a pretty big something to get him going, if you take my meaning. Now?" Rowan shrugged.

Caroline felt an upwelling of compassion for Lord Thomas, although tempered with concern. She had seen glimpses of anger held in check, and it had frightened her. Carefully, she said, "It is said that anger can bring much clarity of thought."

"Yes, ma'am, that I can well believe. Anger can certainly light up one path very brightly, but think of all the others that bright light casts properly in the shadows." And Rowan gazed at her so steadily in the dim room that Caroline knew he knew all about Lord Thomas's plans to marry Melisande.

That subject Caroline shied from. "Thank you for telling me all this."

Rowan nodded. Caroline could tell that he wanted to ask a question and would not, from deference. She said, "I shall do nothing to prevent Lord Thomas from what he sets out to do, but I do not think I can aid him."

"We all do what we can," he said. "Do not trouble yourself, ma'am. The major will find a way for himself.

He would deny it, but he trusts nothing that isn't a challenge."

With that perplexing remark, Rowan excused himself. Caroline left the shop, walked slowly up the street to Mrs. Quigley's house, her students, all that was familiar to her. She felt very much at a loss, and liked it not at all.

Chapter Eight

Thomas had spent the afternoon in his room at the George, ostensibly writing business letters related to his leasing of Bonwood House. He had finished them shortly after Jon Hatcher had relieved him after his morning schooling, so the reality found him coatless, lying on his bed, head pillowed on his arm, following the progress of a spider on the ceiling. He had tried to take a nap, remembered instead a time when he could have slept anywhere, anytime.

Thomas had seen this spider by the window before. Its legs had fine white and brown stripes, although it looked solid from the bed. It was not as large as some of the spiders he had seen in Spain. There the warmer climate had bred any number of formidable species of insect life. This spider appeared devoid of any coherent plan apparent to a mere human. It wandered here and there, often crisscrossing the same "ground."

So perhaps *progress* stated the case too strongly.

"You and me both, sir," Thomas said to the spider.

He forced his thoughts to what should be the most important of his considerations right now—that Jon had not returned from his observation of Righty and Lefty at Bowes's house.

Thomas suspected the storm had persuaded the two lazy villains to linger in Bowes's barn. Bowes's tactics,

Thomas reflected, were as wretched as ever. When it was raining, one was too concerned about keeping one's hat or cloak over oneself to be bothered to remark more than that it was a sure pity someone else had to be out in such weather.

Better now also to be down the road when the rain began and could wash out all traces of where one came from than to cut a trail in fresh mud. The mud would slow them down, possibly cause more of those potholes Righty so justifiably despised, and who knew when the next rain might come and wash their trail out?

Thomas traded arms behind his head. Normal commerce had ebbed outside due to the rain. It appeared to be slackening, more of a gentle, relaxing patter.

What kind of artwork does one ship using two ruffians in the middle of the night, and keep them until the next night so they might scurry back to their holes under cover of darkness?

Artwork one had no business having.

Which left a few interesting possibilities: Bowes was a thief, a smuggler, or a go-between for them.

Which meant that someone was either desperate enough to hire an idiot like Bowes or that Bowes had happened on something and figured out a way to turn it to his advantage. Thomas snorted, not liking either possibility, but seeing their irony.

Who would be the end recipient of this contraband? And, given Bowes's closeness to Miss Wendham and his pointed, although understandable, dislike of Thomas, would there be a way to turn Thomas's knowledge of it to his advantage with Miss Wendham?

God knew he needed some advantage. She had been so cold in the churchyard. She had stood there, magnificent from the proud straightness of her spine to the unflinching angle of her chin, and yet not reproved Bowes for what he had said.

It had fallen to Miss Norcrest to find the middle ground between decency and family honor. That she had chosen to do it by complimenting Rowan and Annie—and under pressure, no less—spoke much for her.

Her face, verdant green eyes shining, rose before him. Thomas took a deep breath, allowed the picture to remain. He had done his best to put off thinking of her until he had thought through Bowes and his mysterious artworks.

Thinking of Miss Norcrest could only be considered a reward.

When she tipped her chin up, Thomas could see her resemblance to her sister. Their different coloring—Miss Norcrest so blond and Miss Wendham so darkly beautiful—diverted attention from their similarities in features, but with determination on her face, Miss Norcrest was every bit as lovely as Miss Wendham. Perhaps more lovely.

Thomas rolled off his bed and paced about, observing with a sardonic eye that the spider had settled into the crevice between the ceiling, the wall, and a beam. Lucky creature, Thomas thought savagely.

For some time, he had not felt the rage that had gripped him during and after his capture. He had thought he had quenched its red-hot blade in the bitter waters of guilt and regret and shame. It was loathsome to find himself indulging in it.

But he wanted to imagine that French colonel's face purpling as Thomas choked the man's life from him. He imagined giving the order to have the guards who had tormented him shot. He wanted . . . he wanted to see Miss Norcrest with her hair unbound, in a transparent white shift with ribbons on it, standing before a brace of candles, her maiden's blush high on her cheeks, but her green eyes inviting him to finally come home and lie upon the fields among the wildflowers.

Thomas inhaled sharply, turned the image around in his mind as though caressing it.

Damn you, Wendham, he thought, *why did you never mention your other sister? Tell me another was as beautiful? I might have been prepared, then. Why were you at El Puente de la Dama Blanca? Why did we ever talk about that damnable bridge?*

Then he forced himself back to reason.

Judging by the vehemence of her reaction to the loss of her brother, it was Miss Wendham to whom he owed reparations, not Miss Norcrest. It was Miss Wendham to whom he had pledged himself, not Miss Norcrest. It was Miss Wendham whom Peter had thought would be the best match for his character and temperament and passion. Not Miss Norcrest.

Wendham had known them both.

Hell, Thomas wondered, *why did I think that saving deliberations about Miss Norcrest would be restful, my reward?*

There was nothing simple about her, and his argument that because she had tried to help him she must not be as upset by Peter's death was fallacious. She had the strange and rare ability to separate out her feelings, to remain loyal to her sister while not hating him.

Thomas leaned heavily against the casement window, watched the rain come down. It was no longer restful patter to him. It was an impediment, forcing him to wait for news to distract him, forcing him to stay indoors and entertain these thoughts.

He had to remember the course he had set, his objective. He could do little for Miss Norcrest except make sure she had the chance to make a better match. She was young, lovely, and well provided for. In short, to any prospective groom she was perfect. She could make a good match without his help.

But Miss Wendham? She was beautiful, too, but the seven years between them would make a difference to many a man.

Besides, he had told his plans to Miss Norcrest. It all came back to that. Thomas could not win her good opinion by proving himself unworthy of it.

He almost wished he had said nothing to her.

This is nonsense, he told himself. Likely he was thinking so of Miss Norcrest because she had been kind to him. She was there, and accessible. It had been a long time since he had found someone friendly. Likely when he got closer to Miss Wendham, he would experience all the good aspects of her character that he had experienced when Wendham had read from her letters. The contrast between her and Miss Norcrest would fade, just as the light outside his window faded and reduced everything to shadows.

There came a knock at his door. Thomas spun around even as he heard the low voice say, "It's me, sir."

"Come," Thomas called, tucking his shirt more neatly into his breeches and straightening.

Rowan entered, looked over the mess of letters, the rumpled bed, Thomas's coat tossed carelessly over a chair back. "Good evening, sir," he said. The *What have you been doing?* came through unsaid.

"Good evening. I did not expect you."

"Annie told me to come fetch you for dinner, sir. She seems to take it personally that you would eat here at the George."

"Your wife is a jewel among women, Sergeant-Major," Thomas said, meaning it. "But unfortunately, I cannot accept." He tipped his head toward the door.

Rowan needed no other hint. The door closed, he

came toward the middle of the room, where Thomas quietly explained why he waited for Jon Hatcher.

Rowan whistled. "Trust you to be in the middle of anything below-board going on, sir."

"I beg your pardon, Rowan."

"Don't take offense, sir. Once you got your promotion, we all said, 'Trust in it, Major Dashley will find any thicket full of French there is to be found.' And you did, sir."

"There were others working on the question, too, Rowan."

"I know that, yes, sir."

Thomas decided not to argue. "What do you make of the business?" he asked.

Rowan shrugged. "Never thought Captain Bowes was much in for the finer things in life, sir. From what I heard, he didn't discriminate, if you take my meaning."

Another knock came softly but urgently on the door. Thomas opened it to reveal Jon Hatcher, cap in one hand, a note in the other, catching his breath. Thomas motioned him in, shut the door. Then he nodded to Jon.

"Lord Thomas, the wagon just left. Mr. Bowes himself came out into the stable to tell them what's what."

Thomas frowned. "And how do you know that, Jon? I told you to watch from the hill."

Jon twisted the cap. "I found a way to sneak inside the barn, milord."

Rowan glanced significantly at Thomas as if to say, *See, you've inspired him, sir.*

Thomas pushed aside his irritation, both from the boy's disobedience and his guilty pleasure in being a source of inspiration to anyone anymore. "Well, what did he say?"

"He minded them be careful on the trip back to Portsmouth, my lord, told them no more accidents, and then they settled on them coming back with 'some more of it' Wednesday next. He seemed in bad temper. I waited until they were gone down the Winchester road, then I snuck out of the barn."

"What do you mean by *bad temper?*" Rowan asked the boy.

"He was in an ugly humor, sir. One of them, the shorter one who sat down a lot—" *Lefty*, Thomas thought "—had asked for extra pay to cover the day they lost last night. Mr. Bowes refused and began giving them the business." Jon grinned. "Sort of like my mum when I've forgotten to wash proper."

"So Mr. Bowes refused to compensate them?"

"Yes, sir. Told them their accidents were their business, and they were lucky to get paid anything for this run since they'd been late and one of the crates had been broken. Then the bigger one sort of glared at the shorter."

Ah, Thomas thought, almost with fondness, *I wonder what Righty and Lefty will converse about on the long road to Portsmouth.*

"I am glad we know when they are coming through next, Jon, that I will not deny. But the next time I set you watching them, you are to follow my instructions to the letter. Is that understood?"

"Yes, sir," Jon said, a little dimmed.

Thomas took a shilling from his pocket, tossed it at the lad. "Get yourself something wet downstairs before you go home. Watching is thirsty work. Then I want to see you at Bonwood House tomorrow morning promptly at nine o'clock."

"Yes, sir." Jon essayed a grin and was half out the door before he stuck out the letter. "Sorry, sir, this is for you."

Thomas took the letter and closed the door on Jon.

"You needed to scold the lad, sir?"

"If you had seen Righty and Lefty, you would not even ask. Bullies both of them, and unpredictable. A moment."

He opened the letter, found it an invitation to dinner from a Mrs. Denbigh for that very evening. She apologized for the lateness of the invitation, but had recently returned from a visit and heard about his leasing Bonwood House.

He showed the invitation to Rowan, who said, "Best to go there, sir. It's as likely as not that Miss Wendham and Miss Norcrest will be there. Miss Norcrest and Miss Denbigh are friendly."

"I am amazed at an invitation after yesterday."

"People saw Miss Wendham does not approve of you, sir, but that Miss Norcrest does."

"Do give my regrets to your wife."

"Yes, sir," Rowan said. "And I won't be telling Annie about those other goings-on, sir. She would be like to scold you for missing your sleep."

Thomas smiled, as he was meant to, but the comment struck him to the core. He dearly wanted to be in a position where his own wife would worry about his missing sleep. It was such a homey thing, so rich in domestic happiness, so unlike the war, so opposite Thomas's situation.

He tried to think of Miss Wendham worrying about his missing sleep. He could not picture the expression on her face.

But Miss Norcrest . . . he could easily picture the gentle frown, the concern like the shade from the oak they had stood under yesterday morning, the sincerity of her. Once politeness no longer barred her from asking, she would ask until she found the very core of him. Domestic happiness indeed. Bliss even.

But there was Miss Wendham, and his promises to keep.

"I shall keep the matter between us, Sergeant," Thomas said.

Chapter Nine

What the Denbighs' house lacked in classical elegance, it made up for in hominess. Some Denbigh ancestor had desired to show off the wealth of the local forest, and had hired carvers to decorate the wood paneling with intricate designs in more wood. Caroline knew that although Melisande appreciated each individual carving, she hated the overall effect.

"I," Melisande had said, "would have at least ended the paneling four or five feet below the ceiling and painted the above some light color so I did not feel as if the walls were closing in around me."

Since Melisande had voiced that opinion, Caroline had tried to feel the same way. She had failed every time. When she was enjoying the company, she found one place very like another, especially after dark in the winter, and convinced herself that she had found one more example of how she would never achieve Melisande's sensibilities, no matter how hard she studied.

Caroline forgot all her self-recriminations, however, when she spied her friend, Peg Denbigh, standing practically at the door, a smile on her cherub-like face, her blond curls bouncing, and her hands out. Caroline took her hands, and was pulled forward into a hug.

"You will never believe who is here," Peg whispered.

The Denbighs' footman came forward to take wraps,

cloaks, and hats. Caroline looked speakingly at her friend while Peg curtsied nicely to Melisande. Then Peg took Caroline's arm, pulling her close again as Mr. and Mrs. Denbigh greeted Melisande in their boisterous tones.

"That new gentleman who is to take Bonwood House. The very handsome and gentlemanly Lord Thomas Dashley. Mama got him this very afternoon. And this is the best part: she engaged him, not just from curiosity, although we are of course all curious, but because she heard how he smiled at you. But I beg you, do not be jealous of me, for I have had a full quarter-hour alone with him."

"Oh, dear," Caroline said.

"But what is wrong?" Peg asked.

"Is Mr. Bowes to be here?"

Peg shook her head. "Lucy is not back yet. Besides, I understand he left for London late this afternoon."

"Thank God for that at least," Caroline said. "I must stand near my sister."

Peg's eyes widened as she began to understand that something would not be right.

Caroline went beside Melisande, but there was no opportunity to warn her, for as Mr. Denbigh led them into the withdrawing room, he spoke of how beautiful the autumn weather had been this year, how mild, and how easy and fruitful it had made the harvest in consequence. Caroline admired Melisande's pleasant countenance, for she knew such subjects held little interest for her.

But at the first sight of Lord Thomas, Melisande paled and lost her composure. He was standing to greet the new arrivals. Of course he had known they would be here, Caroline thought, even as she wished she had worn a better dress than her pale apricot.

His fleeting smile belonged to her alone, sending all thoughts of her dress from her mind. Since her talk with Farmer Rowan that morning, Caroline had such a wealth of detail for her imagination to work upon. She imagined him ranging far and wide, alone and self-reliant upon his horse. She imagined him meeting desperate people and persuading them to aid him. She imagined him bleeding onto the earth, despairing of returning to Wellington with his report.

Then Lord Thomas bowed to her sister, a slightly lower bow, did anyone else notice.

Melisande had herself under control again. Only the flaring of her nostrils and the tightness of her polite smile betrayed her. She dipped the barest curtsy in acknowledgement of his presence. Thank God no one thought they needed to be introduced.

Other neighbors had come as well. Soon the entire room buzzed with conversation. Melisande wasted little time before beginning a conversation with Mrs. DeWitt, a widow with some property nearby. Usually Mrs. DeWitt initiated the conversation with Melisande. She knew enough about art to flatter Melisande's greater opinion and ability.

The thought, come out of nowhere, disconcerted Caroline sufficiently that she did not hear Peg's whispered warning that her mother was bringing Lord Thomas up to her.

Suddenly he was bowing before her, searching her face. Again the room's noise and distractions faded for Caroline, narrowing to become Lord Thomas alone.

Flashes of her earlier imaginations played themselves out, a series of portraits Melisande might have painted when she felt especially bitter. They colored her view of the man before her, but none could compare with the actual man.

Caroline felt as she had felt at her first seeing of him. She had thought he belonged to the sere climes of Spain, judged he would be hot to the touch, much like his sandy hair appeared burnished in the soft candle-light. He was warm. She remembered that from his having carried her. But there was warm, and then there was warm. He certainly made Caroline feel warm, and she felt herself blushing and thankful for the Denbighs' dark paneling.

What must he think of her, to see her blushing at his attention when she knew he had pledged himself to her sister?

The thought made her writhe inside, and she had little time to recover herself, for Mrs. Denbigh said, "Lord Thomas, we are often informal here, but in this case I think I am safe in asking you to take Miss Norcrest in for me."

Caroline did not often remember that her social standing ranked higher than Melisande's. Melisande and Peter's father had been a mere mister, whose name did not stretch so far back that one could count. Caroline wondered how Melisande bore such arbitrary inequities.

"It would be my great pleasure," Lord Thomas said.

Caroline's heart started beating in rapid pace, for he sounded as if he truly meant it. Mrs. Denbigh said a few nice things, then left Caroline, Peg, and Lord Thomas so she could gather up the rest of the party.

"It is very wonderful for us to have you here tonight," Peg said. "I expect you shall be busy putting your new house to rights and shall have little time for visiting."

"I have tried not to let that be so, Miss Denbigh," Lord Thomas said. "In my first letter to Mr. Barnes I asked that I be allowed to put the house in readiness while the business could be concluded. He graciously allowed me to do so."

"If that is the case, my lord, I shall have Mama invite you to come with us to the next assembly."

Lord Thomas bowed to them. "While there is such pleasant company to be found, I should be loath to absent myself."

Peg giggled.

But Caroline noticed that Lord Thomas glanced toward Melisande, who was showing him her back.

He caught her watching him and said, "Miss Wendham is in looks this evening."

Caroline had to wait a moment before she could answer, so startled and impressed as she was by his patience. "I have always thought my sister the most beautiful woman I know." She glanced at Peg and said, doubly mortified. "Do not think—"

"Not for a second," Peg said. "I would never dream of competing with Miss Wendham for looks. That would mean I would have to look even farther to you, dear Caroline, and that I should not like to do."

Caroline laughed at her friend's extravagance. "What fustian you speak!"

"If you will have it that way," Peg said, although she was no longer laughing. "Ah, Mama wants me."

Caroline watched her walk away, troubled.

"You are fortunate to have such a loyal friend," he said.

"I love Miss Denbigh like a sister," Caroline said and bit her lip.

Lord Thomas's mouth puckered, then relaxed. "How long have you known her?"

"All my life, although we did not play together much as children. My mother did not let us far from her."

"I remember Wendham saying she and your father died when you would have been about twelve. Here is my arm, Miss Norcrest."

They were forming up to go in to dinner. Caroline put her hand atop his extended wrist. Her breathing quickened. Even to her gloved hand, he did feel warm to her touch. But perhaps that was merely a manifestation of her own color, which rose with every passing second.

She spied Melisande, with Mr. Denbigh, frowning at her. Few things could have so easily prompted Caroline to recover her wits. Whatever Lord Thomas made her feel, Caroline had to remember his object: her sister. She must control herself to feel nothing for him other than wariness or pity.

But every feeling rebelled against such reasoning and control.

They followed Mrs. Denbigh into the dining room.

"I am sorry, Miss Norcrest, did I upset you. I barely remember my father to miss him, but I still feel my mother's loss quite keenly. She was a gentle woman. I always thought she had spent her days reading poetry. Instead she had been studying metaphysics."

"You would speak of metaphysics with your mother?"

"I knew of metaphysics what any schoolboy would know. She taught me to think past that."

"She sounds a wonderful woman," Caroline said, as he stood by her chair so she could sit down. They would be seated with Lord Thomas to Mrs. Denbigh's side and Caroline one down, the opposite end from where Caroline usually sat.

"She had a fine mind," Lord Thomas said.

A catch in the rhythm of his speech made her swivel on her seat to regard him. She pondered the distinction between being called a wonderful woman and being described as having a fine mind, and said, "My mother, too, had a wonderful sense of aesthetics. It is no wonder Melisande has it." She had almost said Melisande and

Peter. "But like me, she could not produce a piece of art herself."

He smiled as he too sat down, a smile that acknowledged her tact. "I saw your brother drawing one night. He encouraged me to draw and sketch. He taught me a lot about perspective and degree. Did he paint as well?"

"No. Applying the color to something maddened him. It is really Melisande who is the more talented artist. She can paint, but it is not her first love. She prefers sculpture."

The Denbighs' two footmen began serving the fish course. Lord Thomas said, "He told me that once. It was the same trip we took when we discovered Cavalcari's workshop. We had found a little group of artists who had tucked themselves away to stay out of the fighting."

Caroline bit her lip. How much had Peter trusted Lord Thomas? Knowing that would help her know how much she could help him. She asked, carefully, "Did you see the sketch of one of Cavalcari's falcons Peter sent to Melisande?"

"No, but I should have liked to."

"It was from that sketch that Melisande decided she wanted one," Caroline said.

Wanted understated the matter. Melisande had seen the picture and fallen into raptures about the bird's proud lines. Without giving a care to the fine dress she wore, she had gone upstairs and rummaged through the pieces of stone she kept for small projects that might strike her fancy. Melisande hated to wait for a piece of stone or marble to come from London or wherever else it might be shipped.

From her short bench near the door, Caroline had watched Melisande raise dust, her feet crunching on small pieces of stone not yet swept up, and mutter to herself until she found the perfect piece of granite. "Silver gray," she had said, then held up another part of Peter's letter. "Just as recommended. I'm going to begin at once." She had hugged the letter and the granite to herself. "Dear brother, thank you. Thank you."

Three days later, the "Cavalcari" had taken up its place of honor in the Red Room. It was the last piece Melisande had done from one of Peter's sketches, consequently as dear to Mel as her own heart.

The right-handed-left-handed mistake was not like Peter. Usually he had known to reverse the directions so that one looked at a piece of art not as though one saw it in a mirror. Peter had long professed he never made mistakes. Caroline was human enough to have taken some minor pleasure in seeing him wrong, and honest enough to know she did it and chastise herself for it. A weighty mix of emotions.

But she felt an uncomplicated sadness that Lord Thomas had had the ill luck to be the one to point out Peter's mistake to Melisande.

"I wonder when he found the opportunity to send it to her. We were called back soon after that." Lord Thomas raised his brows. "Never tell me your sister is good enough to have made the bird in your red drawing room?"

"Perhaps," Caroline said, and thought, *So, my question is answered. Peter did not trust you enough to tell you that they planned to sell what Mel might produce, if Peter did not make his fortune in the army.*

Mel had hated the idea of selling her talent. If Peter had made the decision not to trust him, one must be loyal to family first. Caroline could not, in good conscience, tell him about Melisande and Peter's plans.

It should not matter that Lord Thomas made her feel at once relaxed and surprisingly tense. It should not matter. She would not let it matter. Her feelings would be her secret. A quick glance around the dinner table surprised a few thoughtful looks in her direction. The observers suddenly found something else to look at. The conversation remained undiminished, but still Caroline was vexed.

Melisande's creamy shoulder did not deviate from its graceful yet implacable turning away.

Before a blush could come back into Caroline's cheeks, she changed the subject. "How do you find Bonwood House?"

Lord Thomas picked up his gleaming fork, flaked off a small piece of fish. Then he put down the fork. "I am sorry, Miss Norcrest. I should not have pried into your sister's business, or reminded you of your brother and myself in Spain."

"Why do you fear recrimination from me?" she asked, and did blush. "I am sor—"

"No," he said, shaking his head. "No. *You* must never apologize for speaking your mind. We are friends, are we not?"

Caroline nodded. "I do believe we are. Still, I was impertinent. It is one of my worst failings."

"Alongside stubbornness?"

"I think one sometimes forces the other."

Lord Thomas smiled. "I think your honesty more than compensates."

"You flatter me too much, my lord," Caroline said.

Again he shook his head. "No. That I cannot do."

She looked her question.

"Because you would not have me fear recrimination from you. You have implied it, have you not, Miss Norcrest? What you say, or even imply, I take to be your feelings. As I said, you are honest. To be someplace where I may leave aside recriminations . . . that is a very good place. You would call it flattery. I call it paying tribute where tribute is due."

Caroline could not help but laugh. "You are absurd,

and sound like you would twist 'render unto Caesar what is due Caesar.'"

"Perhaps. It is justice, though, is it not?"

Although Lord Thomas did not frown, Caroline sensed a troubled note within him. "Should we begin to speak of justice, my lord," she said lightly, "I fear you would talk rings around me. I have not had a mother who taught me the discipline of metaphysics."

"You would trust me on this point, then."

"I shall." Caroline suspected, although she did not want to be so obvious as to look about her, that others noticed the lack of attention she paid to her food. Not wanting to appear rude to dear Mrs. Denbigh, she took a bite of her fish, found it very good. "How *do* you find Bonwood House? You see, that *was* the question I wanted answered."

Lord Thomas held up a hand. "I shall never accuse you of prevarication again. I like Bonwood House very well. It is of sufficient size to contain half a regiment, will have pretty enough gardens within three years or so, and the rooms do not overwhelm. My only complaint with regard to it is the complaint I would have to have with any house: I have no sister or mother to stand as hostess."

"You have a sister who stays with your brother, Lord Dash?"

"No. It is only the two of us. It is as well, for I could not have provided her an alternative while I was away, and Dash does not feel the need of a hostess. Speaking of hostesses, I believe I should turn and speak to ours."

He did, and Caroline turned to Mr. Franklin, the vicar, who was happy to discuss her progress with her pupils. He refrained from any vulgar asking about Lord Thomas, for which Caroline was excessively grateful.

She could tell that everyone around the table knew or had figured out that there was tension between Melisande and Lord Thomas. They might not, however, know why, and Caroline would not be the one to enlighten them.

Caroline recognized that Melisande would not like her business being aired. *Let them judge him by what they see,* she thought. *This is Oxfordshire, not Spain.*

When Lord Thomas could turn back to Caroline, sometime during the third remove, they spoke only of impersonal matters. Caroline knew he had been sensitive to the atmosphere at the table.

When the ladies withdrew, Peg cornered Caroline by the fireplace. "You must tell me all. Why does your sister seem to so resent Lord Thomas? We are all staring. I heard something about her being cold to him in church, but I thought that might have been because he was standing with the Rowans, whom Melisande would not care to converse with. But then he mentioned before dinner that he had met you and Miss Wendham *before* Sunday morning at church. What happened then? Did they quarrel?"

"They did not quarrel," Caroline answered, truthfully. She wished that they had quarreled, for then that would mean Lord Thomas had tried to defend himself. He had not.

"Then it is one of your sister's starts," Peg said. "I suspected as much."

"My sister's starts?"

Peg grimaced. "You will not admit it, but your sister has been known to take people into dislike for no reason that anyone else can see."

"Indeed, I will not admit any such thing."

"I said you would not." Peg shrugged. "You, on the other hand, Caro, do not appear to dislike Lord Thomas, and you are the better judge of character."

"You are a fine friend," Caroline said.

"I shall not be fobbed off with compliments. Do tell me, what do you think of him?"

"Other than not to dislike him?"

Peg gave her the smile one gives when one has been teased and does not resent it. Then she tipped her brows up, asking the question again.

"He is very gentlemanlike. He speaks well and eloquently. I have learned his mama taught him metaphysics."

That had Peg laughing, as Caroline expected it would.

"He was highly regarded by Lord Wellington," Caroline added.

"You enjoy talking to him."

"Yes," Caroline said, hoping she did not appear embarrassed. "I do enjoy talking to him."

Peg grinned.

"And when does Lucy come back?" Caroline asked. "Have you had a letter from her?"

"She said within the week, and that she may be bringing the Sudburys back with her. That," Peg said, fluttering her lashes, "should be an event. I think our Lucy has fond hopes of your yet marrying her cousin. Excuse me, first cousin once removed."

Both young ladies laughed, for Lucy had always introduced John and Sally Sudbury that way. Caroline and Peg had often tried to wriggle the reason why from her. Caroline assumed the importance of that remove had been ingrained in Lucy for so long she no longer regarded it.

"It is always pleasant to speak to Mr. Sudbury," Caroline said.

"Give over, do, Caroline. Mr. Sudbury is all well and fine, a pleasant enough gentleman, but if one were to stand him and Lord Thomas Dashley side by side, I know which one I should pick."

"You have never preferred dark-haired men, have you?" Caroline asked.

"No, never. Besides, you never mentioned, last summer, that you found Mr. Sudbury remarkable."

"It is always pleasant to speak to Mr. Sudbury," Caroline repeated.

"Very well. If you will not say more about the matter, I shall not press you. Here come the gentlemen. Doubtless by tomorrow you shall hear from Lucy. She will be far more interested in keeping you apprised of Mr. Sudbury's arrival than she will me. Mr. Sudbury has never shown the slightest proclivity for me. You know well that Lucy is never happier than when she is arranging someone to her satisfaction."

"You have the right of it, I think," Caroline said.

"Hello again, Lord Thomas," Peg said. "I was just telling Caroline about our friend, Miss Bowes, who may be bringing some houseguests back with her."

"Indeed," Lord Thomas said, his voice smooth and rich. Caroline envied him his ability to move so silently. Likely it had stood him in good stead when he was sneaking about the Spanish plains and mountains. She also resented it, for his surprising her was causing another blush.

"Yes, they are the cousins she has been visiting, Mr. and Miss Sudbury." Peg inclined her head archly. "I hope our neighbors' ability to entice people of such breeding to this area makes you plan to stay indefinitely."

"I find attractions enough here already," Lord Thomas said.

"I think our heads are supposed to be turned, do you not, Caroline?"

Caroline wondered if Peg had also observed his stiffening at the mention of Mr. Sudbury. She wondered why. She settled, however, for a noncommittal smile.

"You must not mind Miss Wendham's head not being turned once in your direction this evening, Lord Thomas. She has been known to take people in dislike, but she generally comes around."

Lord Thomas glanced at Caroline. He said, "You are all kindness, Miss Denbigh."

"My mother does signal to me, my lord," she said, making a small curtsy. "Please excuse me, Caroline."

Caroline stood silent with Lord Thomas for a full twenty beats of her heart. It did not matter that they came more quickly together toward the end. She was waiting for him to ask if she had revealed his secret to her friend, for Peg's comments about Melisande seemed so pointed. Caroline's pride, however, could no more stand to deny such a potential reproof than it could bear to see her sister's back yet turned to them. It also vexed her that Mrs. Denbigh gave the appearance of playing matchmaker, and that she had a willing helper in Peg.

"I did not know until recently that Mr. Bowes had a sister."

Caroline relaxed. "Lucy is a dear."

"Does she often bring friends into the country?"

"Not as often as she would like, I am sure."

Melisande was again conversing with Mrs. DeWitt, although they had added Mr. Denbigh to their group. Mr. Denbigh appeared out of his element, but determined to do the pleasant host.

"Annie Rowan told me something of Mr. Sudbury," Lord Thomas said. "He visited here last summer, I understand?"

Caroline nodded.

"What sort of gentleman is he?"

Caroline marveled over how a question could be at once commonplace and utterly fantastic. "Quite pleasant, my lord."

Lord Thomas's lips moved in what could have been a smile, although it more resembled a grimace. Was it in reference to Mr. Sudbury, Caroline wondered, or to Melisande's back?

"Miss Denbigh and your sister are not friends, are they?"

"Miss Denbigh is a year younger than I am, and none of us was encouraged to play with the local children while my mother was alive. Melisande and Peter were twenty when she died, well past the time when they would be interested in speaking to girls of twelve."

"Your loyalty to her sister does you credit," Lord Thomas said. "Was it kindness to me, or loyalty to your sister, that stayed your telling your friend about El Puente de la Dama Blanca? No, do not answer that." He glanced over at Melisande. "I wonder when your sister will become used to my presence and set eyes upon me."

"You must not regard Miss Denbigh's comments about Melisande's starts."

Lord Thomas raised his brow in surprise. "On the contrary, I regard them as very promising."

"You do?"

"It sounds as if she were following a pattern. Patterns may be predicted, and when one may predict, one may anticipate."

Caroline shook her head. "Melisande has never been predictable."

Mr. Denbigh approached them, looking very grave. "Lord Thomas, we have reports that there is a fire on the outskirts of town, near Mr. Bowes's property. We—" he gestured to the other gentlemen around the room, who were bowing and leaving, "—have all been summoned to help the Watch. I am sorry to have to cut your evening short, but—"

"Do not apologize, sir," Lord Thomas said. "May I also offer my assistance?"

"It would be greatly appreciated, sir, yes, indeed."

Lord Thomas turned to Caroline.

She shook her head. "Do not wait on me, sir."

He gave her a smile, bowed, and left with the other gentlemen. The room buzzed with feminine conversation. Peg sidled up to Caroline and said, "He is all that is—" then broke off as Melisande approached Caroline.

"No one remaining here seems to know where the fire is. Do you happen to know, Caroline?"

"From what Mr. Denbigh said, I think it is the outbuildings for the old town hall."

Melisande became very still, except for her dark eyes, which widened with alarm. She grasped Caroline's wrist. "We have to go. I shall inform Mrs. Denbigh." And she swept away in a rustle of silk.

Peg stared after Melisande, then raised her brows.

"Do not ask me. I do not know," Caroline said.

Shortly she bade the other ladies good-bye and was in the landau with Melisande. The cool night air brushed Caroline's hair from her forehead, brought the tang of smoke and a muffled bustling of voices and calls.

Burkett, their driver, turned the carriage around in an unexpected semicircle so that they headed toward the village, away from Norcrest Manor. Caroline gripped the door's edge for balance. "Where are we going?"

"To the fire," Melisande said, gripping the door closest to her. "I need to see."

"But why?"

"It will be interesting to see how the firelight falls." She smiled at Caroline. "Come, do not worry. We shall not go close. I just need to see."

Although reassured somewhat by Melisande's smile, Caroline yet felt that Melisande had forced it for the occasion. Caroline knew, however, that she would not persuade Mel that she did not need to see how firelight moved. She had some reason, and maybe it was artistic. Caroline had long ago given up the notion that she could understand how Melisande perceived things. It was enough for her to appreciate that however Melisande arrived at her perceptions, they created powerful art.

As they went briskly down High Street, they could hear the rushing and whooshing of the fire, with yells and calls as counterpoint. Its glow lighted up the sky, reflected here and there as dull orange, madly dancing shadows.

Caroline pressed her handkerchief over her mouth and nose, for the smell of smoke threatened to choke her.

"There now, there now," Burkett was saying to the horses, which were shying and trying to skitter sideways. He cracked the whip. The horses plunged forward, almost running over a boy who had darted across the street. "We can't go much farther, ma'am," Burkett said over his shoulder to Melisande.

"Take us around the other side of it," Melisande said.

"Yes, ma'am," he said, as reluctant as his own snorting and rearing team.

Caroline wanted to offer Burkett words of encouragement, but Melisande would likely have reprimanded her for it. The elder sister had spoken. Besides, Caroline did not think he could have heard her anymore.

The scene broke upon them, bright pandemonium writhing against the black, star-studded sky and blacker outline of a thin stand of elm trees. Of the four outbuildings that used to service the old town hall, two blazed high. Sparks flew up in viciously twirling patterns, causing equally vicious twirling shadows of orange light, before caroming away in the breeze.

A spark caught in one of the lesser elm trees.

Melisande gasped.

Men ran around between the buildings, holding buckets and pails and poles that Caroline assumed were axes or shovels, although she could not see clearly enough to be certain. No one, however, appeared to be actually throwing water upon the burning buildings. Then several loud but indiscernible shouts had the men forming themselves into a line stretching out from the closest burning building toward the village.

Lord Thomas appeared, jogging toward their landau. He had shed his jacket, leaving his gray breeches and waistcoat and white shirt, open at the throat. He was using his cravat as a kerchief, but had pulled it down so it hung loosely about his neck. Soot and ash liberally streaked it and the rest of his clothes and face. In the ruddy light, he resembled an illustration of a tiger. Caroline's heart shuddered, so wild and beautiful did he appear.

"Miss Wendham, Miss Norcrest, you should not be here," he said, his gaze lingering on Caroline, although whether in question or entreaty Caroline could not tell.

Melisande tossed her head. He forestalled her. "But I am happy to see your horses and driver. The rope down the closest well there has broken, with the bucket at the bottom, as bad luck would have it. The sergeant-major is forming our neighbors into a bucket brigade to go to the next well, and I understand the village has a Newsham engine, but when the Watch tried to get it out, they saw the traces were damaged and just came here directly instead. If I loaned your driver a few men, they might be able to get it here."

"Of course," Caroline and Melisande said together.

"What do you say, man?" Lord Thomas said to Burkett.

"Yes, sir," Burkett said, touching his cap. "I'll put the landau over there, out of the way, so my ladies have someplace to sit, then take the horses and traces."

"Good man. What is your name?"

"Burkett, sir."

"Dashley. I'll send the men out directly." He set his hand on the rim of the landau, close to Caroline's, but perhaps that was only because she sat closer to him. "If the wind veers, will you promise me to leave the landau and go together—and at once—back to the Denbighs' house?"

"That seems quite sensible," Melisande said coolly. "Do return to fighting that fire, my lord."

Lord Thomas recognized it as an order, bowed to the ladies, and walked quickly back toward the fire. Seeing his authoritative strides, Caroline felt a peculiar ache around her heart. Perhaps the smoke had gotten into her lungs.

"Leave the landau where we can see," Melisande said.

"Yes, ma'am," Burkett replied, and swung the landau neatly around, so Melisande, and not Caroline, sat a landau's length closer to the raging fire. It was catching some of the trees, and that was where the bucket brigade was throwing water. Caroline surmised they had abandoned their efforts to save the two outbuildings.

Burkett jumped down and began unhitching the traces. Melisande was still gripping the edge of the landau.

"He will be all right," Caroline said.

Melisande looked at her in surprise. She folded her hands in her lap and watched the fire. "It is fitting—well and fitting—that Lord Thomas should be helping here."

"Melly," Caroline said softly, proud of her sister's civility and sense of justice. Melisande's face was turned toward the fire, however, so Caroline did not know if Melisande heard her.

Three ash-streaked men ran up, nodded in excited politeness to them, then went away in a clamor with Burkett and the horses, toward the village.

Caroline fretted, watching the fire. She counted fifteen buckets that the bucket brigade had, so that they made little progress—a few gallons at a time—against the inferno. Several men were also formed into another brigade, and were passing large, dripping brown clumps that resolved themselves into burlap bags when hefted against the remaining outbuildings.

Through it all Caroline saw Lord Thomas either cupping his mouth with his hands to shout an order, clapping someone on the back, or picking up a dropped bucket or bag.

Then for quite a few minutes she did not see him and wondered how he fared. She knew how quickly fires could change from roaring madness to roaring death. She wished powerfully that she was the four feet closer to the fire that Melisande was, so that she might see that much better.

"He is more than an attractive man," Melisande said.

Caroline blinked. "What?"

"Lord Thomas. He is an attractive man. So often attractive men can live on the luck their faces provide. Like beautiful women. But he was right. Lord Thomas is more, dangerously more."

"Dangerously, Mel?" Caroline asked, but perhaps Melisande had not heard her. She raised her voice. "Mel, who was right?"

But Melisande shook her head. "Do not mind me."

Caroline noticed Melisande's hands remained tightly upon the landau's edge and did not press, although her curiosity had started its own fire within her. What was dangerous about Lord Thomas and who had said so?

Burkett and the other men pulling the Newsham engine within its cart up the street distracted her. They veered off High Street down Old Hall Lane, toward the fire. Then Caroline saw Lord Thomas again, and could tell he was smiling as he met Burkett, if only because his teeth appeared as the only white thing left in his face. He gestured, and the lot of them backed a canvas hose from the engine toward the end of the bucket brigade and the well. More gestures from Lord Thomas brought almost a score of other men running, Mr. Denbigh and Mr. Quigley barely recognizable among them.

The Newsham engine moved from Caroline's line of sight, but soon she could hear a rushing unlike the rushing of the fire. Then over the buildings that blocked her sight, a stream of water soared onto the fire. Caroline had seen a Newsham engine before, and readily imagined the men working the treadles.

A great whooping cry rose from the men by the fire.

"They will put it out, Mel. They will put it out." Caroline scooted along the landau's seat and reached for her sister.

"They will," Melisande said, hugging Caroline. "Oh, thank God, they will."

"Melisande, you're crying," Caroline said in amazement. She had not seen Melisande cry since the day she had read Peter's name in the casualty lists.

"And if I am?" Melisande asked, pulling away and regaining that coolness she wore as closely as she wore her shift.

"I would have hugged you all the more," Caroline said.

Melisande snorted and shook her head. "You are the most tender-hearted of creatures."

Melisande's calling her *tender-hearted* had ever been her way of calling Caroline's character weak.

"Do stop biting your lip. It is most unladylike," Melisande said.

They sat there for some time, silent at the outskirts of all the yelling and carrying on by the men fighting the fire. Caroline's bewilderment grew into anger even as the orange glow faded from the sky, and a cloud of dark gray smoke blocked the stars, leaving only spots of light from the odd occasional impromptu torch or lantern.

Why did Melisande always feel the need to correct her? When was tender-heartedness not a bad thing to have?

And when had Caroline decided to question her sister's every judgment?

That question set her back, and she shivered in her cape. The carrying-on became more organized. Caroline pulled herself from her angry thoughts to see a procession of soot-streaked men, torches and lanterns in hand, coming toward them up Old Hall Lane. They were bearing Lord Thomas on their shoulders, slapping at each other, and calling and cheering.

"Damn fine job, lads. Damn fine job," Lord Thomas said, which caused another round of cheers. Then he saw Caroline and Melisande, started, looked as deeply pained as any man covered in soot could, and lifted his hand to the two women, his expression grim, as the crowd bore him away from them down the street.

Then Farmer Rowan came running over to them, his face black and blotchy with soot. "Miss Wendham, Miss Norcrest, the fire's out, all right, and you'll have Burkett back presently with the horses. Major—I mean, Lord Thomas, ma'am, he thought Burkett was already back. We had to send 'em around by Front Street, since some of the first building fell over and blocked the way back. He said to thank you for letting us use your horses." He ran his hand over his face, leaving a streak that made him look far worse.

"You are quite certain the fire is out and for good?" Melisande asked.

"Yes, ma'am. Lord Thomas had us rake over the embers, and we soaked the lot. We'd wet the other buildings enough, too."

"The trees behind?" Melisande asked, more sharply.

"Singed, ma'am. Singed well. But nary more. Next spring, they'll look a little lopsided. Year after, you'd never know."

"Where are they taking him?" Caroline asked.

"Down the pub," Rowan said, grinning. "Where Bill Little is like to pour him drinks for free. 'Twasn't for Lord Thomas, ma'am, likely the whole village would be feeling the threat. You feel how the wind's shifted? He got 'em pulling together, ma'am, gentlemen and us regular folk, just like he always does. Ah, there's Burkett coming. Half a moment, and we'll have you on your way."

"Would you please convey our gratitude to Lord Thomas?" Caroline asked.

Melisande eyed her sharply, but did not argue.

Some of the exhilaration left Rowan's face as he measured Melisande against some internal tape. Caroline wondered if Rowan had realized, as she had realized from Lord Thomas's consternation, how much it galled Melisande to see Lord Thomas receiving the villagers' praise. "Be my pleasure, ma'am." He went to lift his cap. "Bless me, but Annie shall have my hide. I've lost my new hat. Hey, there, Burkett, let me give you a hand. Ma'am. Ma'am."

Burkett and Rowan had the carriage hooked up and turned around in a trice. Then Rowan bid them goodnight with a wave and disappeared up the street.

"We'll have to walk them, ma'am," Burkett said over his shoulder. "Poor brutes are that done for."

"That shall be fine," Melisande said.

They passed the George, where it sounded like Bill Little poured free drinks for more men than just Lord Thomas. The smell of smoke remained strong, but it did not require Caroline to keep her handkerchief pressed to her face.

Slowly, as the horses walked toward home, the noise abated, leaving only the clop of their shoes against the stones and the intermittent moaning and susurration of wind through the trees.

Caroline thought she had never been so relieved to see Norcrest Manor. As they passed through the large, ivied pillars that marked the entrance to the drive, she took a deep breath and said, "Burkett, you may take a horse back to the George if you would like. You deserve to celebrate, too."

Melisande raised her brows, and her eyes glittered dark and white in the lantern light.

"Why, thank you, ma'am. I would like that."

"Good. You are welcome."

They alighted a minute later, both walking slowly toward the house. Griggs, on the lookout for them, ushered them inside with considerable concern. Melisande forestalled him with a raised hand. "Baths, Griggs. Tell our maids to arrange for baths. I cannot possibly sleep smelling of smoke."

"At once, ma'am," Griggs said.

When he was gone, and Caroline and Melisande started alone up the main stair, Caroline said, "Do you know, it occurs to me that we did not see Mr. Bowes this evening. He is no great friend of the Denbighs. I could understand his being missing there. But the fire? So near his own property?"

"Mr. Bowes is away," Melisande said, and her flat expression said she would not welcome questions on the subject.

"Oh, that is right. Peg said something to me about his going to Town. I wonder if we shall learn what started it."

"I am tired, Caroline. Let us leave off further discussion."

Chastened, Caroline said, "Of course, Melly." They were

close to her sister's rooms. Caroline gave her a little hug and bade her sister good night.

Then Caroline closed her own door behind her and flung the windows wide. She leaned out as far as she could. She could see the lights from the village below and to her left. She pictured Lord Thomas, blackened and sooty, hoisted on the shoulders of her neighbors. She imagined what he looked like now. Although she suspected he did not mind what he looked like, hopefully someone had given him a cloth to wipe his face. There would be back-thumping, singing, cheering, carrying on.

She wished she could be a part of it. She wished she could be near Lord Thomas.

She chided herself. Doubtless everyone in town would feel that way.

Well, most everyone.

One side of Caroline's mouth twisted up. It would be very awkward now for Melisande to continue her open dislike of Lord Thomas. Very awkward, indeed.

Chapter Ten

Thomas walked away from the flurried activity of Bonwood House. He did not need to look back to see the white-aproned manservants carrying items to and fro, some from the house, some into the house from a laden wagon standing in the drive. Some maids carried pails. Others opened windows and flicked cloths vigorously to release their dirt. A flock of sheep under the sleepy eye of their shepherd obligingly nibbled the front lawn into respectability.

Better by far to have before him the meadow fading in the new October cool, leading up a broad hill toward gently bronzing woods. Better to be alone.

Thomas felt like the world's biggest fraud. The entire morning, when not speaking to his new staff about what specifics needed doing, he had taken visits—if only carriage-side—from his new neighbors. Their lips had spoken congratulations and well wishes, their eyes had gleamed their admiration.

Did they live in Bucks, where the 52nd drew from, they might be as easily reviling him.

He reviled himself, not for what he had done last night, but for enjoying it. For those hours, he had again tasted the joy of commanding men, of organizing them into one force to do no one's bidding but his. He had not realized how much he had missed that opportunity, that heady feeling of power and usefulness.

He and the other gentlemen from the Denbighs' party had rushed up to find all confusion, men running around and into each other trying to find the well, get the bucket from it, to find bags to wet and other buckets for a brigade, to find axes and pikes to hack away pieces of the buildings beyond saving, and to avoid killing each other while doing it.

Denbigh became paralyzed with confusion. Mr. Quigley had kept inquiring in a loud voice where the damned Newsham engine might be had. No one had listened to him.

Then Rowan had appeared at Thomas's shoulder, saying, "Your orders, sir," just like old times. And just like old times, Thomas had given him orders, and together they had rallied their troops. Thomas did not know why they had listened to either of them. Although Rowan was now a local, he had not been a local very long. Thomas's status balanced upon the lips of Miss Wendham and Mr. Bowes, no stable perch.

Thomas pushed himself up the hill, letting the stretch within his legs, especially the right, that had been shot, remind him that he was nothing more than flesh and blood, no better than his fellow men, however they might obey him in a crisis.

Then, somewhere before him along the path, he heard young Norcrest's piping voice say, "But the fire was all the grooms spoke of this morning. See, the Quigleys have been by paying their respects. You and Melisande went to see it. Why could I have not?"

"I did not choose to go there. Melisande did. Then we got caught up in it." Miss Norcrest was here, too, her voice sweeter and more enticing than any sound Thomas had ever heard. He stood still, letting fate bring them or not. He realized he craved another sight of her. He also writhed with embarrassment. She had seen him, as had Miss Wendham, being congratulated by the villagers. She had seen him take pleasure in being responsible for other men.

How much that must have pained Miss Wendham!

How much had it pained Miss Norcrest?

Norcrest's voice came closer. "The grooms said Lord Thomas saved the village."

Thomas winced.

Suddenly, around a bend, they came. Miss Norcrest gasped.

"Miss Norcrest," he said, composing his face. If there was something worse than to be thought well of by people far better than he, it was to be caught wallowing in his self-loathing. He bowed. "Norcrest. I am sorry I startled you, ma'am."

"Dashley," Norcrest said, with that peculiar intonation Thomas recognized as an attempt to will his boy's voice into deeper accents. Norcrest held out his hand.

Thomas shook it.

"I was merely surprised to find you away from Bonwood House today," Miss Norcrest said.

Thomas looked left toward the house, although they could not see it for the trees along this section of the gently undulating path. "We have attracted many visitors this morning, and I believe my staff feels its consequence lessened by not being able to invite anyone inside yet. With me from home, the staff may politely refuse admittance to chaos without shame."

Miss Norcrest smiled. Thomas caught his breath to have that bright green gaze turned on him with such a smile. Autumn had surely come to England, but Miss Norcrest would ever make one remember its warm summers.

"From the hilltop back there," Norcrest said, turning and gesturing, "we saw the Quigleys pulling out. The fire last night is all everyone is speaking of, your part especially."

Thomas shook his head. "No, Norcrest, if you must commend someone, commend yourself on having two excellent sisters. They lent us horses, traces, and Burkett to get the Newsham engine. Without the Newsham engine, we should have lost more buildings, maybe even some along Mr. Bowes's property, maybe more within the village. Then they sent Burkett back so that we could make him very much the worse for wear."

"Melisande did not send Burkett back, sir. 'Twas Caroline alone."

Thomas had known that. Another villager had wondered aloud at Miss Wendham's permitting Burkett to come back, and although Burkett would not say anything against Miss Wendham, he had allowed that Miss Norcrest had encouraged him to take a horse.

Miss Norcrest gave her brother a warning look. "Melisande did not demur, Norcrest."

The situation and characters of Wendham's sisters puzzled Thomas excessively. To remember Wendham's telling of Miss Wendham and the letters from her he had read, she displayed all the grace and kindness of Miss Norcrest. It was difficult to reconcile those memories with her neighbors' impressions of her, difficult and unsettling.

He had not pictured his atonement this way. He had pictured that if he could win back Miss Wendham's heart sufficient unto agreeing to marry him, he would have won back some measure of his own esteem.

Miss Wendham no longer seemed quite the prize, however.

An awkward pause followed.

"You were walking into the village?" Thomas asked. "If so, I should not keep you."

"No, sir," Freddy replied. "We are merely out for a tramp before I must go back to school. We were about to turn back." He smiled brightly, tipping his head in invitation.

Thomas bowed to what he wanted to do. "Then our paths run together."

The broad path allowed them to walk abreast, young Norcrest in the middle. Thomas wanted to ask Miss Norcrest how her sister did, but Norcrest's presence kept him silent on that subject.

Instead he asked Norcrest some pointed questions about how he liked school. It sounded as though an upper former were making the boy's life miserable, and Thomas tried to come up with some way of giving him advice without wounding his pride.

The problem distracted him from his larger problem of the deeply aggravating solace he felt whenever he was near Miss Norcrest. He could not deny he took comfort from her presence. She could calm any tempest, he thought, just by standing and smiling it into submission. He had meant what he had said to her at the Denbighs' about a place without recriminations being a fine place indeed.

But Thomas had not come to this country for comfort and solace. Nor had he come to be tempted by a body as lovely as Miss Norcrest's. He half wished Miss Norcrest were cruel to him.

They finished their descent of a hill, and came out upon the road running up from the village. The ivied pillars that flanked the drive to Norcrest Manor stood about two hundred yards up the road.

Miss Norcrest looked about her, and her face beamed with satisfaction. She met his gaze, including his presence in her satisfaction.

Thomas gave up his half wish. He could never offer for Miss Norcrest, whatever direction his desire might lie. He acknowledged, however, that he never wanted Miss Norcrest to be cruel to him. Miss Norcrest's cruelty would feel like the surgeon cutting off one of his limbs.

A carriage bowled out of Norcrest Manor's drive, carrying two ladies and a gentleman. "Look, Caro," said Norcrest, "there is Miss Bowes. She is back. And are those the Sudburys?"

"Yes," Miss Norcrest said. "Would you wait here a moment with us, Lord Thomas? She will have Tinker pull up."

"I would be honored to meet your friends," Thomas said. He would not have missed meeting the man Wendham had not considered well-off enough for a sister he had not seen fit to mention.

Miss Norcrest anticipated Miss Bowes to the foot. The driver did not have a chance to let the horses kick up a dust before they were stopping and a plain-faced girl with a vivacious smile was alighting and hugging Miss Norcrest warmly.

"We have been up to the manor," Miss Bowes said, "in hopes of your returning. We were to leave with despair in our hearts of seeing you today. But now here you are. How are you, Freddy?"

"I am well, thank you," said young Norcrest, failing to maintain his dignity. He grinned. "I am glad I should see you, Lucy, before I must go back to school."

Miss Bowes patted his cheek. "Scamp. You will not pine away for lack of seeing me, but maybe——" she held him at arm's length "——you are growing more quickly than you can eat. Your sister and I shall double your rations now that I am returned."

Norcrest blushed, and Miss Norcrest held her hand

over her mouth. Thomas realized he was trying to contain a smile when Miss Bowes turned her satirical expression upon him, and his face had to form itself back into polite blandness.

She then looked at her friend, who now had an excuse to perform the introductions.

Now that he could see her full face, he realized she looked very little like her brother except for the dark hair. Although Jack Bowes would have everyone believe he knew everything, Thomas had learned long ago there was little spine behind his bluster.

Lucy Bowes belonged to a different species entirely— the general officer species. A man who desperately wanted to be managed would snap her up in a heartbeat, Thomas thought, if he could overlook her slightly protuberant eyes and overbite, which she gave no indication of hiding behind a decorous smile. No, Lucy Bowes would tweak the world full in the face, saying be damned to it.

"So you are Lord Thomas Dashley. Hm. The entire village is gushing about you. On behalf of myself and my brother, I am happy you saved some of our connecting buildings. The village sold that land near the old town hall to my father, and why he did not take those buildings down I will never understand. Here. I have some friends I brought back with me. Please let me introduce you to Mr. John Sudbury and Miss Sudbury. They are my first cousins on my mother's side, once removed."

Thomas could not help but glance at Miss Norcrest as Miss Bowes said this, and share the joke with her. Then he stepped forward to bow to Mr. and Miss Sudbury.

Miss Sudbury gave him a smile that matched her curled blond hair for sprightliness. Had Thomas been in the mood for a brief flirtation, he could not have found a more likely partner. "Very pleased to meet you,

Lord Thomas," she said, making his name sound like a delectable chocolate. Thomas decided he would do well to avoid letting her maneuver him into a corner at an assembly or dinner party.

Mr. Sudbury had been watching Miss Norcrest the same way an infantryman would look toward the spirits keg. His sister's pleasantries concluded, he inclined his head stiffly to Thomas, his gaze flat. Thomas would not have laid a bet on whether he and Mr. Sudbury became friendly.

Like his sister, Mr. Sudbury dressed in the first stare of fashion and had the features to make them worth the cost and effort. Although they did not alight from the carriage, Thomas suspected Mr. Sudbury would be a few inches shorter than he was, and the thought gave him satisfaction.

Still, the lack of a few inches did not disqualify him from being an eligible suitor for Miss Norcrest's hand. That would be a matter of character, Thomas decided, and he would be the one to decide it. He had deprived her of Wendham, so he would stand *in loco fraternis*.

"The three of you were out walking?" Mr. Sudbury asked Miss Norcrest.

"We met upon the path," she answered tranquilly, to Thomas's relief. He wondered if she had recognized Mr. Sudbury's dislike, and had, like Thomas, no wish to enflame it.

"I had heard today was the day you took possession of Bonwood House?" Miss Bowes said, and turned to explain to the Sudburys. "You remember Bonwood House? We walked along its park several times last year."

The Sudburys remembered it. Mr. Sudbury said, "It is a very decent property."

"Thank you, sir," Thomas said, meaning it. "I think I shall be happy there. But to answer your question, Miss

Bowes, yes, today is the day, but—" He broke off, to come up with an excuse for being in the woods for politer company. With Miss Norcrest he could come as close to the truth as possible. With others, he did not know.

Miss Norcrest stepped up so her elbow practically brushed his. He imagined himself feeling her warmth through her cape, the cool autumn air, and his own heavy brown coat. "After last night, Lord Thomas finds himself something of a personage."

She turned her clear gaze upon him, and within it he saw the very definition of grace, beauty, and charity. For a moment, he was the man he had been before El Puente de la Dama Blanca. That she, who knew what he was and what he had done, could look at him that way!

Miss Bowes grinned. "Are our neighbors deluging you with invitations, Lord Thomas, which you have no place to put?"

"You have put your finger on my trouble," Thomas said. "I have been pressed to attend an assembly tomorrow evening."

"Indeed. It is for that very assembly I wished to return with my friends," Miss Bowes said.

"Dancing," Norcrest said, and could not quite contain his shudder.

Thomas glanced at him with amusement, and the boy returned his look. "I should be honored if you, Miss Bowes, and you, Miss Sudbury, would stand the second and third dances with me."

Miss Sudbury accepted with an eager nod.

"I would be pleased," Miss Bowes said, then her expression turned shrewd. "Do I hazard a guess with whom you shall be dancing the first?"

Before Miss Norcrest could say anything, Mr. Sudbury said, "Then I would like to claim the second, Miss Norcrest. If I may."

"That would be very pleasant, sir," Miss Norcrest said with a little dip of a curtsy. "Thank you."

Mr. Sudbury straightened, looking pleased with himself.

"We must let you fire off Freddy," Miss Bowes said. "We saw the gig being hooked up. Come, Freddy, another hug. It shall have to last me until Christmas."

Norcrest obliged her, looking half embarrassed, half pleased as punch.

Thomas handed Miss Bowes back into her carriage.

"Lucy," Miss Norcrest said, drawing up to the carriage, "have you seen your brother since returning?"

"No, he has been to Town. I expect him back tonight. Why?"

Miss Norcrest shook her head. "I wonder if anyone has told him of the fire."

"No one was home to send off an express," Miss Bowes said. "Do not worry, Caro, I suspect it will be the first thing he hears of upon entering the county. Again, our thanks, Lord Thomas. We shall see you tomorrow."

Miss Bowes's driver sprang their horses, and everyone waved. When the carriage was well down the road, Thomas said, "Miss Norcrest, would you do me the honor of standing the first dance with me tomorrow?"

"You must not feel compelled to act upon Lucy's assumption."

"Very well. Would you do me the honor of standing the first and fourth dances with me tomorrow?"

Young Norcrest laughed.

But now Miss Norcrest studied him. Thomas had the disconcerting feeling she was engaged in some internal study, too. Then she nodded.

"Excellent," he said. Then, "I should take my leave of you here. Norcrest, I shall look forward to seeing you again at Christmas." He held out his hand to the boy, who shook it with pleasure. Then Thomas leaned forward and said, softly enough so that he hoped Miss Norcrest would not hear, "Get a group together, sir, and stand up to them."

Norcrest looked startled. "It can be done?" he asked.

Miss Norcrest watched them with wary interest, but she did not ask.

"I am still here," Thomas said by way of answer.

Enlightenment lifted Norcrest's expression. "I am glad, sir."

Thomas turned to Miss Norcrest. "Until tomorrow evening."

Chapter Eleven

The Quigleys were hosting the assembly, and from the size of the gathered crowd, Caroline believed the entire town had shown up for it. Caroline had dressed carefully in a square-collared peach gown with lace overslip. She had had it made for the Season a year ago, before they had learned of Peter. Caroline had looked forward to wearing it this past Season, but a spring illness had laid Melisande quite low. They had canceled their plans, and the dress had never been worn.

Melisande had not wanted to attend the assembly. She was not a great one for dancing on the best of days. Her disdain for the proceeding and the necessity of her attending caused her to hold her chin at an elevated angle, and an interesting sparkle lighted her eyes.

Thus Caroline did not pay much heed to her comments on the way over about the placement of the pearls in Caroline's hair, or the way she fidgeted with her gloves and reticule.

Lucy was at her side directly their being announced. Melisande moved off, bidding Lucy good evening and Caroline not to embarrass her.

"What did she mean by that?" Lucy asked, drawing Caroline toward a carved and gilded wall.

But Caroline shook her head. Melisande wanted Caroline to stay as far away from Lord Thomas as an assembly room would permit, so Caroline had considered it prudent not to mention her promising Lord Thomas the first and fourth dances.

"You were certainly right about Lord Thomas's becoming a personage," Lucy said. "He is in the other room, although one can barely tell for the gentlemen there have him quite surrounded. I suppose that shows some native cunning on the part of the other sex, for shortly we shall have him for dancing. He did secure your hand for the first dance?"

"And the fourth," Caroline said.

"Sly puss," Lucy said. "Is Mr. Sudbury to be quite cast away?"

"Please do not be drawing air castles. Lord Thomas will not be offering for me."

Lucy frowned.

Caroline cursed her loose tongue. "I am . . . like a sister to him."

"Well, that is as may be." Lucy considered her, decided to let the matter pass. "You were right about another thing. My brother was very interested in the fire. *Frantic* would be more like it. He inspected those outbuildings before he even came to the house, and has been quite unaccountably out of sorts. He even put on his regimentals this evening, and I swear he hates his regimentals. Caroline, what is wrong?"

"Your brother also dislikes Lord Thomas excessively," Caroline said, trying to keep the anger from her voice. "Putting his regimentals on is his way, I suppose, of expressing it." She held up a hand. "I would tell you why if I could."

"Mystery upon mystery," Lucy said, tapping a finger against her lips. "But that Jack would try to rub Lord Thomas wrong makes you mad? It seems you have taken your adoptive brother to heart, Caro. Has one fire so turned your head, too?"

Talking of turned heads was making Caroline's ache. "You know what shall do that."

Lucy looked about her until she saw Melisande, who was standing within a circle of Mrs. Denbigh, Mrs. De-Witt, and two other local ladies. Melisande looked as perfect as she always did, although Caroline worried that the slight frown she had taken to wearing in company did her looks a disservice.

It would all be so much easier, Caroline thought, if Melisande could but tell Lord Thomas she understood that sometimes bad things happened in war, bad things that no one intended or planned.

"Hm," Lucy said. "Was Lord Thomas a cavalry officer, then, and my brother wishes to promote the infantry's superiority?"

Caroline did not want Lucy digging into Lord Thomas's past, although she was very much surprised Mr. Bowes had not told Lucy everything. Very much surprised indeed. She tried to imagine a graceful way to decline to answer when Peg Denbigh came up to them and solved the problem for her.

Peg linked arms with both of them. "Here you are, Lucy dear. And here are we, the most eligible females in the room—well, local eligible females, anyway. Miss Sudbury is in looks tonight, Lucy. Do not, Caroline, I beg you, insist I include your sister in my reckoning. You know she has refused everyone local who has asked her, even Lucy's brother here, and I'm that sorry, Lucy.

"Did you have a pleasant trip back? And have you been asking Caroline about our oh-so-very-dashing addition to the neighborhood? He has asked me for the fifth set. Mama is in alt, although he does it from politeness rather than interest. Mr. Sudbury has asked me for the third. Do you have his first, Caroline?"

"The second. How was your trip, Lucy? We did not get around to it when we met."

Lucy knew when she was being handled, for Peg would not suffer a mere, "Fine."

Caroline watched the room for a precious minute. Miss Sudbury *was* in looks in a blue gown of the first fashion, and Mr. Sudbury might have dressed solely to coordinate with her, in a dark blue coat and cream breeches. Captain Bowes, in his bright regimentals, had come up to Melisande and kissed her hand. Caroline observed that Lucy followed this interplay as well while she answered Peg's questions about her trip.

Caroline knew the differences between the uniforms of Mr. Bowes's 52nd regiment and Lord Thomas's 43rd lay solely in insignia and the color of the collar and cuff facings—yellow for the 52nd and white for the 43rd.

What importance did Lord Thomas place in that small difference? Perhaps none at all.

Caroline remembered how Peter had derided the obsessive pride other officers took in their uniforms. Did Captain Bowes seek to wound Lord Thomas's pride, or make certain he did not forget his shame in the midst of a success? Either way, Caroline resented him for it.

The musicians began tuning up. Caroline's two friends fell silent as a crowd of gentlemen entered from the other room, Lord Thomas in the middle of them. No one could have told he had only moved into a new house, for in his dark green jacket, buff breeches, and stockings, he looked immaculate.

But Caroline knew that although he might look immaculate, he was aware that Mr. Bowes paid court to Melisande in his regimentals. He knew it and yet contained his distress. Without thinking, Caroline curtsied, although half the room yet separated them.

Peg giggled under her hand. "You are subtle, Caro."

Lucy said, "Far too subtle."

Caroline turned to them, surprised and confused.

Lord Thomas bowed nicely to all three ladies, and drew Caroline away to where the set was forming. "You look very lovely tonight, Miss Norcrest."

"I am sorry," she said, inclining her head toward Captain Bowes. "I did not know."

Lord Thomas did not need to look over his shoulder to know to what she referred. "It is his right, and nothing for which you need apologize."

"It feels uncivilized to me, like he would slap you in the face if he could."

"I am quite certain he would," said Lord Thomas, then set his mouth grimly. "If he thought he could."

"Oh, no," Caroline said. "They are joining the set. But Melisande never likes to dance. Lord Thomas, I am not apologizing, but I am sorry."

"Do not be. It will be good to dance, however briefly, with your sister."

Caroline bit her lip. "And Mr. Bowes?"

"Captain Bowes does not have it within him to intimidate me. Not even in his regimentals. Smile, Miss Norcrest. Your smile could light a man all the way home."

The sudden intensity of his tone held her gaze to his in a way his words alone could not have done. An expression unlike any she had yet seen softened the hard planes of his face. It thrilled her, made her shiver in the warm ballroom, ringlets of curls tickle her shoulders. Suddenly she wanted Lord Thomas's hands there instead. Even his lips.

The wanton thought startled her. She had danced

with other men, even handsome men like Mr. Sudbury, but she had never wanted them to touch her more closely than propriety decreed. Lord Thomas's eyes had widened while she had felt herself blush from the toes up. He had become very still.

The music beginning startled both of them afresh. They barely had time to do honors before he took her hand and led her around in a circle to start the dance.

"What position are we in?" Caroline asked, for she could not tell with the entire set circling.

"I do not know," he said, and suddenly they both laughed. "Ah, we are seconds."

"It would be horrible not to know what one was supposed to do," Caroline said.

"Tonight especially, I believe."

"Everyone will keep track of you tonight," Caroline agreed.

They separated, came back together, but were closer to Melisande and Mr. Bowes. Caroline knew Lord Thomas was watching for them, but he smiled at her as, hands joined, they stepped toward each other in the balancé.

She caught a whiff of some spicy scent that she could not attribute to any perfume, and it went to her head like wine. Again her gaze found his. She entered some strange space where one part of her reveled in the notion that if she just stood still, she could retain this heady feeling.

The other part of her imagined herself stepping out of position and being trampled by her neighbors. The second thought sufficed to bring her back to the dance.

They kept on with the figures, but as they came closer and closer to Melisande and Mr. Bowes, Caroline had to work harder and harder to keep the smile on her face. She felt it flickering out like a moving candle.

"Courage," Lord Thomas said to her, and squeezed her hand.

Then they were next to them. Melisande nodded to Caroline, who raised her brows pointedly at her, saying, "Melly," her tone a plea for moderation.

Melisande met Lord Thomas's gaze squarely. "Lord Thomas."

Caroline smiled her relief.

"Dashley," Mr. Bowes said.

Lord Thomas acknowledged both of them with calm urbanity, then complimented Melisande on her deep blue dress. Then they were moving past them, and Lord Thomas gave her hand another squeeze. "That went very well," he said. "You were marvelous."

Disappointment deflated Caroline. She cursed herself for it. She should be glad that despite those heart-stopping moments on her part, they were solely on her part. She had imagined any reciprocity within Lord Thomas's feelings. He was not flirting with her. He was treating her gently, with all gentlemanliness, as befitted her status as his ally in his pursuit of her sister.

"I must protest such praise. I did nothing."

He studied her while they did the balancé again. Then, "Very well, Miss Norcrest. I shall let you get away this time."

This comment unsettled Caroline, but she could not question him, as they were coming down to the bottom of the line. The dance ended. Lord Thomas bowed as she curtsied, then he took her hand to lead her from the floor.

They were met immediately by Miss Bowes and Mr. Sudbury, who were their partners for the next dance. The gentlemen bowed, summing each other up in the way men seemed to do. Mr. Sudbury seemed blatant about the matter, quirking an eyebrow. Caroline felt certain, however, that Lord Thomas's bland gaze saw more than his face let on. She wondered what he thought of Mr. Sudbury, and marveled that here, in their second meeting she had witnessed, she still did not know.

"Miss Norcrest is my partner now, sir," Mr. Sudbury said.

Lord Thomas blinked in seemingly good-natured perplexity. He looked to Caroline, then down to her hand, which he retained. "I commend you on your next partner, sir. If she dances as lightly for you as she did for me, you may not realize when you have stopped."

Caroline bit her lip. She could not decide whether she should be happy or deeply unhappy. To be so close to him, have him say such things, made her feel as if she were indeed still dancing. She had to remind herself what she was to him, and why.

Despite her efforts to throw Caroline and Mr. Sudbury together, Lucy showed no such attempt at tact. "A very pretty compliment, my lord."

"I find your friend's company agreeable." He glanced at Caroline, but let go her hand. "She has a lively mind, which shows to advantage whether manifesting what she calls stubbornness or the ability to extricate people from uncomfortable situations."

Mr. Sudbury was shifting his weight from one foot to another, not as though he were dancing, but regularly enough to signal his annoyance.

So, to make him feel better, Caroline shook her head at Lord Thomas. "Pretty compliments aside, sir. That was positively unorthodox."

"I wondered if it should be uncomfortable to dance with my brother and Caroline's sister," Lucy said.

Mr. Sudbury stopped shifting, and Caroline sensed

Lord Thomas's sudden tension from that bland, shuttered expression he sometimes wore.

"Miss Denbigh has been telling me Miss Wendham gave you quite the cold shoulder the other day. What a shame, Lord Thomas, especially if you find my friend's company here so agreeable. One cannot be easy if one's friends constrain one from meeting together."

"Lucy," Caroline said with a lightness she did not feel, "you know how Peg will make mountains of mushrooms. For my sake, would you please not repeat her aspersions on my sister?"

"Very well, Caroline. For your sake. There, Lord Thomas, you must add loyalty to your list."

The music was beginning for the second dance. Lord Thomas stepped forward and offered Lucy his hand. "It was there, ma'am, only Miss Norcrest will call it stubbornness, you see."

Lucy's lips twisted in an appreciative smile.

"I protest," Caroline said, even as Mr. Sudbury offered Caroline his hand and withdrew it, affronted. "Not you, sir. Your cousin."

"There is no cure for me, I am sorry to say. Come, then," Lucy said, "we shall stand together for the beginning."

And so Caroline spent the second dance listening to Mr. Sudbury's compliments, watching Melisande and Mr. Bowes speak to each other across the room, and containing her agony over what Lucy might be saying to Lord Thomas.

Thankfully, Mr. Sudbury confined himself to complimenting her rather than disparaging him. By the end of the dance she felt sufficiently grateful to him for his tact that the old camaraderie between them had reestablished itself.

She also realized how ludicrous it was for her to fret

about Lord Thomas. Whatever he might say, he *was* a capable gentleman. Besides, she could do nothing from where she stood.

Lord Thomas lifted a brow at her, but allowed Mr. Sudbury to make sure he had no further conversation with the ladies before the next dance. They left to find Miss Sudbury, Lord Thomas's partner for the third dance.

Lucy hooked her arm through Caroline's and drew her aside toward what Caroline was beginning to think of as the interrogation wall. She recognized the inevitability of Lucy's questioning, and were the subject not so close to heart, Caroline would have prevaricated.

But the subject is *close to my heart,* she thought, although she did not try to fix the line where her loyalty to Melisande and Lord Thomas lay. That it lay somewhere between them, and that she would draw a protective circle about both of them, was enough. They both deserved it.

"Do you dance this one?"

Caroline shook her head.

"Then you must tell me something of what goes on. I cannot bear not to know when there are deep and mysterious goings-on under my very nose."

"Why must there be something deep and mysterious?"

Lucy rolled her eyes.

"Lucy, do be a dear and tell me what makes you think there is something deep and mysterious going on."

Lucy sighed. "When Jack came home and made such a fuss, I asked him why he did not ride out to Lord Thomas immediately and thank him for his part in putting out the fire. He told me, 'Dashley will not be wanting to hear anything from the likes of mere me, and if you want to keep your . . .' well, never mind that, exactly. He told me that I should be careful around Lord Thomas, as he lives by charming people into doing things for him.

"So you should look grave, Caroline, for I see how coolly your sister treats him, and one could not say that Melisande lacks in discernment. Indeed, Melisande practically breathes discernment. I do not know the man alive who could succeed with your sister on charm alone.

"But you, Caroline? You are too accommodating by half. So I pressed him—Lord Thomas, that is. He spoke compliments, none unorthodox, mind you, and said that you were a worthy ally." Lucy sighed again with exasperation. "These military men and their insistence on putting everything into military terms. I hope he meant *friend,* for I shudder to wonder for what purpose he would need an ally."

"Do go easy, Lucy," Caroline said. "He has been fighting a war these last four years, and unlike our brothers, doing it far closer to the place where one must see any number of messy and unpleasant things. I shudder to wonder at the things he has seen. As for needing an ally, who would not wish for a friendly face when one moves into a new neighborhood?"

"My trouble with you, Caro, is that I suspect you of not telling me everything, and of having too intricate an imagination. You can invent from whole cloth any number of reasons why those you care for are never wrong."

"A fine friend *you* are," Caroline said, pretending mock indignation. She felt shaken to the core by Lucy's assessment.

Lucy shook her head. "Mayhap you do not know everything. But I shall tell you this: my brother not only dislikes your Lord Thomas, he fears him. It was in his eyes. And while I have none too fine an opinion of the straightness of my brother's spine, it does give me pause."

Caroline thought of how Mr. Bowes's eyes had flashed when he had denounced Lord Thomas to herself and Melisande. She had not seen fear there then.

But remembering the next time they had met, in the churchyard, she realized Mr. Bowes had stood behind Melisande. Mr. Rowan had also accused Mr. Bowes of being less than a proper officer. Did something go on there beyond Mr. Rowan's loyalty to Lord Thomas?

But except for Lord Thomas's intent to persuade Melisande to marry him, there was nothing that Caroline knew of that Mr. Bowes needed to fear from Lord Thomas.

Did Mr. Bowes think Melisande more likely to capitulate than Caroline did? Caroline did not like that thought, and now that she considered the matter, she realized Mr. Bowes and Melisande spent a lot more time together than they ever had. They also stopped conversations abruptly when she entered the room. Although Caroline would not have wanted Mr. Bowes for a brother, she wished she could attribute such conversations to romance.

Melisande and Mr. Bowes yet stood together. Melisande's back was to the room, and Caroline sighed a little at her stubbornness. Mr. Bowes, however, surveyed the room warily.

"Now you are frightening me," Caroline said slowly.

"It is well I should, I think."

"What would you have me do?" Caroline asked.

"I do not know, except that it would help if you knew some reason why my brother should fear Lord Thomas."

"The only thing I know, Lucy, and this must be within the strictest confidence, promise me—"

"Promised," said Lucy, holding up her hand, her face intent with excitement.

"—is that Lord Thomas would discharge a weighty obligation to Melisande. Why your brother would fear him, I do not know. I cannot imagine one matter causing or even influencing the other. Do not question me further on the matter, either, for I shall not say."

"I shall not press *you* for details, but answer me this: does my brother know what your 'matter' is?"

Caroline nodded.

"And he is not talking, either. Very curious."

With trepidation, Caroline watched her friend think. Usually the soul of well-balanced reason, every now and again Lucy displayed a streak of stubborn adherence to one side or another. Caroline also suspected that Lucy had had quite the tendre for Peter, although she had joked about how vulgar it would be for her brother to marry one twin and she the other.

It would be all too easy and understandable for Lucy to dislike Lord Thomas if she heard about El Puente de la Dama Blanca. Easy and understandable, but Caroline would hate it.

"As a kindness to me, do not press your brother for details, either, please, Lucy."

Lucy regarded her with some surprise. "You mean that, don't you, Caroline? Hm. Well. Perhaps you are right. He might misrepresent it, and then I should be in a bigger stew than I am now." She laughed. "You see, I tease myself. I am all over my curiosity."

"Fustian," Caroline said, but did her best to laugh with her.

Then the music ended, and Lord Thomas was coming toward her, Miss Sudbury on his arm.

Chapter Twelve

Thomas had an urge to check his pocket for the compass he continued to carry, although he rarely used it these days. He wanted to know if the compass, like him, had developed a new north. During the dance, he had been uncannily aware of where Miss Norcrest was suffering interrogation by Miss Bowes.

Perhaps it was merely that Miss Wendham, he felt sure, would stay where she was. She had shown little liking for the company, less for dancing, none for meeting him.

He wondered why she tolerated so much of Bowes. Wendham had, to be sure, but Thomas had regarded it as regimental pride, since they were both of the 52nd. From what Thomas gathered from neighborhood opinion, however, it may as likely have been Wendham's taking what he thought was due him from his sister's potential suitor. No one gainsaid that Bowes desired Miss Wendham. Nor did anyone gainsay Miss Wendham's emphatic refusals, at least while Wendham lived.

But Miss Norcrest—he never knew quite what she would do. Her curtsy when he had first entered the ballroom had surprised and gratified him. Nor could his head convince his heart that he should feel ashamed or guilty.

Then, when she had cared enough to apologize for Jack Bowes wearing regimentals, he had thought he might kiss her in the middle of the assembly. Something of his thoughts must have spoken to her, for he had not mistaken her awareness of him, not as someone she pitied, but as a man.

Because of that awareness, he had felt like a man in a way he had not felt for over a year. He had not felt like a man when Wellington had refused his resignation. He had not felt like a man when he had delivered messages up and down Navarre and Catalonia in northeastern Spain, sending guerrillas after the retreating French to harry them. He had certainly not felt like a man, indeed anything human, when looking upon the bloody fields of Toulouse and Bayonne.

Miss Norcrest's opinion of him had been like armor against Bowes's snide pronouncing of his name as they had passed in the dance. As for his dance with Miss Wendham, he had felt nothing when he had touched her hand, and the shock of that had been as great as the French musket ball that had taken him down.

Thomas had felt so much upon finally meeting her. During their subsequent meetings, he had hoped she might soften. If anything, she had seemed, if not angrier, more hardened.

Perhaps it was her artistic temperament that made her appear cold, or so overly passionate about her brother's death. Preoccupied with her passion, she would notice little around her. How then could she care about it, not noticing it? How then could she give back?

Thomas had noticed that absorbed air about Peter Wendham, too, especially when Wendham was doing one of his sketches. He remembered one night he had gone over to Wendham's tent and found him outside alone, hunched upon a hassock before a fire. His sketch-pad lay open on his lap, revealing a detailed picture of a delicate but hauntingly human Madonna.

When he had praised Wendham about the Madonna, Wendham's reactions had been swift and surprisingly savage.

"Go away," he had snapped, standing and covering the sketch as though it were a baby and the skies had opened up. "What do you mean, sneaking up on me like that, Dashley?"

"I beg your pardon, Captain," Thomas had said, drawing himself back. He was tired, and had ridden most of the day to return, and had been required to report to Wellington in his dusty uniform. He had not eaten or slept much in two days.

The blunt reminder of their relative ranks served to calm Wendham, or at least remind him of his manners. Although he continued hugging the picture to his chest, his face relaxed into the eccentric, elongated smile that could mark him as an individual even when a shako covered the rest of his face. "Sorry. Times are I forget where I am."

"Hard to do in a camp of 15,000 men," Thomas said. "Although, I must confess, it is decided quiet around here."

"Had my sergeant watching. I'll flay him if he's drunk. So, you're back in. You can tell me all about it."

Thomas blinked away his memory of the rest of that night, of Wendham plying him with drink, and he having to say, gently as he could, that he could not talk about what he had seen, or where the army might be moving. He had asked instead if Wendham had any news from home.

And Wendham, obliging chap that he was, had read his sister's latest letter, only arrived two days before.

Thomas tried to remember the substance of that letter, but failed entirely. But he remembered the precise tone, the assured manner of the phrasing. It had remained only for Thomas to imagine the patrician features Wendham had drawn speaking those words for Thomas to lose himself in a haze of longing.

Now, standing in a ballroom in England, Thomas reminded himself that that longing had been as real as the longing he felt for Miss Norcrest. The one then had been prompted by a need to believe in something, to believe his risking his life had a purpose. This longing could not be described so succinctly, mixed and tempered as it was by duty, honor, and regret.

So with Miss Sudbury on his arm, chattering away, Thomas walked across the ballroom toward Miss Norcrest, entertaining himself with the dismal notion that Wendham was doing a jig in heaven over Thomas's attraction to the unexpected sister while he had committed himself to making the known his wife.

Whatever happened, he thought darkly, he must not permit lust to distract him from his purpose. He needed Miss Norcrest as an ally. He would keep her as an ally and nothing else. He had so often prided himself on his control. He would not let it fail him.

Still, when he saw Miss Norcrest laugh, he knew she was merely putting on a good front. That Miss Bowes had upset Miss Norcrest, and likely over him, caused a painful mixture of ire and guilt to bubble within him.

Miss Sudbury glanced curiously at him, and recalled to himself, he put on his public face, and wished the ladies well.

Miss Bowes tipped her head, studying him with her bright eyes. "My cousins and I were out walking this afternoon, Lord Thomas, and we passed by Bonwood House. There is a little path that runs along the back of it toward the village."

"Yes," Thomas said, "I have walked it myself."

Miss Bowes nodded. "I wondered—or did my eyes

deceive me?—that I saw that the Athena had been damaged?"

"Yes, an arm has come off. My gardener found it, and put the arm away so it may be repaired."

"Goodness," Miss Norcrest said, "Melisande will—" She broke off, bit her lip, and stared at Miss Bowes.

"Come with me, my lord," Miss Bowes said. "I would help you."

Miss Norcrest shook her head at Miss Bowes ever so slightly, but Miss Bowes pretended not to see her.

Well, Thomas thought, he should go once more into the breach. He nodded to Miss Bowes, and Miss Norcrest and Miss Sudbury followed in their wake, both unhappy, although for different reasons.

Miss Wendham and Captain Bowes looked surprised and not pleased to see their party approaching.

Miss Bowes was barely within polite speaking distance when she said, "Miss Wendham, did you know the Athena at Bonwood House is damaged?"

Miss Wendham said, sharply, "How?"

"An arm has come off. The right, I believe." Miss Bowes looked to Thomas, who nodded back. "Lord Thomas says his gardener found it. It has been stored away so that it may be repaired."

"I believe you favor the statue very much," Thomas said to Miss Wendham.

"Indeed. It was one of my first local favorites. I saw it within a week of coming here when my mother married Norcrest."

"I brought Lord Thomas to you, Miss Wendham, so you might give him an opinion on how to repair it," Miss Bowes said.

"It may be very difficult to repair," Miss Wendham said. "It depends upon the damage."

"If you are willing, I should certainly like to consult

with you on its restoration," Thomas said, keeping his voice mild. He would not permit a trace of the hope he felt.

Still, Miss Norcrest's proximity to Miss Wendham made her concern impossible to ignore. Then she had her polite smile in place again, leaving Thomas strangely moved.

"That may be possible," Miss Wendham said.

"Miss Wendham has always felt strongly about preserving art," Miss Bowes said. "It was a passion she and her brother, Peter Wendham, shared. Mr. Wendham was, unfortunately, one of the casualties of the war, my lord."

Thomas felt ambushed. Miss Wendham's eyes began to glitter. Miss Norcrest tucked her arm through her sister's. Bowes frowned at his sister.

Miss Bowes realized she had said something indelicate, although Thomas did not think she knew what. "Well, I am glad that is settled," Miss Bowes said. "It is such a shame that things are damaged. Miss Sudbury and I just toured Lord Elgin's marbles. To see such hacks and cuts in their edges, why, it makes me wonder what he left behind."

Miss Wendham released Miss Norcrest's arm. "I applaud Lord Elgin's decision, Miss Bowes. No one who cares about keeping artwork whole and entire could reach any other decision. The Venetians certainly cared for nothing more than to lob a few cannonballs at the Acropolis whenever they happened by, and the Turks did little about it. Indeed, their officers used the buildings to house their own cannonballs. They whitewashed their houses from the burnt remains of priceless statues. What else could any man of feeling do?"

"Elgin could have stepped away with his drawings," Miss Bowes said. "Instead he retaliated by taking the marbles."

"Lucy—" said her brother.

But Miss Wendham did not want to give up the subject, either. "Looting and pillaging would be retaliating," she said. "When one has to take a year, hire innumerable workers, and incur almost £30,000 in costs, one cannot be accused of looting and pillaging. Lord Elgin did not go to Greece to loot."

"True. He started out commissioning drawings," Miss Bowes said. "I will grant you that not many people set out upon a journey intending to loot and pillage, to be sure."

Except, perhaps, Peter Wendham, Thomas thought suddenly, astounded at himself for thinking such a thing. It could not be denied, however. Wendham had told him on more than one occasion that he had bought his commission as an investment, that he wanted to find the supply wagon of gold that could be captured and brought home as Wendham's personal nest egg.

The times Thomas had tried to dissuade Wendham from thinking along such paths could not be counted. Wendham might be laughing at himself by the end of the conversation, but he would not put aside his goal of setting his sister in her own establishment.

It was always for Miss Wendham. Thomas needed to remember that.

"I repeat," said Miss Wendham, "Lord Elgin did not loot, or pillage."

"I am sorry," Miss Bowes said. "I had no idea your feelings on the subject were so strong. What do you think of Payne Knight, and the Dilettanti Club's own opposition to Elgin's scheme?"

"Payne Knight is a pompous toad who—" Miss Wendham lifted her chin. "Perhaps that is all I should say of Payne Knight."

"What of one of Elgin's ships sinking with some of the marbles aboard?"

"He raised them. At some considerable cost."

"But if he had not?"

"I would be as angry at him as I already was at the Venetians and Turks."

It was a fine answer, Thomas thought. Here was the Miss Wendham Peter had so often described. Here were the animated features, the keen intelligence, the fierce passion. How could he help but admire her?

Even Miss Norcrest followed the conversation with a smile. She was proud of her sister, and Thomas felt excessively in charity with her for it.

"It is fortunate that you do not have to be angry at him, then, Miss Wendham," Thomas said.

Startled, she nodded.

"That is right," Bowes said, an edge to his tone. "You once hanged a British soldier for raiding a Spanish woman's family strongbox, did you not, eh, Dashley?"

Miss Wendham's full attention was suddenly upon him. "But that was Wellington's policy, was it not?" she asked.

"Yes," put in Bowes, "to keep the locals friendly."

"That is right," Thomas said, feeling again like he was creeping into an ambush. For Miss Wendham to bring up the war made him anxious in the extreme. Or perhaps his agitation was only uneasiness at hearing so many of the people who had sheltered him, given him information, and in some cases had died helping him, described dismissively by Bowes as "locals."

Thomas continued, "He—Wilcox, his name was—also injured her badly. These were good people, whose country was overrun by the enemy. We did not need to add to their suffering. But I had no objection to someone taking valuables from the French army. That was our duty and responsibility, to deprive them and starve them out whenever possible."

"So when duty and pillaging run together, that is all right with you?" Mr. Sudbury asked. His question bordered on insult, and Thomas idly sized up his stomach and potential for damage and dismissed the notion of taking offense. It would not be a fair fight.

Miss Wendham fanned herself, effectively hiding her expression as she waited for his answer.

"War and peace have different standards, sir, and if you want to know more about them, I suggest you apply to your cousin." Thomas singled Bowes out with his superior-officer look, and wonder of wonders, Bowes almost saluted before settling into a sulky frown that encompassed his entire body.

"But in short," Thomas continued, "pillaging in peacetime is heinous, for there is no reason for it other than greed. Or sheer meanness of spirit. Pillaging from your enemy in war is good tactics. It might keep you alive tomorrow."

"Has Lord Elgin profited from bringing the marbles to England?" Miss Norcrest asked.

Miss Wendham frowned at her, and Thomas wondered why. Her question had released some of the tension, brought them back to their original subject. Should Miss Wendham not be thanking her sister instead of frowning?

Miss Norcrest blushed. "I do not know much about the marbles, Melisande. I am sorry."

"The short answer is no, he has not," Miss Bowes said. "I hear, in fact, that he is considerably in arrears over the matter. There has been some speculation that he will try to sell them to the Government."

"Would he make a profit?" Miss Norcrest asked.

"It would be highly unlikely, I do believe," Miss Bowes said. "There is no reason for the government to give Elgin more money than what he expended. He transported the marbles courtesy of His Majesty's Navy, and was in the position of taking them because he was Ambassador to Constantinople."

"Money and profit are not the point," Miss Wendham said. "You have heard Lord Thomas here say that the only motivation for pillaging during peacetime is greed. But if one's motivations are not from greed, but love, such removal of art and artifacts is not pillaging, but preservation."

That Miss Wendham should quote him as an authority! Thomas felt such a glow of satisfaction that he compressed his lips, lest he betray himself with a smile.

But Miss Norcrest tensed and said, "We cannot know what was in his mind, though, can we, Mel? Do I not remember hearing that he had wanted those marbles for his own home in Scotland? Would that be love, or greed?"

"He wanted drawings for his home in Scotland," Miss Wendham snapped. "It was only when he saw the deplorable conditions they faced, that he decided to bring the friezes back."

Miss Norcrest looked aside. "I will trust you to know more about it than I, but I hope that the government will buy them, so everyone might see them."

"The people who can appreciate them can see them now," Miss Wendham said.

Miss Norcrest opened her mouth, then shut it.

"But that is a conversation for another day," Miss Wendham said, smiling at him. "Thank you, Lord Thomas, for your evenhanded judgment."

Miss Wendham smiled at him.

Miss Wendham had actually smiled at him. Thomas could not believe it. He stood there, feeling thick and bemused and dazzled. Every paean of praise for his sister that Peter Wendham had ever uttered sounded in Thomas's ears.

As Thomas blinked in the sudden light of her smile, he thought, *Finally, finally, I am making progress.*

Miss Norcrest was biting her lip. Thomas wondered what she was restraining herself from saying. She met his gaze, green eyes wide and shadowed. That look cut through him, and he did not know why, or what it meant.

Then Miss Wendham held out her hand, and Thomas took it, all amazement and, yes, he must admit it, delight.

"Why, Miss Wendham," said Mr. Sudbury, laughing, "your smile has quite overpowered Lord Thomas."

Miss Wendham looked down, dark lashes partly covering her beautiful dark eyes. "Do not worry about Lord Thomas, sir," she replied coolly. "For I am told, most notably by my sister there, that Lord Thomas is quite stout of heart."

A flush of anger or embarrassment crept into Miss Norcrest's cheeks. Thomas hoped it was anger, and not anger from being embarrassed, for he found himself hating the notion of Miss Norcrest ever describing him as stout. But she would not look at him, so he could not tell. And how to reply?

He bowed, said, "However stout my heart may be, ma'am, I shall always be pleased to receive your favor."

Then Miss Norcrest did look at him, but her green eyes no longer resembled England's green fields, but her Channel's dangerous crossing. Somehow he had upset her, but he could not ask her in this company. Nor was he entirely convinced he wanted to, if he would be honest with himself, for the description of *stout* stung.

"We have missed the fourth dance over our conversation," Miss Bowes said. "Caroline, who was your partner? He did not come."

"He is here," she said, nodding to Thomas. "So you see, it does not signify that we did not dance."

Chapter Thirteen

Caroline had much to endure before she could speak privately with Melisande. She was promised to other gentlemen, including Mr. Sudbury again, for dancing. She talked to most of her neighbors, all of whom were glowing with admiration over Lord Thomas.

Caroline spent this time brooding. *How ironic,* she thought, *that he, who can supposedly charm the birds from the trees, could in turn be bewitched by a single smile.*

She tried to feel happy for him. She knew she should be happy for him. Lord Thomas had been very honest in his desires and goals. He had made her a gift of his intentions, and by doing so, given her the gift of his very honor. But she could not feel happy.

She tried to remind herself that she had never been more than a tool to aid his plans—an outlying building, perhaps, that he had taken so he could better fire on the larger fort.

The thought could not comfort her, because she could not forget that moment when he had looked at her, not as an asset, but as a man looks at a woman. Caroline knew the look, understood it, had received it before from other men. Receiving it from Lord Thomas, however, had made her want to return it.

She thought to speak to Melisande in the carriage, but Melisande had agreed to take Peg home. Peg chattered happily all the way there, and then the moments before they would reach home seemed too few to begin a conversation Caroline suspected would take some time.

Arriving home, Griggs took Melisande aside to ask her about some correspondence that had come, and Melisande had gone at once to read it.

So Caroline finally caught up with her sister in Melisande's bedchamber. Decorated in austere shades of blue, it was as neat as her workshop was chaotic. Caroline had long found herself distracted by the dichotomy between Melisande's most private spaces. Melisande had lighted two braces of candles, each of which stood in the dead center of the tables holding them.

Melisande had taken down her hair and was brushing it, doubtless counting the requisite hundred strokes. "You," she said, "have been simmering all evening. What has you so upset?"

Caroline had thought through any number of approaches to the subject. But Melisande's light tone made her forget them. "I know you will never forgive Lord Thomas for what he did, but at least he did not do it from cruelty."

Melisande lowered the brush to her side, becoming very still, black hair making her look armored, rather than vulnerable. "You accuse me of cruelty?"

"I do. I do, for you enjoyed seeing how happy he was when you smiled at him."

"And how is that cruel?"

"I have heard you rant about Lord Thomas for upwards of a week. What made tonight so different?"

"I liked his opinions about preserving art." Melisande smiled fondly at her, but Caroline did not miss the trace of condescension that usually accompanied Melisande's fondness. It had been different with Peter, Caroline thought suddenly. Peter had received the truly fond looks, the deference, the respect.

Caroline shook her head. "Please tell me, Melisande, that you do not intend to get some kind of revenge upon him by raising his expectations, then dropping him."

"That would be cruel, would it not? And clichéd."

"Then what are your plans? You have some plan, Melisande. You always do."

Melisande turned and put the brush down on her dressing table, but she could not thus hide her emotions. The mirror revealed her animosity, frightening in its reined intensity. Melisande saw herself, turned away from her image, shook her head so her freshly brushed hair switched about her shoulders.

"Whatever else I have said about you, Caroline, you are a fine judge of character. You must have realized that Lord Thomas's help with the fire makes it disadvantageous for me to be at daggers drawn with him. I must do the pretty, and continue to do the pretty while he has the stomach to remain in the neighborhood. But I do not have to like it."

"But smiling at him, Mel?"

"He wanted to atone," Melisande said between clenched teeth. "Let this be his atonement. Let him be like Prometheus. He may receive smile after smile, but the stone will always fall down the hill."

There was nothing else Caroline could say, no words she could use that would persuade Melisande to see. She understood that, even as her stomach roiled with anger, fear, and a sadness so intense she wondered how her eyes could possibly be dry. "I see," Caroline said dully. She went to the door.

But Melisande's cold words stopped her. "What expectations does Lord Thomas have?"

"I do not know what you mean."

"Tell me."

"Puzzle it out for yourself. I am done helping you. I am told by my friends that I am too loyal, and I begin to think they are right."

"You think that is what you have been doing?" Melisande shook her head, derisive again. "Helping me? Poor Caroline. You really have never understood what is important, have you?"

"I now know I am glad I am not you. That is important." And with that little rebellion, Caroline fled Melisande's room for her own, where she threw herself on the bed and sobbed.

The weather had shifted again, not unsurprisingly for early October, although this reversion to soft breezes and warm sun could only be welcomed. Thomas found Miss Norcrest where she had written in reply that she would be, upon a bench at the far part of Norcrest Manor's gardens. The bench, sheltered by vines bedecked in thick, late-summer leaves, balanced at the edge of cultivated and wild, for the woods began a bare twenty feet and a gravel path away.

Miss Norcrest looked at her hands, twisted in her lap. She resembled a slender white sentinel of a statue set in the garden. Looking upon her, any walker would think carefully before braving the woods.

Thomas's heart twisted with her hands. He stopped on the gravel path, deliberately kicked up some stones to warn her he was near. Alerted but not startled, she watched him approach her with the same wariness he had detected in the note she had sent back, agreeing to meet him.

He had hoped he imagined her caution. She had never been wary around him before. Stubborn, yes;

quick-witted and honest, certainly. Never wary and all it implied.

"Thank you for meeting me," he said.

"Do you have some question for me?" she asked.

Were it not for the wariness, her pointedly business-like tone would not have irritated him. But it did. "I first wanted to thank you for describing me so favorably to your sister."

She frowned her question.

"Stout of heart," Thomas said.

"Lord Thomas, I have known better than to argue your case before my sister. If she has decided to flatter you, I have had nothing to do with it." She looked away. "And 'stout of heart' would not be one of the phrases I would use to describe you."

Immediately Thomas felt a weight lift from him he had not realized he carried. "Miss Norcrest, you wound me."

"Indeed I hope not, sir. For when I think of stout, I think 'rhymes with gout,' and that I should not associate with you."

She was holding something back, that much was certain. He said, "May I sit down?"

Miss Norcrest nodded. There was enough room on the bench for him to sit next to her without her moving, but when he did and found himself so close to her, he felt a sudden awareness of her that tugged at him with innumerable small fingers all over his body.

The breeze plucked wisps of her honey hair from their resting place by her bonnet and drew them across her face, alternately hiding and revealing a small mole near her jaw. Although soldiers under his command could have taken lessons from the straightness of her back, her neck was bowed and at such an angle that he wanted to run his hand down its soft length. To comfort? To enflame?

How was it that, even after Miss Wendham had smiled at him, he could still feel this way?

Miss Norcrest drew a hand toward her face to hold back the blowing curls. He felt his anger seeping away.

"I did have a question," he said, and, now that she was here, he did not know how to ask it. "When your sister and Mr. Bowes saw us coming across the ballroom, they were neither of them happy to see us."

"I begged Lucy not to intervene," Miss Norcrest said.

"You misunderstand me. I do not intend to criticize you. Or Miss Bowes, either. I am grateful to Miss Bowes."

Here Miss Norcrest bit her lip.

"Here is my question: is your sister softening toward me?"

Miss Norcrest caught her breath. Then she said, "Before I answer that, there is something I would like to know."

"You, Miss Norcrest, may ask me anything." But his heart sank. Miss Norcrest would not prevaricate if she could say yes to his question. How clear, how easy everything would be if Miss Norcrest could only say yes!

"Lucy says her brother greatly dislikes you. You must understand—she does not know about Peter. Mr. Bowes has not told her. He has given other reasons for his dislike. I would like to know why you think he would dislike you—for some reason other than Peter."

"You do not ask the easy questions," Thomas said. He stood, removed his hat, and ran his fingers through his hair.

"Then there is another reason."

Thomas nodded. "There is indeed."

Lord Thomas braced one booted foot against a notch in the bench. Not a fashionable pose, perhaps, Caroline thought, but a practical one. He even revealed a bit of mud mixed with leaves that clung to the bottom of the boot, from walking the woods.

But the position showed off his strength. Peter had been a man, but Caroline had never thought of him as being strong physically. Peter's strength lay in the force of his will, which he regularly employed.

Lord Thomas possessed both, but seemed reluctant to use either. He tended not to lean forward and crowd her, yet Caroline never felt that she had anything but his undivided attention, and that she held his interest.

He rubbed one hand absently against his raised leg. The right, Caroline thought, remembering his slight limp after he had carried her all that delicious distance. If she thought even a moment, she could recall how thrilling it was to be carried in those strong arms.

"There is a military truism," Lord Thomas said, then stopped and gazed into the wood. Caroline did not follow his gaze, but traced the line of firm jaw and brow against the blue sky. Lord Thomas looked full at her, and there was nothing of the apologetic about him. It was as though he had shed his humility like a cloak, revealing what he truly was.

"There is a military truism that the best-laid battle plan rarely survives first contact with the enemy. We were all drawn up on the heights above Fuentes d'Onoro. This would be back in May of 1811. We, the Light Division, ma'am, were ordered to come up to the lines and cover the retreat of General Houston's battalions across a broad plateau. Captain Bowes's company was supposed to have joined us. They came with us, but when we arrived, he was nowhere to be found.

"Now there was some very thick fighting in the woods nearby. Very thick. It's not surprising that his company got separated from the rest of the division.

"The papers write of charges and withdrawals, breaches

made, flanks turned. But the truth is, nothing is as simple as the descriptions would have it. Hundreds of things happen at once, and it can get very confused. While you can never mistake a formal advance, a retreating force can move in any direction except toward the other line."

He held up one hand, palm and fingers flat, put his other hand perpendicular to it, then moved it around to show the angles. "And a force advancing after a retreating force, well, sometimes the men's bloodlust makes them throw off their discipline. Even if there were no bloodlust taking over the men, in the smoke and confusion, when you cannot see the landmarks you are aiming for, you can make mistakes."

"What mistake did he make?"

"No one could agree. But while the rest of his regiment and the division took heavy casualties, the majority of his company survived."

"So is that what Mr. Rowan meant when he said Bowes was not a proper officer?" Caroline asked. She frowned. "But could it be said that he saw the situation as hopeless and acted in the best interest of his men?"

Lord Thomas shrugged, more from perplexity than impatience. "Had it only been so simple. But gossip is an ever-present evil in army life. The officers can sometimes button their lips, but the enlisted talk among each other like they're all still in some pub with hours before last call. We were not done more than a few hours before some of Bowes's men claimed Bowes had never started correctly when the rest of the division left, did not know where he was once he did start, then lost his head in the thick of it and ran. One man in Bowes's company even told Rowan that Bowes had not given an order to retreat, but had run himself, effectively letting his lieutenants figure out that they were alone and how and where they should advance or retreat."

"That is horrible."

"It would be if it's true."

Caroline looked her question.

"When questioned, Bowes produced an order that was in Colonel Gaddington's hand, telling him to retreat immediately and shore up Sontag's Brigade, which was on the right flank. Gaddington was on Wellington's command staff, but outside of the captain's line of command. No one could ask Gaddington about the order, unfortunately. He fell in another part of the engagement. Good man. Another loss that day."

"So you think this soldier who talked to Mr. Rowan mistook the matter?"

"It was possible, although no one in the company could remember seeing a courier bringing the order. That alone might not be enough to keep me suspicious, but I had the opportunity to look at the order. It did look like Gaddington's hand. I had received several orders from him myself, although they had been passed down to me through my major and colonel. Of course, I never received orders from him in the press of battle."

Caroline knew that he was being fair, and that the effort did not cost him anything. Lord Thomas, she thought, credited her with being impartial, but that was likely only because he was. He would be determined to be fair, she believed, unless something definite could persuade him to think otherwise.

Still, something seemed out of balance to Caroline. "What was your opinion?" she asked quietly.

"I could not decide," he replied. "I wondered, though, how Gaddington would know where to find Bowes's company above all others, especially if they were not where they were supposed to be. I wondered as well at Gaddington's breaking the line of command. He was a veritable stickler for the rules of military conduct. But it was not my place to volunteer opinions. That was for the others who considered the matter. When questioned under oath, all I could say was that the phrases in the order did not sound like Gaddington, but perhaps were written in the heat of things." He shrugged. "I do not know."

"There was a court martial then?" she asked.

"A formal inquiry."

"And you were one of the ones to testify?"

"I was, at that time, of the same rank as Bowes, within the same division, and had had experience with Gaddington."

And people trusted you, Caroline thought. "So Mr. Bowes was cleared?"

"Whatever suspicions there were, he had the order from Gaddington. No one could prove otherwise. Of course the men were not satisfied, and several sobriquets followed him around. I could not repeat them to you."

Caroline smiled, then asked, "Did you know Peter then?"

He nodded. "We had met, briefly, before, but we became friends over the matter. Bowes called him as a character witness."

"They had known each other since childhood, when our mother's remarriage brought Peter and Mel to this neighborhood."

"So I was given to understand," Lord Thomas said dryly.

"What was his opinion?"

"He supported Bowes at the inquiry."

Caroline could hear the "of course" in his voice. *Of course,* she thought with a sudden sinking feeling, and, had she been by herself, would have thumped the heel of her hand against her forehead.

How could she have forgotten a triumphant Peter at

fifteen crowing over how he need never worry about failing an examination because he could imitate his headmaster's handwriting? He did a fine imitation of Caroline's handwriting, too, and Mel's he could dash off as though he were Mel.

How far might Peter's loyalty have extended?

Caroline felt chilled through and through. She had long thought of Peter as a rascal, but a rascal who would cut corners to have a little harmless fun, no more. The more she heard, though, the more she felt certain Peter had crossed the line from harmless fun into harmful mischief.

Remembering that even Lucy doubted her brother's spine, Caroline felt sure Jack Bowes had panicked under fire, and had compounded his cowardice by enlisting Peter to help him.

Why had Peter helped him? Childhood loyalty was all well and good, but Peter had always been such an example of all that was noble and right.

It meant, too, that Peter had omitted mentioning things to Lord Thomas. He had actively lied to him. Had Peter made that a practice? Caroline dismissed the notion, for what would Peter have needed to lie to him about again? Surely such an incident would be idiosyncratic in the extreme.

El Puente de la Dama Blanca. The White Lady's Bridge. She found her own imaginary picture of it coming into her head. Lord Thomas had said he and Peter had discussed it one night.

Caroline did not like where those thoughts might lead.

The sinking feeling hardening in the pit of her stomach, Caroline asked, "Did Peter have a private opinion about Mr. Bowes's conduct, outside the inquiry?"

Lord Thomas did not appear to notice her discomfiture. "It would have been awkward for us to have spoken of it. When he told me he had recommended to your sister that she not marry Bowes, however, I had my answer to what his true opinion was."

Caroline wondered if Lord Thomas and Peter had ever discussed Lord Thomas's marrying Melisande. She thrust the thought away, then one more horrible replaced it.

Lord Thomas had spoken of casualties, casualties Caroline presumed would have been lessened had Mr. Bowes shown up with his company to reinforce the retreat. If he had not come because of cowardice, for how many lives was he directly responsible?

Would he have apologized to grieving family members as Lord Thomas had done?

No, in every respect, Lord Thomas was the superior man. He did not deserve the treatment he would continue to receive, and she should be no part of it.

Besides, she would grow to love him. She knew that she could, and her stubbornness always led her to reveal her feelings. Discipline and control had never been her happy cousins. It would be an unmitigated disaster.

Caroline contemplated a world where the only future she knew was the future she could not have. Peter, she thought. It all came back to Peter and what he had been doing at that bridge. Had he not been there, Lord Thomas would not feel the need to marry Melisande.

Maybe Lord Thomas would have wanted to marry Melisande regardless. Maybe he had fallen in love with her listening to her letters to Peter. Caroline remembered the hungry expression on his face that first afternoon he had seen Melisande. Perfectly natural, Caroline conceded.

She should send him away. It would be a kindness to him, whatever he thought, and however her heart might break never to see him again.

But how could she possibly tell him he should go?

Chapter Fourteen

"Why did you ask me about Bowes?"

Those penetrating eyes of his saw through her, Caroline was convinced. Despite his apparently insane desire to throw himself against Melisande, Caroline could not believe, not for one teeny, tiny second, that Lord Thomas did not see everything around him that there was to see. She imagined him giving witness against Jack Bowes. Had she been in Bowes's position, she would have wanted anyone but him giving testimony. One looked at Lord Thomas, and one believed, because one knew that he had figured it out, and *he* believed.

So Caroline hesitated. "Melisande has been much more in his company since he returned this spring. I was curious what you would say about him. I wanted to know whether knowing something more about him would help me understand. But I do not think so."

"Something has happened to make you doubt the wisdom of helping me."

To her surprised dismay, tears welled. Ashamed of herself, she tried to look away from Lord Thomas, but he saw. He dipped his head as though conceding something within himself, and drew her gently to him. She crushed one side of her bonnet against his broad chest and shoulder, but she did not care. She wanted only to be in the place that felt true for her.

"You must trust me to make it right," he said. "I will make it right." Awkwardly he patted her shoulder.

Caroline recognized the pat for what it was: sympathy offered at an emotional distance. Struggling inside, she pulled herself together, lifted her head from his shoulder, and offered him all she had to give. At least, she gave him all she could give that he would accept. "I trust you," she whispered.

An expression she could not identify flashed across his face. "Miss Norcrest—" he said.

"I trust you that you would try," she said. "But it never matters, for I can no longer help you. I do trust you, Lord Thomas. I trust and respect you. But Melisande is my sister. I have looked up to her all my life. From the time I was a little girl, my mother would say to me, 'You watch your sister, now, and mind, and you will become every bit the fine young lady she is.' So I watched, and minded, and although I have none of her artistic talent, I hope I may have become a fine young lady."

"You have. Without question or demur."

"Perhaps," Caroline said, but her smile faded quickly. "But I cannot be both a worthy ally and a worthy sister beyond saying this: leave Melisande alone. Leave her entirely alone. I do not like the person she is becoming."

She could feel the chill from him as he said, "So my first question is answered. I suspected as much. Once I thought on it, it was too good to be true. And you, you are too generous not to congratulate me immediately."

Caroline winced. "I thought it might be Mr. Bowes—who has made her act so out of character, that is—but I do not think so anymore."

"And I have put you in the unpleasant situation of forcing you to choose between your loyalties. I should not have traded so on your accommodating nature. Do not frown, Miss Norcrest, I beg you. I would be blind not to notice how you do whatever you can to keep those around you happy. Did I not remark upon it in your schoolroom?"

He straightened, again reminding Caroline of a broadsword poised to strike. "You have only to command me—one word will suffice—and I shall not opportune you again."

"You would leave the neighborhood?" Caroline asked, hope and dismay warring within her. "You would give over this notion of—" she stumbled over the word *marrying*, "—persuading Melisande to forgive you?"

"No. That I cannot do."

She shook her head. "You are more stubborn than I am."

"It is quite possible."

Caroline smiled in resignation, both to her hopes and her dismay. She clasped her hands together, and walked about a few steps. "I cannot give you one word. Go. Stay. They are too stark a choice. It would be unfair."

"No," he said, suddenly right beside her so she had to look up at him. "It would not be unfair. I am responsible—"

"How many people did Mr. Bowes kill by his cowardice?" she asked.

Immediately his face shuttered. "Cowardice was not proved."

"Very well. Were you not acquitted during your own court of inquiry? Did Lord Wellington not refuse to accept your resignation? Did he not then continue to attach you to his staff and trust you to carry secret messages for another year?"

"You have been speaking to Rowan."

"I could not very well speak to Mr. Bowes," Caroline said, putting her hands on her hips in her frustration.

He bowed, which served to goad her.

"You would tell me that it is a military truism that plans never outlive first contact with the enemy. You would tell me that for him and ignore it for yourself."

"You may try to accommodate those you like, but I pity anyone who makes the mistake of thinking you some die-away miss." He attempted a smile, speaking lightly. "If you were one of the heroines in these fashionable novels, I should not believe that you would creep secretly up the dark staircase, flickering candle—madly flickering candle, I should say, since all those old castles are drafty—in hand, to reveal the horrible monster. No, Miss Norcrest, you let a man know you are going first, and that you carry a stout stick."

Despite his light tone, a muscle twitched in his jaw. Caroline took pity on him. "You would distract me with unorthodox compliments, and that horrible word again?"

"Horrible word?"

"Stout."

He digested that. Then, "You know that the substance is sound, whatever the form of it took."

She choked back laughter, feeling its hysterical edge, and said, "Do you now accuse me of being sensible, Lord Thomas?"

He held his hand over his heart. "It is a lowering thought to a fashionable young woman such as yourself to be thought sensible, I know. I would not presume to be *that* unorthodox, if unorthodox I am. I shall instead say that I value your friendship."

Caroline felt herself at an impasse. He would not go. She did not want him to stay under such circumstances. But although she had told Melisande she was glad she was not like her, the rift between herself and Melisande troubled her deeply.

Melisande perceived her as taking sides, and Melisande was spending a lot of time with Mr. Bowes. Neither fact could make Caroline happy. One removed all her influence over the other.

"Very well, Lord Thomas. I shall not importune you to leave, and you will not importune me about Melisande's feelings. You must judge those for yourself. Nor will I plead your case to her. 'Tis the best I can do."

Caroline felt her own dissatisfaction acutely and was fairly certain of his, but he said, "It is a fair compromise."

He bid her good day after that, and Caroline turned heavy feet toward the manor, where she sought out Melisande and found her in her workroom.

Ordinarily Caroline would have tiptoed past the workroom door. She, like everyone else in the house, knew better than to disturb Melisande while she worked.

But although Melisande had a dusty, paint-smudged apron on over her fine white dress sprigged with blue, Caroline knew she was not creating anything. Melisande was in her maybe-this, maybe-that mode, picking up first one piece of stone, considering it, then putting it down for the next one.

Caroline sat down on the battered chair Peter had usually occupied, waiting for Melisande to greet her. However unwritten, workroom rules were nonetheless firm.

Besides, Melisande would be justified if she remained angry at Caroline.

"What do you think of this?" Melisande asked, hefting a piece of marble the size of a man's head.

"Would that dark vein on the bottom give you trouble?"

Melisande turned the marble over, made a moue with her mouth, said, "You're probably right." She turned her back on Caroline, set the piece back down, and began rummaging through a pile of like-sized stones.

"What are you thinking of?" Caroline asked, although she had a feeling she knew.

"Of making a falcon with its legs the proper way," Melisande replied tartly.

Caroline sighed. "Why are you letting Lord Thomas's comment bother you so much, Melly?" she asked gently.

"If he is correct, he is correct, no matter who he is."

Caroline looked around at the brushes, washed and standing bristles-up in jars, the blank canvases nailed to frames stacked by the far wall, the containers of paints, the chisels hanging in marching precision from smallest to largest near the worktable that pointed stolidly toward the north wall.

Melisande had not proven herself readily able to handle suffering. She had carried on for months after Peter had died, with private fits of weeping and melancholy that stained her face in public.

Finding Melisande here, hunting purposefully amongst her stones, filled Caroline with happiness. Melisande so lived for what she did here. Although Caroline usually found the workroom too jumbled for serenity, today it felt warm and comfortable.

"What will you do with the bird downstairs?" she asked.

Melisande tipped her head to regard two pieces of stone she had set upon the worktable, one a gray granite like the one the other bird was made of, the other, although also a granite, of a much lighter hue, more white mixed with black. "I do not know. But I shall replace it."

"May I have it?"

"Whatever for? It is wrong."

"Wrong or not, I like it for what it is."

"You do have strange notions, Caro."

Now was not the time to debate that, Caroline decided. "May I have it?"

"If it will make you happy."

I shall have no further use for it echoed in Melisande's

tone, but Caroline did not care. She said, "It is beautiful. I loved it the first time I saw it."

"The lighter granite, I think," Melisande said, setting the gray back on the pile, "so I do not confuse the two."

"Are you going to begin work right away?" Caroline asked, knowing she would have to give up any notion of conversing with Melisande if she were going to start work.

"No. There are other matters that demand my attention today." Melisande picked up a cloth, and wrapped the piece of stone in it.

"I wanted to say I am sorry I said those things to you last night."

"Do not regard it," Melisande said. "My dear, soft-hearted sister. You have always hoped the creature less likely to win will win. We never thought that way."

Caroline knew Melisande referred to herself and Peter. "I only wanted to be fair, Melly. There *is* doubt."

"We will not debate this matter again, Caroline," Melisande said, but her voice was not sharp.

"Very well."

"I have said all I will on the subject."

"All right, Mel."

Melisande was gazing again at the cloth-wrapped stone. "I have been doing some thinking on the matter we discussed last night, and maybe you are right, Caroline. It would be tiresome to have to keep smiling at Lord Thomas. I have decided instead to be civil—no more, no less. Perhaps," and here she gave a little snort, "he will begin to regard me as an unassailable castle wall and give up."

"I think any action that does not give him false hope is wise and good."

Melisande washed her hands in a chipped basin. Peter had made the chip when he had dropped a box of paints while putting them away. Caroline wondered if Melisande remembered that every time she washed her hands.

"I wish I could begin work today," Melisande said, "but there is much to be done. For you, too, Caroline. You have received a note from Miss Bowes. I think she will call you over there to discuss the dance."

"Yes, Mel," Caroline said.

Thomas did not notice the woods he walked through except in the most perfunctory way. Usually the simple screen of brown and green touched his soul in some elemental way, but leaving Miss Norcrest this time had left him surprisingly depressed.

Despite his professed admiration for her impartiality and loyalty, it upset him to find himself on the losing side when their skirmishing finally came to formal lines of battle. His conscience did not appreciate his disquiet, either. That she should be concerned with her sister first and foremost was the most natural thing in the world.

But Thomas was honest with himself: he could have let his conscience work him back to appropriate nobility were it not for the insidious notion Miss Norcrest had put forward about Bowes. Thomas had never thought of other officers' blunders as being equally reprehensible as his own had been.

How easy it would be for him to succumb to the call of that line of reasoning, especially when accompanied by those green eyes, drowning in their tears. Did they look to him as if for a rope? It was impossible and unsettling. She made him want to be St. George fighting the dragon. He was at best Scaramouche the clown, laughable only because in his mocking way he could yet laugh at himself.

Deriding himself, he had to rate his blunder worse than Bowes's. Even if Bowes had panicked in the press of a heated battle, how could one attribute one soldier's death to Bowes's actions? It was an impossibility. Bowes had then made it through other battles, with, if less than grace, at least competency.

By comparison, Thomas had given information before he had endured anything close to what could break him. He had thought the intelligence he had gathered was supremely important, and he had taken the easy way. He could count all his dead.

He tried to recall some of their faces, saw instead Miss Norcrest's. He did not deserve her fighting for him. He did not deserve the confidence and trust she showed in him. He could still feel the soft, wonderful length of her against him when she had cried. He had needed to offer some comfort. How could he not? But he had known that had he put his arms about her, he would not have been able to let go of her. What awkwardness would have followed then? What loss of honor!

Thomas shook his head, seeing Bonwood House spread below him, and started down the hill. Home. In some strange way, it had begun to feel like home. Not even Dashwood felt like home.

He would stay here. He would atone.

But maybe, once he had gone tomorrow on the picnic Miss Bowes had invited him to, he should try to avoid Miss Norcrest's company. Duty, honor, and responsibility were best served when they had nothing beautiful and seductive distracting them.

Caroline had mixed feelings as she approached Lucy's house. She would always consider Lucy a friend, and the house the place she had visited countless times for parties, tea, dinner, or just a comfortable coze. Its walls held many of her girlhood secrets. But it was also Mr. Bowes's home. Caroline wondered how she would meet him again, knowing what she knew now.

She stopped before the large stone pillars that supported an overhanging roof and considered the knocker. A maid had seen her, would likely be letting the butler know she was without. So Caroline shook her head at herself, for she was doing just what Lord Thomas told her she was wont to do: arrange herself to everyone else's happiness. She would grit her teeth and sound the knocker despite wanting to run someplace and hide her head. She would do it because Lucy wanted to see her.

Inside there was no sign of Mr. Bowes. Caroline breathed a little easier as his butler showed Caroline upstairs to Lucy. Lucy rose from a mahogany escritoire that stood out as one of the only furnishings in her room not painted white. She held out her hands, her eyes sparkling, and dismissed the butler.

"You will never guess," she said as Caroline took her hands. "I can barely believe it myself."

"If you can barely believe it, I am certain not to be able to."

"You have to see. I need your opinion. Keep your bonnet and cape on." Lucy dropped Caroline's hands, reached for her hat, cape, and reticule. "I am going to show you."

"Outside?"

"In those same outbuildings so recently threatened by fire," Lucy said with an excited waggle of her brows.

That excitement communicated itself to Caroline, although she also felt a tremor of trepidation.

They went right back downstairs, and Lucy said to her butler, "If my brother should want me, please tell him we are going for a long walk."

"Very good, miss," replied the butler.

Lucy swept them outside, holding Caroline's arm

tightly against further speech until they were quite far from the house. "They are going to be remarking on my second long walk of the day, but it cannot be helped. My cousins are visiting an acquaintance today, so I had the time and I chose to take it."

Lucy took a deep breath, went on. "Jack likely does not remember that he gave me keys to all the estate buildings when he left for the Peninsula. But I remembered, although I had to dig around for the blasted things. He acted so oddly about the fire that I had any number of peculiar notions about what might be in those buildings."

"Good God, Lucy, of what did you suspect your brother?" Caroline was shocked that Bowes's own sister would express such thoughts. Then she remembered that this was Lucy, after all.

Lucy raised her brows, continued walking. They were passing over a wooded crest. "That never matters. But what I found was not what I expected, certainly."

"How long are you going to keep me in suspense?"

"I could not describe such things to you, Caroline. You shall have to see them. Then you shall understand why my brother acted like the veriest Bedlamite about the fire. He had made provision for dust and flooding, as you will see, and we will not find a lantern within. But he had not calculated on threats made by fire in the village."

Caroline resigned herself to Lucy's anticipation of her surprise. She saved her breath for walking more quickly, and soon they approached the three outbuildings along a path rutted with wagon wheel tracks. From this side, the screen of elm and pine trees separating the buildings from the town looked tall and untouched by fire. All was private and quiet.

Lucy put her finger over her lips and then fished out

her keys. She opened the padlock to the building farthest from the trees. The door swung open without a sound.

"It has been oiled," Lucy said.

Caroline had noted that, too. In the sunlight from the open door, she could see dark gray dust tarps covering the tops of wooden crates. Protection from wind and water, she thought. Farther inside, away from the light, Caroline saw the impression of other large, cloth-covered shapes.

"I brought a candle," Lucy said. She produced it and a flint box and striker from her reticule. At Caroline's raised brows she said with a roguish smile, "When sneaking about, it is best to come prepared."

Caroline remembered Lord Thomas's comment about her carrying a stout stick. "I say 'amen' to that."

Lucy gestured with her head over her shoulder for Caroline to come with her. They stepped inside, and Lucy closed the door. "You will see better without the light in your face."

She held up the candle. By its dim light Caroline determined the entire center of the room was filled with crates covered by dark gray tarps. They stood on wooden pallets to hold them off the floor.

Lucy led the way around the crates. "Here," she said, handing Caroline the candle. Then she threw back a tarp.

Caroline's jaw dropped. Before her were three pieces of art, each depicting a different Christian scene.

She hunched down, moved the candle close so she could see the detail. The first, a mosaic lifted whole from its embracing stone so that its edges looked lacerated, showed Christ upon a boat surrounded by other fishermen on their boats. Fish leapt willingly from the sea toward the fishermen. The earliest Christians would have done this, Caroline thought, still closely influenced by their Roman roots.

The second, a painting, showed Christ upon the cross,

with all the closed, anonymous quaintness Caroline considered the hallmarks of medieval artwork. The third, likely painted some three or four hundred years ago, showed a Madonna with child with all the fulsome, glowing attention to detail characteristic of the Renaissance. Her white veil rendered her expression radiant as well as blissful.

Lucy chuckled, although there was a nervous edge to it. "I thought you would be impressed. *I* was impressed, and I have not your sensibility to art."

"I cannot believe it," Caroline said. "They are beautiful. I cannot believe them." She shook her head, gestured with her free hand around the dark room. "Do you think these other crates have similar pieces?"

Lucy shook her head. "I do not know, although I surmise so. These were out of their crates, under the tarp, just as I showed them to you. I would not dream of touching the crates. What if I were to break something within them?"

"It could not be borne," Caroline said, nodding. She stood, her candle illuminating the Madonna, and contemplated it. The Madonna possessed such an arresting expression Caroline could feel the Madonna wanting to whisper something to her, although whether secret wisdom or a warning, Caroline could not decide.

"I know what question you will ask next," Lucy said. "It is the one I asked myself when I was done gawping at them. Where did my brother come across such beautiful things?"

"And what are they doing here?" Caroline said.

"That, too. And why would he bother with them? If my artistic sensibility does not come close to yours, I suspect all of his artistic sensibility could be found in the little finger of my left hand." Lucy hesitated. "Caroline, I must ask you, why did you think Jack would be so interested in the fire? Had he said something about these buildings?"

Caroline looked at her blankly, trying to think of why she had asked Lucy that. "Well, the fire was near his land, and Melisande . . ."

"What about Melisande?"

Caroline's eyes widened. "Melisande was frantic that the fire should be put out. When she heard about the fire, she insisted on driving out to watch it."

"Oh, that is why. I wondered why it was your driver who helped get the Newsham engine out."

Caroline bit her lip, stared at the paintings. Even if every crate contained only one piece of art, there were likely fifteen to twenty other pieces.

Did Melisande know Mr. Bowes had this artwork? Caroline wondered. If she knew, likely she also knew where it was stored. She had recognized the threat to these buildings from the fire. That explained how intent, how frantic she had been, why she had clutched the side of the landau so hard, why she had cried and clung to Caroline when they had learned the fire was well and truly out.

"You think your sister knows about all this," Lucy said, waving her hand over the whole.

Caroline nodded before she could help herself. She compressed her lips.

"Do you think she also knows it is here now?"

"I think it is safe to say that if she does not, she knew it was intended to be here at some point."

"You think she knows what it is? Oh, what am I saying? To say your sister does not know art is like saying spring does not follow winter."

"I can identify the periods, but I could not give any opinion about whether they were genuine."

"They look genuine enough. When I think of the

times I have told Jack that I thought he would sell his soul to have your sister accept him . . ." Lucy shook her head. "I never thought he would go to such lengths. Good God, what must this cost?"

And what, Caroline thought, did Lucy think of Melisande for agreeing to have such things purchased for her? What did Caroline think of Melisande agreeing to have such things purchased for her?

"We do not know that anything dire or desperate is going on," Caroline said. "Maybe she is merely advising your brother."

Lucy snorted, wiggled the fingers on an upheld hand. "We are back to my little finger."

"Which is quite lovely, but not proof of anything."

"One of these days, your defense of your sister will be less than charming."

"Why are you and Peg so annoyed with Melisande these days? Peg even tried to persuade Lord Thomas she was taken to fits of public ill temper. I had to ask you to leave off your criticisms of her only last night. Besides, if what you suspect comes to pass, she will be your sister, too, and you will owe her some loyalty."

"Some, perhaps. Not the amount you think she deserves. And public temper, hm? As opposed to private?" Lucy sighed. "Poor Caroline. Melisande has never been an easy person to know. She has changed since Pe— since Mr. Wendham was lost. It is not unremarkable. To be expected, even. But she *is* harder, less forgiving."

"Do you not think that makes her deserving of sympathy?"

"I do not want to argue with you. You are becoming very outspoken, do you know that, Caroline? First you speak up loudly for Lord Thomas, to *my* brother's detriment, and then you insist on berating me for expressing my opinions of *your* sister."

Caroline colored. "You are right, of course. I am sorry."

Her point made, Lucy laughed it off. "It is all this mysteriousness. Your sister. My brother. Lord Thomas. All this artwork." She shook her head. "What are we going to do?"

"I am going to ask Melisande about it. We can assume your brother does not want anyone questioning him about it."

"That we can take for granted, yes." Lucy's lips twisted in exasperation. "Normally he is quite content to leave any little detail to my care. It quite stretches credulity to believe he would put himself through this much exertion for something aboveboard. The letters alone he would have had to write!"

"So I shall ask Melisande?"

"Yes. Do. But do be careful how you go about it."

Caroline rolled her eyes, and Lucy grinned sheepishly. "I had to say that, did I not?"

"You are incorrigible."

Caroline took a last look at the three pieces before Lucy covered them back up with the tarp and smoothed down the edges. They moved around the central pile to the door, where Lucy blew out the candle. The darkness lasted only a moment, for Lucy had her hand on the door handle and pulled it halfway. Still, Caroline shielded her eyes with a corner of her cape.

"You go first, up the hill to that maple," Lucy said. "Then I shall come out and lock the door and join you."

"You think that is necessary?"

"Be prepared, remember?"

Caroline managed a smile and did as she said.

Lucy joined her under the shady maple a few minutes later. "There." She took a deep breath. "It is a pity, though. I had planned to make this my picnic spot tomorrow. Lord Thomas has agreed to come, and I thought to have it here to remind him of his gallant work. Now I shall have to go east, and I do not like the picnic spot east. Well, regardless, Sally will have something to do." At Caroline's raised brows, she added, "You said he would never offer for you."

"Yes, I did say that. It happens to be true, so you need not try to prick me into some indiscretion."

"Really, should I ever do that?" Lucy asked, and laughed. Then she sobered. "When you have spoken to your sister, write me a note straightaway, all right? The suspense will surely do me in, otherwise."

"As soon as I can. I promise."

They walked back together, for the path to the Boweses' house and Norcrest Manor lay in the same direction. Then Caroline bid Lucy good-bye, and hurried home.

When she reached Norcrest Manor, she learned that Melisande entertained Mr. Bowes in the drawing room.

"We were told not to disturb her, ma'am," Griggs said.

"I see." Caroline wished she could be a fly on the wall, or at least find some excuse to loiter outside the door. "Would you please let me know when Miss Wendham is free?"

"With pleasure, ma'am," Griggs said, and bowed.

Caroline waited upstairs for over an hour before a maid brought her news that Mr. Bowes was leaving. She smoothed her hair and her skirts and went downstairs in time to watch, from the landing, Melisande see Mr. Bowes out. When Melisande turned around, Caroline descended quickly, saying, "I need to talk to you, Melly, right away."

Chapter Fifteen

Melisande said, half-exasperated, half-indulgent, "What start have you gotten yourself into now, Caroline?"

"Please, Melly."

"Very well."

They went into the drawing room. Melisande's brows rose when Caroline closed the door behind them. "Has someone importuned you or given you insult?"

"No, no. It is nothing like that." Caroline bit her lip. "Lucy called me over today to show me something she found. Artwork, Melly, a whole room full of crated artwork."

Melisande regarded her gravely, then walked along behind a cream-colored divan, her fingers grazing its back. "Did you see this artwork?"

Caroline nodded. "There were three pieces uncrated."

"And what did you make of them?"

They might have gone back in time ten years, when Melisande had lectured her in art history. Caroline responded as if she were reciting. "Three distinct periods, but I do not know their provenance. They would be priceless, just those three, and there were many other crates." Caroline took a breath. "This is no surprise to you. You knew they were there. What is your involvement with them?"

"Why do you think I know about this?"

"The fire. You knew the pieces were threatened by the fire."

Melisande quirked her brows.

"And you would not have just asked me to describe them in more detail, had you not already seen them yourself."

Melisande paused. "What is your concern?"

Caroline's heart sank. Melisande did know. "They are valuable pieces. Why are they sitting in an outbuilding?"

"They are protected," Melisande said.

"Yes, we noticed that. But you must admit it is strange. It looks like they are being hidden."

Melisande's hand gripped the divan, but she said, "What could possibly make you think they were being hidden?"

Caroline sighed her frustration, and pushed back wisps of her hair from her face. "If they were not being hidden, why did you not have Lord Thomas and some of the men break open the padlock and secure the pieces well away from the fire?"

Melisande's head tipped back as though someone had struck her. Then she said, her voice frosty with anger, "It is nothing you need to concern yourself with, Caroline. Nothing, do you understand? You are to forget you saw it."

"How can I know what to forget if I do not know how you are involved with this artwork? Melly, please tell me how you are involved. Are you giving Mr. Bowes your opinion on them?"

"What did I say?"

"But—"

"But nothing. Do as I say." Melisande drew out each word for punctuation.

Caroline gestured helplessly. "But Lucy knows of it."

"I am certain Jack will speak to his sister. This is a very sensitive subject. I—we—cannot have either you or Lucy talking about it. To anyone, do I make myself clear? Not even each other. There is too much at stake."

"You cannot leave it at that," Caroline said.

"That is just what I am going to do."

She made to pass Caroline, but Caroline stepped in front of her. "Why will you not trust me? I can be trusted."

"I will have no more discussion on the matter," said Melisande with icy disdain. "Excuse me. I have to speak to Griggs."

Melisande swept around Caroline, who stood there blinking with surprise and perplexity. Melisande disappeared around the corner in a swishing of skirts. Then Caroline sat down on the divan and tried to think.

Melisande knew the artwork was there, and why. She and Mr. Bowes worked together, although what part Melisande took, Caroline did not know. Nor did Caroline know how long this had been going on. Had the artwork been there a week, or a month? That it had not come into the neighborhood before last May, when Mr. Bowes had returned from the army, Caroline did not doubt. Besides, Melisande would have wanted to find a better place for it over a wet fall and winter. The protection of roof, tarp, and crate would do well enough for summertime, but they were temporary measures at best.

The fire had made both Melisande and Mr. Bowes frantic, and Melisande had seemed particularly upset just now over the notion that Lord Thomas and some of the men remove the artwork—even in its crates—to safety. Would there have been a point at which Melisande would have done that? Caroline had to believe that she would have, or Caroline would have to believe that something entirely havey-cavey was going on.

Perhaps it was just the mention of Lord Thomas that had put Melisande's back up. Caroline frowned, suddenly remembering Melisande's cryptic comments that

Lord Thomas helping to put out the fire was fitting. Yes, those were the words she had used. *Well* and *fitting*.

Caroline fished back for other cryptic comments about Lord Thomas. There had been Mr. Bowes saying he was dangerous, although Caroline had thought at the time he had meant dangerous only to Mr. Bowes's ambitions toward Melisande. Then there had been Melisande's comment about him being charismatic, not merely handsome. Caroline had had the undeniable impression that Melisande feared him for it.

Still, it made no sense. Why would it be well and fitting for Lord Thomas, specifically, to be the person fighting the fire? Had Melisande considered it well and fitting for Lord Thomas to atone by protecting something valuable to her?

Or, and here Caroline sat straight up, or, had Melisande considered it well and fitting for Lord Thomas to protect this particular artwork?

If so, the connection could not be more obvious. Spain. The artwork was Spanish. Melisande and Mr. Bowes would have suspected that Lord Thomas could identify its provenance as easily as he had identified the flaw in the faked Cavalcari falcon. He had been there. With Peter.

Peter! Caroline thought. Had Peter purchased this artwork and Mr. Bowes become responsible for getting it home? Or had Mr. Bowes learned that Peter had wanted it for Melisande and arranged its purchase and removal?

Now Caroline remembered that some of the letters Peter had sent to Melisande had contained sketches. Some Melisande had shared freely. Some she had not. If Peter had seen some painting or sculpture he had coveted, he would have sketched it and shared his enthusiasm with Melisande.

Where were those letters? Would one contain a sketch

of one of the three pictures Caroline had seen only an hour ago?

They were in Melisande's workroom. Caroline remembered seeing them there once, in the flat basket that stood on the table before the chisels and other carving tools. If there was a place in the house that could be considered sacrosanct to Melisande, it was the workroom. Maids were not even permitted to clean the room unless Melisande was present, hovering over their shoulders lest they dust something not to be dusted, or swept up some valuable sketch or piece of stone.

Or threw away some essential sketch.

Caroline felt dazed by the implications. But first things first. She would stay up past Melisande this evening and look for those sketches. Then she would decide what to do.

She passed from the room and into the library, where she put pen to paper.

> *Dear Lucy:*
>
> *Likely by now your brother has told you not to speak of anything we discussed today. I will try to have another opinion by tomorrow. I am sorry I cannot be more use right now. You understand.*
>
> *Yours,*
Caroline

She folded and sealed the letter, then summoned a footman to carry it immediately to Lucy's house.

Now it only waited until this evening.

The letters had moved since Caroline last noticed them. She had brought a brace of candles and set them on the central worktable, and could see immediately that the basket contained only a couple of pieces of paper. Closer inspection revealed them as a few dusty receipts for stone. Caroline steepled her fingers before her mouth and looked about her.

Besides the long wall of tools, there was the table holding the chipped basin and rags underneath; a couple of stools around the battered, paint-splotched central worktable with its drawers full of brushes and paints and long drawers for sketching paper; the easel before the north windows; a sturdy table, equally pitted with paint next to that for holding a palette and whatever paints Melisande was currently using; a rack holding canvases on frames between the easel table and the central table where the wall jutted into the room; and finally, the bench by the door reserved for visitors.

The drawers of the central worktable, Caroline decided. She started forward, only to have her eye caught by a candlelight reflection from the northern-facing windows. Yes, there was a drawer in the easel table that faced toward the windows, away from the center of the room. Caroline had never noticed it before, and it certainly did not seem functional to have a drawer facing away from the side one would be working from.

With shaking fingers, she reached for the drawer, only to freeze as a sharp noise came from the hallway. A few dozen frantic beats of her heart later, Caroline decided it was safe. She opened the drawer.

The drawer did not hold letters, but their accompanying sketches, unbound. Caroline glanced through them, saw some she recognized, remembered thinking how beautiful they were. She had told Melisande how much she had wanted to visit places where there was such art. As she continued paging through them and got to the very last one, she saw the Madonna.

She could not mistake the serene, tender expression,

and shook her head. *Peter*, she thought sadly, *you were so good*.

But Caroline could not ignore the implications of having her suspicions proved true. Peter had known about this artwork, had written to Melisande about it.

Holding the sketch and the brace of candles, Caroline walked downstairs, knocked on Melisande's door. "Come in," Melisande said.

Book in hand, Melisande reclined in her night shift and blue robe, her toes stretched before her fireplace. She had plaited her hair for the night, and the long, dark rope lay across one shoulder. She set her book aside on a small table that also contained a brace of candles, three lit.

"What is the matter now, Caroline?" she asked.

Caroline set her candles down on a table next to her, and stepped forward, extending the sketch. "This is one of the pictures I saw today."

Melisande drew her breath in sharply, almost a hiss. "You invaded my privacy?"

"Yes," Caroline said, although she felt her bravery oozing from her.

Melisande stood, snatched the sketch away, and held it to her breast. "What could possibly justify your invading my privacy? Have I not always been a good sister to you? Have I not always made sure you knew right from wrong? Have I not always taught you everything I know?"

Caroline swallowed. "Yes, Melly, you have. But this goes beyond you and me. Beyond you and me and Mr. Bowes, too. Those pieces in Mr. Bowes's outbuildings, they come from Spain."

When Melisande did not answer, Caroline pointed to the paper. "That sketch came from Peter. Peter was in Spain. Where else could they come from?"

"What does it matter?"

"What does it matter? Melisande! It must matter. They are priceless."

"You have said so already, Caroline. Why are you repeating yourself?"

"How did you find the money to buy them, or how did Mr. Bowes, and from whom?"

"We did not buy them. The only money I paid was in transport."

Caroline believed her. "And Mr. Bowes?"

"He contributed his property for storage and arranged the transport."

"They are from Spain?"

"Yes," said Melisande.

Caroline sighed in frustration. "How were they available to be transported from the country? Those pieces must belong to someone. They might be stolen."

"They are not stolen."

Caroline found herself exhausted. She sat down in the mate to the chair Melisande had occupied, and said, "Mel, I told you before that I could be trusted. I can be trusted. And now you have to trust me. You have to tell me the entire story."

"Are you threatening me, Caroline?" Melisande asked, a sharp look about her eyes, although her tone remained mild.

"No. I could help if I knew what this is all about."

Melisande sat down as well, although she did not sit back. "Peter found it, a cache in the mountains, a shrine in a cave, abandoned and unknown to everyone. Whenever he had the chance, he would go there, make some more sketches, send them back to me. It was all just sitting there, collecting dust, and who knew when the cave might collapse and destroy it all? He wanted to bring it home, preserve it."

"Just like Lord Elgin," Caroline said, understanding.

"Just like Lord Elgin," Melisande said. "After Peter—
I arranged with Jack Bowes to get it home, in memory of
Peter."

With understanding also came staggering incredulity.
"How do you expect to appease the Spanish government? They are bound to assert their rights."

"Peter had a letter from a local grandee, giving him
permission to move them to save them."

"Where is it?" Caroline asked, with another sinking
feeling. She did not like mistrusting any letter that came
by way of Peter, but she could neither deny the feeling
nor the logic supporting it.

Melisande raised her brows imperiously, then went to
her desk and pulled out a rolled piece of paper bound
with an impressive ribbon of white and red and gold.
She handed it to Caroline. Caroline unrolled it, saw fulsome addresses and equally fulsome titles. In English it
granted to Captain Peter Wendham of His Britannic
Majesty's 52nd Foot permission to excavate and remove
artwork from his environs. A passage of similar length
next appeared in Spanish. It was signed "Don Luis de
Almarez y Santiago," and contained an imposing seal to
match the ribbon.

Caroline handed it back.

Melisande replaced it, turned, and stood facing
Caroline, arms crossed. "Are you satisfied now?"

Caroline did not shake her head. She did not want
to give herself away so blatantly. But something still
bothered her.

"What is the trouble?" Melisande asked.

Then Caroline said, "Why, if you have the permission,
do you yet keep the artwork hidden?"

Melisande snorted. "Do I want every blasted thief
from here to Spain thinking that I am transporting treasure? No, I will wait until I have the place in London set

up, move the pieces there, display them as they should be displayed, then tell the world."

It seemed reasonable, Caroline decided, but she yet felt suspicious. She sighed, then fished about a little more. "I wish you had told me. I could have taken some of the burden from you."

Melisande smiled, shook her head. "Soft-hearted Caroline. You are not fitted for secrecy." She raised her finger, held it up, not pointing, and her voice became firm. "But you will keep the secret now. We are almost at an end. There is one more wagonload coming—then we confirm our place in London before the weather begins to grow bad. We will open our exhibit during the Season next spring. No one will forget Peter's name then. And oh, Caroline, what attention you will attract! This will more than make up for the two Seasons you have missed."

"And you, Melly?" Caroline asked, feeling tears spring to her eyes at her sister's enthusiasm.

"You let me shift for myself," Melisande said. "Now do go on to bed, Caroline. I cannot keep my eyes open much longer."

Caroline handed Melisande the sketch and left the room. She walked slowly down the hall to her own bedroom. She felt the pull of Melisande's dream, understood how round and full and sweet it would taste to her sister.

But to Caroline, it tasted burned. However ostentatiously real that permission seemed, with its beautiful ribbons and gold embossing, Caroline could not think of it as any more real than the orders Peter had doubtless written for Mr. Bowes.

She did not know what to do. She could not call in the local magistrate. She could not do that to her sister. Mr. Bowes, she thought, could fend for himself.

That left the subject of Lord Thomas. Caroline had known better than to ask Melisande if Lord Thomas could identify that artwork, or Don Luis de Almarez y Santiago. Melisande would have stopped talking immediately. Indeed, Caroline was somewhat surprised Melisande had kept talking. Caroline reflected that she had asked the easy, obvious questions and been satisfied with the easy, obvious answers.

She wanted the easy, obvious answers to be the only ones. She knew it was not so. There were enough gaps in what she knew to fit several wagonloads of artwork through abreast, sideways, and, Caroline thought wryly, one atop the other.

So although Caroline had not asked Melisande about Lord Thomas, it did not mean she could disregard what he might know or what Melisande and Mr. Bowes might do to prevent his knowing anything about their plans. Caroline hoped it would not come to that, but she could no longer believe that Melisande would act civilly should her project be threatened. Caroline wanted there to be no more heartache, on either side. If she needed to be the bridge between them, so be it. And so be it that she was building a bridge whose boundaries she did not know. She would figure it out. She would talk to Lord Thomas tomorrow at the picnic, delicately probing.

It never mattered that she would enjoy it, too.

Chapter Sixteen

For her picnic site, Lucy Bowes had chosen a pleasant, grassy field well mowed by someone's flock of sheep. The field ran up a gentle slope into the woods that sheltered the road where, about a half mile to the northeast, Thomas had seen Righty and Lefty and their mysterious wagon. A large copper beech tree stood out in the field, about forty yards from the wood, proclaiming its independence from its fellow creatures. Its uplifted arms provided a wide ellipsis of shade, although not for long. The edges showed signs of brown. Once the leaves turned full brown and fell, Thomas thought the tree's majestic branches would make a wonderful sight covered in snow.

Snow would not fall anytime soon, but Miss Bowes had also chosen to settle her array of blankets at the edge of the shade, where the sun might warm them. The day, although neither cold nor crisp, nevertheless had altered from the previous day's warmth.

Walking across the field, Thomas was thankful for the dark gray cape he had shrugged on after his brown coat, and could not help but remember all the times he had worn a similar, lighter gray cape over his red regimentals as he had snuck, slunk, and skulked around the back ways of Spain.

Today, however, he walked tall and did not mind

being so exposed. Perhaps that indicated that he was finally thinking less like an exploring officer, and more like a gentleman landowner. That should be considered progress.

Thomas was the last to arrive, which meant that he could observe Miss Norcrest and the others. Miss Norcrest and Miss Bowes both wore their cardinal cloaks, which made them easy to pick out. Miss Norcrest stood with Mr. Sudbury, while Miss Bowes and Miss Sudbury sat upon the blanket, Miss Bowes shading her eyes with her hand and gazing toward him.

Thomas wished he did not have Mr. Sudbury to contend with today. Sudbury struck him as the kind of man who did well enough in unmixed company. He would have no trouble being either rough or smooth. But mixed company confused those elements, resulting in an unappealing, blotchy surface.

Then Miss Bowes waved her arm above her head, and Thomas smiled wryly and waved back as the other members of the party watched him walk across the field. As he came closer, however, he could see that they wore very different degrees of welcome. Could he have harnessed the energy in Miss Sudbury's smile, he could have pulled heavy artillery through mud. Miss Bowes seemed right pleased to see him. Mr. Sudbury appeared resigned to not feeling welcoming.

But Miss Norcrest's troubled, tentative smile surprised him. They had parted amicably yesterday. She had appeared happy until he had arrived. What would have caused her to be troubled by him?

Thomas wanted to think he had imagined her discomfort. While playing the gallant with Miss Sudbury, he continued to wrack his mind for anything that would have contributed to her manner. He could not. All the time, Miss Bowes watched him and the others with barely veiled speculation over the cold chicken and fall raspberries.

It seemed no surprise to her when Mr. Sudbury asked Miss Norcrest to take a walk with him up to the woods. Miss Norcrest agreed pleasantly, although her gaze fell upon Thomas and a line appeared between her brows.

Mr. Sudbury took her hand and helped her rise. She stumbled a little on a root, and although Thomas pushed himself to his feet, he could not assist her faster than Mr. Sudbury, who held her hand already. Still, she smiled at Thomas genuinely for the first time since he had seen her that day, and Thomas was reminded of his comment that she could light a man's way home. He realized how much he had meant it then, still meant it now.

"You do look after my friend," Miss Bowes remarked to Thomas when he sat down again and Mr. Sudbury and Miss Norcrest had walked a bit away.

"Knowing her as you do," Thomas replied, "I am certain you would want her well looked-after."

"Oh, indeed," she said, but Thomas knew she was not satisfied.

"Dear Jack," said Miss Sudbury, eyes lambent, "implied that you and he were in the same division in the army. How I do so admire all you gentlemen who risked life and limb for King and Country."

Thomas wondered if she had worked hard to construct the parallel phrasing and congratulated herself on it, at the same time reflecting that he could stand Miss Bowes's eventual disappointment in him better than he could Miss Sudbury's hero worship. He stood and offered her a hand. "Ladies, why do we not follow Mr. Sudbury and Miss Norcrest's example and take a walk?"

"A fine idea," Miss Bowes murmured, looking very much like she had won a bet she had made with herself.

They walked after Miss Norcrest and Mr. Sudbury, toward the woods. Above Miss Sudbury's chatter about how beautiful the woods would be in a week or two, Thomas noticed that Miss Norcrest seemed content in Mr. Sudbury's presence despite his accents becoming more and more ardent. With a decided internal growl, Thomas decided that Miss Norcrest did not rebuff him.

"Yes, the woods will be beautiful," said Miss Bowes. "Just like a picture."

Had she raised her voice? Either that or they had come within earshot of Miss Norcrest and Mr. Sudbury, for Miss Norcrest abruptly turned back to them.

"It is a different landscape for you this year, Lord Thomas," Miss Bowes continued. "How would a painting of these woods compare, say, with those of Spain?"

"The land is very different," Thomas said, trying to catch the compliment Sudbury was giving Miss Norcrest. It had something to do with her hair.

"Yes, but would the difference merely reflect the varying landscapes of the two countries, or the more subtle issue of styles of painting?"

Thomas frowned. "I am not sure what you are asking, Miss Bowes. I am sorry."

"I think," said Miss Norcrest, "that Lucy is wondering whether there is some distinctive style of Spanish painting that you would be familiar with and recognize. Is that not it, Lucy?"

Miss Bowes smiled. "It is. Very nicely put. One can always trust Caroline's family to be able to form the proper question whenever it comes to matters artistic."

Miss Norcrest looked unhappy, although Thomas did not understand why the subject discomposed her. Perhaps she merely reacted to any mention of him and Spain, as she had reacted so to Bowes wearing his regimentals at the assembly.

"I am not familiar enough with Spanish art to know its hallmarks."

"But you know what you like?" Mr. Sudbury said.

Thomas wanted to plant him a facer. It had been a long time since anyone had derided him to his face. He probably had Rowan and other loyal friends to thank for that over the last year and a half. Before that, he had gotten along quite nicely.

Realizing it, however, did not make it any the easier to take. From such a one as Sudbury, who had been trying to court Miss Norcrest while he was being captured by the French, it was almost past his endurance.

Thomas also found himself caught by the novel idea that he resented Bowes much less than he did Sudbury. For all their differences, he and Bowes spoke a similar language, shared similar circumstances, and had had a similar goal—to go home as unscathed as possible.

Thomas tried to recall that these were supposed to be gentler circumstances, that it was well not every one of England's sons had fought.

And Miss Norcrest was biting her lip.

"As you will have it, sir," Thomas said with exaggerated politeness.

Mr. Sudbury smirked again, no doubt thinking he had made Thomas back down. "You must not feel apologetic for having the sensibility of a soldier, sir."

Thomas was about to ask what Sudbury's sensibility might be when Miss Norcrest said, "Lord Thomas has a fine eye for art." Despite her not meeting his eye, the comment warmed him through.

"How fine?" Miss Bowes asked, lightly, although again Thomas sensed some undercurrent between her and Miss Norcrest.

"Enough to tell that the carved falcon in the Red Room had been copied from its true sculptor. It is Melisande's own creation," Miss Norcrest said, "after she had received a sketch from Peter. While he was in Spain."

This news surprised everyone else, even the Sudburys, who had not seen the falcon. They exclaimed over Melisande's talent, while Miss Norcrest and Miss Bowes exchanged another speaking glance.

They had all come to an open grove along the path from the woods. The path would run straight into the road, Thomas determined, unless it unexpectedly doubled back on itself, and there was no reason for a path here, with a road in front of it, to double back unexpectedly.

Roads, after all, were not ladies.

"I am still amazed at your sister's talent," Thomas said to Miss Norcrest, "and still wonder when your brother had time to send back a sketch. Cavalcari's workshop was one of the last places we visited before being called back."

He had Miss Bowes's instant attention. "You knew Mr. Wendham?"

There was nothing for it, Thomas decided. "With the 95th Rifles, ma'am, my regiment and his and your brother's were formed into the Light Division, under Craufurd."

"But it is too peaceful a day for Lord Thomas to want to speak of the army," Miss Norcrest said. "We were speaking of art you had seen in Spain."

"Let us do keep walking," Mr. Sudbury said, and tucked Miss Norcrest's hand through the crook of his arm. "It would not do for you ladies to become chilled." He and Miss Norcrest led the way along the path.

Miss Sudbury looked to Thomas for an arm, but he had to offer one to Miss Bowes as well. The path's surrounds quickly became thick with undergrowth.

"What else did Mr. Wendham take you to see in Spain?"

So Thomas described some of the little studios Wend-ham had found—the details, frescoes, and mosaics in various castles and towns, and the churches.

"Did you ever happen across a picture of a Madonna in white?" Miss Bowes asked. "I do swear one of Mr. Wendham's letters ran full of it."

"I do not think so," Thomas said, "although I could not be sure. I was detached from the regiment fairly often, so my experiences differed."

"Oh, we are at a road," Miss Sudbury said, setting foot upon it. "Is this the same road we took in, John?"

But Sudbury either did not hear her or pretended not to, his head bent toward Miss Norcrest, and Miss Bowes appeared to be thinking hard.

"If you came in from the north, ma'am, this would be the road," Thomas said. "You would then turn off about a mile and half to get to Miss Bowes's house."

Miss Bowes attended. "You have not been idle, Lord Thomas, in your short time here. I daresay you know the land around here as well as I do."

"I would not make any such claim," he said, smiling.

"You are too modest, sir," she replied, and, with a nod, called to Miss Norcrest, who, with Sudbury, came back to them. Miss Norcrest stood to Thomas's other side, Sud-bury next to her. "How far should you all like to walk?"

Thomas glanced measuringly at Sudbury, then said, "I am content to leave myself in your hands, ma'am."

Sudbury, not to be outdone, said, "You decide, Lucy."

"Shall we walk toward the crossing, Caroline, or should we turn back? We could make a neat circle at the crossing."

"I have always liked that walk," Miss Norcrest said.

"Excellent," Thomas said, offering her his arm before Sudbury could again.

Miss Norcrest's clear gaze took his measure, he was

convinced, but she also took his arm, leaving Sudbury to offer to the other ladies. Then Thomas deliberately allowed himself and Miss Norcrest to straggle behind.

Again she knew what he was doing and allowed it. Her very agreeableness, treating him the same way as she did Sudbury, put him in a devilish temper. He took a few deep breaths, and tried to remember all the things he had told himself yesterday. One charge upon the breach had been rebuffed, but he had not lost all his ground. He must tread carefully.

Caroline had not had a chance to speak to Lucy that morning before the picnic. She did not know what Lucy knew, what she had pried out of her brother. Whatever Jack Bowes had said or had not said, though, Lucy had centered on Lord Thomas as another likely source of information about artwork coming from Spain.

Had she also put together Mr. Bowes's fears of Lord Thomas with the artwork?

All these questions burned inside Caroline. She also knew Lord Thomas had not missed her rather speaking looks at her friend. Lord Thomas was far too attentive by half.

Then she derided herself, for she also appreciated the ease with which he had plucked her from Mr. Sudbury. She had listened to Mr. Sudbury's compliments with only half an ear. Behind her she had listened intently to Lord Thomas's deep, thrilling voice talking about the artwork he had seen.

She had noted with deep interest that although he named villages, towns, cities, castles, and homes, the name of Don Luis de Almarez y Santiago had not been among them. Could she be so bold as to ask for his name specifically?

"You shall likely consider me wildly ungallant, Miss Norcrest, to remark that you seem a trifle low today, but I would consider myself a poor friend not to ask if there is anything I may do for you."

"I do not consider you wildly ungallant, Lord Thomas," she said, watching where she walked. "I am not low, however, merely a bit distracted."

"Is it something I can help with?"

"No."

"Are you certain?"

"Yes." She tried to smile. "Lucy asked you many questions. I hope you did not feel uncomfortable."

"Not at all."

"I am glad. I enjoyed listening to your telling about the various pieces you saw in Spain."

"You heard me over your conversation with Sudbury?" Lord Thomas asked.

"I was not really listening. It was dreadfully rude of me."

"I would never have thought your attention was elsewhere. Doubtless neither did he."

"Well, I am glad of that."

"You are kind to treat him politely, Miss Norcrest. But if you do not wish to fix his interest any further, you would do well to treat him with more distance."

Caroline's stride broke. "You believe I encourage him?"

"I believe he believes you do. Your accommodating nature, Miss Norcrest—"

"I do believe I am weary of hearing you speak of my accommodating nature, sir," Caroline said.

Lord Thomas's brows rose. "Your pardon, ma'am. I wanted only to warn you as Wendham might have, were he here."

His comment roused her as few things had roused

her. "No, sir, that will not do. You may not take refuge there. Stop trying to be my replacement brother. I do not want one."

Caroline wanted a husband. She wanted Lord Thomas as her husband, and every mention of Peter served only to remind her that he had bound himself to Melisande.

No. The word echoed around her mind. *No, no, no, and no.* Melisande would never agree to have him. Melisande would never love him.

Caroline did. She loved him with a passion she had barely dreamt possible.

The abrupt thought startled her. She concentrated on not tripping over her feet while she wondered when such feelings had begun.

She had known since she met him that she found him attractive. Confined as she had been to this small section of England, with only the occasional eligible visitor such as Mr. Sudbury, she could not have helped but find Lord Thomas's keen, handsome features attractive. His character, too, had drawn her. For all his professed culpability, people yet followed him, did what he said. Even Mr. Bowes backed off when pressed. Everyone thought him grand. Except Melisande, that is.

But Caroline loved him, every inch and foible. She loved the way he could stand still and somehow command everyone's attention. She loved the way he could look at her and make her feel warm clean through. She loved the way he could tease her gently about metaphysics. She loved the loneliness she sensed inside him, for it made her identify the hole she had also felt inside her all her life.

She loved Lord Thomas.

Why had her heart decided to inform her head of it at the moment when he yet seemed determined to drown in his professed responsibility? She shook her head. She did not know.

Lord Thomas would never put aside that responsibility. Whatever Caroline said about not wanting a brother made as much difference as telling the stars not to shine at night.

And she had been unpardonably rude in her discovery, for his face had taken on a wooden expression, not quite the shuttered look, but close enough. It hurt her to be the cause of such pain, hurt even more to know that she could not possibly share hers with anyone. Her dearest friends were closed to her on this subject.

Interestingly enough, she also realized that she would not have been able to discuss these feelings with Melisande, even if they had had a different object. Melisande would give her that little smile that said *Caroline, you are so tender-hearted*, which meant, of course, *Caroline, you are a fool.*

No, she would not discuss such feelings with Melisande. They were too precious to be dismissed.

"My apologies," he said.

Caroline grimaced, shook her head. "I will accept yours if you will accept mine. And no fustian, please, about my not having to apologize. I shall take responsibility for my words like a gentleperson."

"Very well," he said, "if you must have it so."

"I must. Not everything, Lord Thomas, is your fault." She bit her lip. She could no longer profess to herself that she did not know where that thought came from. She wanted him to stop taking responsibility for everything. Maybe then he would stop taking responsibility for Peter. Maybe then he would stop taking responsibility for Melisande.

Maybe then he would take responsibility for Caroline. Wanting it to be so, however, did not make speaking it any the less rude. Caroline wondered what this beast love was, that it could so provoke her to rudeness and depress her all at once.

"I beg your pardon?" he asked.

"Do not, I beg *you*. I must be out of sorts today," Caroline said. "I do not know how it would have happened. The day is lovely, the company agreeable—"

"Caroline! Lord Thomas! Do come quick," Lucy called.

Thirty yards or so ahead of them, the others were poised by the side of the road. Miss Sudbury stood back from the edge with her gloved hand over her mouth. Mr. Sudbury was hunched over, arms braced on legs, looking down. The steep leaf- and fern-covered incline, almost a ravine, meandered along both sides of the road beginning about a quarter-mile back. It gave the road a sense of remoteness, and was one of the features of this stretch Caroline liked the most.

Lucy was waving Caroline and Lord Thomas on, and also looking down the incline.

Lord Thomas took Caroline's hand, and together, they half walked, half ran up to the others.

"There is a man down there," Lucy said.

The bracken hid some of him, chiefly his head, from the edges farther down the slope. The bracken between him and the road looked trampled. He had rolled down, Caroline surmised. Now that she had taken that initial assessment, she could see that his clothes looked prosperous, if rumpled.

Lord Thomas produced a rather long and wicked-looking knife from his boot and handed it to Mr. Sudbury, who took it with wide eyes. "Stay with the ladies and watch about you."

"Good God, sir—" began Mr. Sudbury.

But Lord Thomas did not heed Mr. Sudbury. He ran lightly down the hill in a semicircle well around the fallen man. Miss Sudbury whimpered and edged toward her brother. Lucy took Caroline's hand, and together they watched Lord Thomas approach the fallen man. He studied the man from several angles for what felt like a tense half-hour, but was likely half a minute, before carefully going forward and lifting a broad fern branch from over the man's face.

"Who is he?" Lucy asked.

Lord Thomas whisked off his cape and laid it over the man, then began running his hands over the man's arms and legs. He was feeling for broken bones, Caroline realized.

Then Lord Thomas looked up at them. "I do not know. Your house is closest, Miss Bowes. I would like you all to go and arrange to have a wagon brought back here."

"I say, Dashley—"

But Lord Thomas anticipated Mr. Sudbury's protest. "Take care of the ladies, sir. The person or people who did this may yet be about."

"How do you know he did not just fall down the slope?" Lucy asked.

"He has been coshed on the head, ma'am, and all these plants and bracken are disturbed. Had he fallen, the top section would be intact. He was rolled from the top, ma'am. Likely that is why you noticed him at all. You saw the gap in the undergrowth first."

Caroline raised her brows at Lucy, who nodded. Then Caroline said, "The man is injured. Let us do as Lord Thomas recommends."

Lucy nodded again.

"Go carefully, sir," Lord Thomas said. "And keep your knife hand free."

Mr. Sudbury nodded and gathered his sister to his left side. Lucy and Caroline were going to follow. But before she took a step, Caroline looked down at Lord Thomas.

She hated the idea of leaving him alone, but of all of them, he was the most suited. Had he not survived so long by himself? Did she not trust in his strength, in his very self?

Perhaps some of what she felt appeared in her face, for he tipped his beaver hat to her and smiled slightly. She firmed her courage long enough to give him an encouraging nod. Then she turned quickly away before she could betray too much concern.

Chapter Seventeen

"You say he's Spanish, sir?" Rowan asked.

"I would stake my life on it," Thomas said.

Rowan set his tankard of ale down awkwardly and hard on his dining room table. It sloshed over a little, spilling foam on the wood. Rowan scowled, swiped at the spill with the end of the lace-edged table runner. "What Annie don't know, won't hurt," he muttered. "But what's a Spanish gentleman doing here?"

Thomas took a sip of his own ale, which Rowan had served after he had invited Thomas in. "That is the question. He had not come around by the time I left him at Bowes's house. All we know of him is what we can see from his dress. The others—Miss Norcrest, Miss Bowes, the Sudburys—they did not recognize him as Spanish. Not that I would expect them to."

"Right. Any tracks around and about?"

"An overabundance of them."

Rowan nodded glumly. "Ain't it always the way? 'Tis a pity, too, sir, that Bowes's house was the closest to the spot. You did remember 'tis Wednesday?"

"According to Jon Hatcher, Righty and Lefty came through early this morning and left by the north road. But I considered it. It is Wednesday. Bowes is getting another shipment of artwork no one seems to know anything about."

"Or they'd be talking about it."

"I could not imagine Miss Wendham not talking about it," Thomas said, remembering her passionate advocacy of Lord Elgin.

"I cannot stop thinking, sir, that Mr. Bowes was in Spain. This gentleman is Spanish."

Thomas nodded. He thought along those lines, too.

"You weren't expecting anyone, were you, sir?"

Thomas shook his head. "I have corresponded with some of the local grandees and counts who helped me. This man is not one of them."

"A relative?"

"No letter of introduction has come, nor been found on his person."

"Stolen?"

"Could be, although why anyone would care who came to visit me is beyond me."

"A right mystery through and through."

"One that I fear will not be resolved until he regains his senses."

"What chance he will speak English, sir?" Rowan asked, and took a draught of ale.

"He got this far," Thomas said. "And the Spaniards have never conquered our British trick of merely adding an 'eh' to everything they say in hopes we understand them better."

Rowan smiled, but it seemed perfunctory.

They drank their ale, Thomas aware of Rowan watching him. Finally he said, "You still appear dissatisfied, Sergeant-Major."

"It is not over the Spaniard, sir. You're right about needing to wait it through."

"Then you might as well get out what is on your mind."

"I do not want to pry, sir."

Thomas smiled ironically, which prompted Rowan to

grin. Then Rowan sobered. "It's like this, sir. I wanted to ask you how you fare with Miss Wendham."

"As well as can be expected," Thomas said and hoped that would be the end of it.

It was not. "I thought you would say something like that. We talked about this, Annie and I. I have something to say to you, sir, and I know you're not going to like it, so I suppose before I say it, I'll also say that no matter if you're mad enough to wish me to the devil, I will not take offense. If you needed me tomorrow, at your back, I would be there. No questions asked, no quarter given, just as I have been before."

Dread in Thomas's belly thickened, like heavy cream being churned into butter. Although Rowan was more gentleman farmer than gentleman, he had the perspicacity to see what was what, and the courage to say it. From his reluctance, Thomas suspected he was not expected to like what he heard.

"I will always be proud to have you there."

"Thank you, sir." Rowan cleared his throat. "It's like this, sir. Going after Miss Wendham, it's like enlisting for the forlorn hope. You remember seeing poor Lieutenant Maidenthorpe of the 3rd at Badajoz, sir, and Captain Burney of the 88th at Ciudad Rodrigo? Did he survive to earn his promotion? No. Did any of them, poor bastards? And at what cost to their men?"

"Someone had to do it," Thomas heard himself say with lips that felt stiff. "The 3rd cushioned our way."

"I'm that grateful to them. It's what you accept. In war. But this is not war, sir. Here, there's no one to give you the 'promotion' if you make it, no one to say your honor has been redeemed. There's only the other fallen you'll take with you."

Thomas thought Rowan had dropped a brick upon

his head. He felt stunned, dazed, by this view of what he had considered a noble effort.

Then, unbidden, a memory of green eyes threatening to overfill with tears came to mind. He pictured them overfilling in truth, recalled the tender feel of her body against his. He realized he ran his thumb against his fingertips, searching for that feeling again. It could not be, however. He should never touch her again.

He knew that, yet he could no more resolve that it be so than he could forget that moment when she had left him with the Spaniard by the roadside. She had given neither demur nor any female exhortation to be careful. Thomas knew that had been a gift of her trust, and he valued it as he valued nothing else.

Still, Thomas cursed himself. It was bad enough that the Rowans seemed to care. No one should care for him. It was worse that he wanted someone as pure and lovely as Miss Norcrest to care for him.

"Miss Wendham has the right to her anger," Thomas said. "I need to give her time to come around. If you must call it a forlorn hope, Rowan, call it a forlorn hope that lasts however long it lasts."

Rowan screwed up his lips and shifted the ground of his attack. "Why was Captain Wendham there, sir? Why are you responsible for what happened to him?"

"You know why," Thomas said tightly. He should get up and leave. He should not be listening to anything else that might make him waver in purpose. He had made a pledge.

"I know what you think, sir, but you know there are questions out there. Who gave the captain his orders? Why did anyone think there was anything to hold onto at the White Lady's Bridge? It did not even figure into our later advance on Vitoria. It made no sense."

"Sense does not matter. It still happened. Because I was weak."

"No, sir, that's where you've just decided to be stubborn." Rowan sighed. "What has ever induced a man to lead the hope? Remember Maidenthorpe? Remember what you said about him? 'Damned prideful boasting,' you said, 'thinking he can get up there alone.' I remember, sir. I remember thinking, 'Thank God I have a reasonable, capable officer commanding me, one who isn't throwing away my life on his own honor.' Sir, Miss Wendham will not fall. Not if you waited a year. Not if you waited ten years."

Thomas shook his head, realizing his former sergeant accused him of the sin of pride. He should stomp from the room in high dudgeon at Rowan's presumption. The part of him yet in that French prison and the part of him that had learned what had happened at El Puente de la Dama Blanca dearly wanted to. But there was a part of him that had begun to smile again. Whatever its source, however it had formed, that part of him kept him firmly in his chair.

Besides, he conceded, loyalty and courage deserved like treatment.

Thomas put his palm flat down on the table. "Your assessment of the likelihood of my chances matches mine."

The front door opened, and a gust of wind jangled the small bells hanging from a broad beam just inside. Annie Rowan swept in, carrying two small, paper-wrapped parcels.

Thomas rose and bowed, and she came over, set her parcels down, and wished him welcome. "Please, my lord, do not interrupt your important conversation." Then, cocking a brow, she regarded each man in turn, and Thomas had the uncomfortable feeling of being called onto the carpet.

Rowan must have, too, for he winced and looked out the window to the apple tree, heavy with red fruit, adorning their small grove.

"You *were* telling him, weren't you? Or are there other, weightier matters to discuss?" She borrowed a mouthful of ale from Rowan's tankard.

"She has not always been so rude, sir. My long absence—"

"There's no hope for you trying to apologize away my question. It's there, on this table." Annie put her hand palm down on the smooth wood, rubbed it. Her fingers grazed the runner. She frowned, looked suspiciously at her husband, then said, "Did you tell him, husband, or should I?"

"Do be quiet, woman," Rowan said.

To Thomas's surprise, Annie smiled and folded her hands.

"If you know she will not have you—Miss Wendham, Annie—then what do you plan to do now?"

"Stay here. Do what I can. Things change. Circumstances change."

Rowan grimaced before saying, "How do you pay back lives by breaking others? Sit down, sir, and look at the question the way I know you can."

Thomas had half-risen, then realized he had likewise moved his hand before his body, in his old gesture of resting his hand upon his sword. Rowan had seen that gesture, but seemed unfazed by it. Thomas, however, was appalled. "My life is forfeit already," Thomas said.

"What about Miss Norcrest?" Rowan asked.

"What about her?"

"It is hoped in the village that the two of you might make a match," Annie said.

"Miss Norcrest knows what I am here to do," Thomas said harshly. He took a breath, tried to moderate his voice. "I told her. Local feeling may be local feeling, but how could I tell her I have given up on her own sister? Would she want the kind of slimy, dishonorable creature I would be then? No."

"What is Miss Norcrest's opinion of your undertaking?" Annie asked.

But Thomas was not about to touch that line of questioning. "It is better that I remain as I have been: a stand-in brother. I pledged myself to Miss Wendham. It was thoughts of Miss Wendham that enabled me to get home."

The Rowans exchanged a look that spoke much of how they had expected this conversation to go. Thomas had the funny, dislocated feeling one gets when one has to realize people have been discussing one.

Then Annie shook her head and addressed the ceiling. "I do not think I can ever understand how men think."

Rowan touched his wife's cheek with a knuckle. "Do stop trying, then, my girl."

"You would plead acceptance?" Annie said with a snort. "Who goes happily into acceptance? Nay, it would not be for me."

Thomas went still, and cold. Acceptance had to be the last thing he felt. He remembered the way Miss Norcrest had looked back at him before leaving him in the woods with the Spaniard. All her trust in him had pooled in those green eyes and reached out a vine that circled his heart, making it stop within him.

Then his heart had begun pounding within his chest as if he were about to go into battle. Who would have imagined that after all he had gone through, all he owed, he would find love in this small village in England far from his home, farther from the place where he had thought he had left his heart.

He wanted to see Miss Norcrest's pride of him shining in her eyes every day, year after year. He wanted to hold her in his arms, feel her supple body against his, drink of her mouth, kiss her senseless, and beg her to fly to Scotland with him before he could let thoughts of his duty work on his mind.

Or she could change hers.

Even more, he wanted to turn back time, to have not spent the night at that comfortable house in Spain where his host's brother had betrayed him.

But then, likely it was he would never have met Miss Norcrest. He would never have known the fire he felt burning within him. He could not stay by that fire, but he thought if he could but hold onto its smallest spark, he could be, if not happy, at least content. Miss Norcrest could not be his. No damn the muskets and cannons, and into the breach. No carefully creeping behind enemy lines. In battle one died only once. To serve honor, death could happen a million times.

Annie Rowan nodded, as if he had confirmed something for her. She stood, placed a kiss on her husband's cheek, said, "Milord." She bobbed a curtsy and disappeared into the kitchen.

Rowan took another gulp of his ale and brooded upon the kitchen door.

"She is a fine woman," Thomas said.

"That she is."

"You are an exceptionally lucky man."

"That I am." Rowan smiled and patted the runner. "She knew anyway. Somehow she always seems to know. If that isn't one of a man's greatest hardships, I don't know what is."

Thomas took another gulp of his ale, yearning for the woman he would have and could not. "I appreciate all you and Annie have tried to do for me, Rowan."

"Sir—" Rowan began, half exasperated, half pleading.

"But I came here to apologize, to atone. It would be easy to propose to Miss Norcrest. She is everything I could ever want. But paying for one's sins should not come so easily."

Disappointed resignation set in Rowan's mouth and jaw, causing a furrow between his brows. "Like I said, sir, I'll be there any time you need me. Truth is, Annie has threatened to lock me from the house do I not persuade you to see the error of your ways, so I may need to be closer than you expect. Sir."

"And you would let a lock stop you?" Thomas asked.

"No, sir." Rowan grinned. Then he looked apprehensively over his shoulder. "But who said a lock would be the only barrier?" He sighed. "Enough of that. Your mind is set. I can see that plain. Will you stay to dinner, sir?"

"Yes, thank you. I would like that."

"Likely Annie is already giving the orders."

"I am sorry, Rowan."

Rowan made a face. "No, sir, for this I am entirely to blame."

Then Annie herself came into the dining room, a letter in her hand. "Jon Hatcher just brought this. It is an urgent note from Miss Norcrest for you, Lord Thomas."

Thomas opened it.

Dear Lord Thomas:

Please accept my apologies for summoning you on such short notice, but if you would ever wish to do service to my sister, please come to Norcrest Manor at once.

Yrs very sincerely,
Caroline Norcrest

Thomas handed it to Rowan, who read it with Annie tiptoeing to look over his shoulder.

"The Spaniard, sir?" Rowan asked.

"I would be willing to bet on it," Thomas said grimly.

Chapter Eighteen

Lucy's note to Caroline did not read with Lucy's customary succinctness. The poor, strange gentleman they had found off the road had started to regain consciousness, but not coherence. He also spoke in Spanish, to Lucy's surprise and amazement.

For Caroline, however, his nationality possessed an unsettling symmetry. Then had come the part that made the note drop from Caroline's nerveless fingers onto the Persian carpet of the Red Room.

I do not know Spanish. He is certainly speaking with less than perfect diction. But he has been repeating a phrase over and over again. I wrote it down. It has the words "dama blanca" in it. If my Latin teacher is to be believed, and Spanish is as close an offshoot to Latin as is French, "dama blanca" means white lady, Caroline. The artwork. This must have something to do with the artwork. What are we to do?

Caroline did not know what to do beyond the minute. She sat, stunned. She had not thought much about how the white-veiled Madonna's name would translate into Spanish. Of course it would be "Dama Blanca." That phrase in turn belonged to another of painful familiarity: El Puente de la Dama Blanca. The White Lady's Bridge.

All her suspicions about Melisande, Peter, and Mr.

Bowes crowded her mind. She had to know the truth for once and for all.

She stood, and then sat down again. The Caroline of two weeks ago would have done what she had done only last night. She would have spoken to Melisande and taken her assurances as though they were the truth. She would have supplied all gaps in logic herself and trusted. She would have been accommodating.

Caroline decided she could no longer be accommodating.

She went to the library, rolled back her desktop, pulled paper toward her, and wrote to Lucy.

> *Stay near the Spanish gentleman yourself, and let no one else by him until you hear from me.*

Then she wrote a note to Lord Thomas and brought them both downstairs to the footman for immediate dispatch. "Have someone else take the second note to Bonwood House. They are both very urgent. Do you know where my sister is?"

"I think she is from home, miss."

Caroline confirmed the footman's opinion with Griggs, then asked him to have Melisande come to her in the Red Room as soon as she returned.

Caroline paced a half-hour between the ticking grandfather clock and the spot where the flawed falcon had been. She wished she could see the bird. The open, empty pedestal seemed like a bad omen. Caroline touched it, found it cool, and frowned. Surely something so alive-looking should have left behind some warmth.

Finally she heard Melisande come in. A murmur of voices, then Melisande stood at the doorway.

"What is it, Caroline?" she asked, irritation ringing in her voice. She glanced at the pedestal, at Caroline's hand. "I had the statue removed, of course. But do not worry, I have it set aside for you."

Caroline took her hand away. "Earlier today we found a man in the woods. He is at Lucy's house. He is mumbling on about a white lady. Who is he, Mel?"

Melisande raised a shoulder in a wordless rebuff.

But Caroline was done with humoring her sister. "Answer me, Mel."

"You will not take that tone with me."

"He is speaking in Spanish, Mel. 'Dama blanca,' he says, as in El Puente de la Dama Blanca."

Melisande's beautiful eyes widened. "You will not ruin it. You will pretend you never heard about this."

"How can I? The man was hurt desperately. Someone set upon him, Mel. Someone bashed him on the head. Then someone rolled him down the verge, off the road, so he would not be discovered."

Melisande's eyes widened. "He was hurt that badly?"

"Yes," Caroline said, her voice urgent.

Melisande's expression turned stricken. "He wanted to ruin it. Jack said he would deal with him, but I did not know he would be so hurt. Where is he?"

"The Spanish gentleman? He is at Lucy's house."

"Then Jack can still take care of him," Melisande said, and smiled a strange, twitching smile that Caroline realized yet contained as much agitation as relief.

Caroline had seen her sister worked into a passion before, but nothing like this. It frightened her, and she felt tempted to run away.

But she knew she could not. "No, Melisande. Mr. Sudbury and Miss Sudbury know of him. This man cannot disappear now."

"The Sudburys are nothing," Melisande said, twisting her hands together. "You want to ruin it, just like he did. But you won't. I won't let you."

"Melisande, listen to me. Lord Thomas knows of him, too."

Melisande's jaw dropped, and tears pooled and dripped down her face unheeded. "It *is* ruined forever. All for nothing. Oh, Peter, Peter!" She whirled, a fist poised in the air. "Damn you, Jack. And you, Lord Thomas Dashley."

Then Melisande turned, strode over to Caroline, and took her by the shoulders, so Caroline could see the glistening tracks of her tears, and the wild sparkle in her eyes.

Caroline stiffened, but did not try to pull away from Melisande's fierce grip.

"You. You have his ear. He listens to you."

"Whom do you mean?" Caroline asked. But she suspected, for she was already shaking her head.

"Dashley, of course," Melisande said, confirming Caroline's dread. "Maybe if you talked to him, made him understand."

Caroline was astonished at how such a beloved, familiar person could suddenly appear so strange and alien. She took a deep breath, thought of Lord Thomas, and all the varied facets of courage. "First let go of me, Mel. Then we can talk about it."

Melisande blinked, let go.

Caroline rubbed her arms where Melisande's fingers had been. "What were trying to do, Mel? What scheme had Peter involved you in?"

"Scheme? Scheme! It was no scheme. It would have been a victory for preservation. Those, those peasants!" Melisande exclaimed, and began walking furiously around the room.

Caroline sank down on a settee, arms still about herself. Her upper arms had begun to pulse with renewed feeling.

"They had as good as walled up the shrine, but not quite. Instead they let it sit with the dust and rain blowing in. Peter told me he barely recognized what it was when he first ventured in. There had been a Roman temple near there, Caroline, in the mountains along the Roman road, a temple to Athena. When the Moors conquered the land, the peasants must have taken the marble statue of Athena in her counselor's robes. They had draped it with white linen, and brought it to the nearby cave. With the statue and other pieces, they remade the cave into a shrine for the Virgin."

"You are speaking of El Puente de la Dama Blanca," Caroline whispered. "The artwork came from the White Lady's Bridge."

"Can you imagine how Peter felt when he went in there? How beautiful everything was! The colors, the proportions, the sheer history of the place. People had added to it throughout the years, then suddenly forgotten it. A converted temple lost for centuries, long enough for every native peasant to believe it only a place to go to and wish for a happy marriage, or the birth of a child." Melisande shook her head. "He was overcome with joy. He wrote me and told me our futures and fortune were assured. He made arrangements for men in his company to remove some of the artwork and crate it up. Then he had it shipped to Lisbon. It sat there until the war was over."

"Only some? Where was the rest?"

"The big pieces remained. At the shrine." Melisande was nodding her head as if Caroline would find this the most normal thing in the world. "There was the statue to Athena, most of its linen drapings disintegrated into dust. And a cross, painted with Christ's own image, inlaid with rubies and sapphires. The peasants never pulled those stones out. Papists," Melisande said in amazement.

And Caroline found herself nodding back, even

though a notion, horrible in its very inevitability, was overcoming her.

"There was also a beautifully carved reliquary, still locked. Peter wanted me to be the one to open it."

Caroline did not want to ask the question, confirm her dreadful thoughts. She forced her lips to form the words. "That is why he went there at, at the end?"

"His last letter to me said he had heard Major Dashley had been captured and mentioned the bridge, that the French were sending men to investigate overland from Madrid. He was afraid they would look too closely, for although the peasants rarely went there, he could not rest easy that there were no signs of his earlier work. So he wanted to get there first, see if he could take off anything else, or frighten the French away. He begged me to take heart, that he would not fail us." Tears again dripped freely down Melisande's face. "I received his letter after I saw the army list."

Pity replaced some of Caroline's horror. She went to her sister, and took Melisande's hands. Melisande did not resist. "Oh, Melly, I am sorry." And she thought, *Poor Peter. You poor, blind, ambitious man.*

"You understand why I had to bring it here, to England, do you not?" Melisande asked. "You understand that I needed to finish Peter's work?"

Caroline squeezed Melisande's hands. "Of course I do. But it is smuggling, Mel, and theft."

Melisande pulled her hands away, lifted her chin. "I have the letter from Don Luis. And you will speak to Lord Thomas. Among us all, we will make this work."

Caroline knew her doubt showed in her face.

"We will do it for Peter," Melisande said, her own expression hardening. "He will do it for Peter. He said he would atone."

"Atone, atone," Caroline said in exasperated frustration. "I am sick of hearing about Lord Thomas's atoning."

"Indeed?" Melisande said at her most frosty.

"Think, Melisande. Lord Thomas could not cover up the disappearance of a Spanish gentleman."

"One Spanish gentleman does not count. I have the letter from Don Luis."

"You have a letter from Don Luis written by Peter, and you cannot convince me otherwise."

Melisande took the surprise in stride, although her eyes narrowed. "Very well, I shall not try." Her smile had that bright, encouraging expression one gives a precocious child. "I ask you, what else were we to do? The Spaniards would claim it."

"Of course they would," Lord Thomas said from behind them. "They would be fools not to."

Caroline and Melisande turned and watched Lord Thomas and Sergeant-Major Rowan come into the room. Lord Thomas would have appeared inscrutable, but for the muscle twitching in his jaw. Despite her despair, despite her disappointment over how easily he had turned her aside, Caroline acknowledged that she loved him with a ferocity bordering on pain. Her heart beat quickly, preparing for whatever might come.

"What did you hear?" Caroline asked.

"Enough," he replied grimly. "Miss Wendham?"

"I do not want to answer any of your questions. I do not have to answer your questions."

"Melisande, please. You cannot avoid this now."

"I have nothing to say. The pieces are on Mr. Bowes's property, and you can do nothing about it."

"Very well," Lord Thomas said. He tugged the bellpull and watched Melisande with grave consideration until Griggs arrived and bowed low. "Miss Wendham and Miss

Norcrest would like you to send someone around to Mr. Bowes requesting his presence here."

Griggs looked to Caroline, who nodded, and Melisande, who shook her head. Then Caroline stepped forward. "Immediately, Griggs."

"Certainly, miss," the butler said.

As Griggs left the room, Melisande turned away from them, toward the windows.

"Melisande, who is the Spanish gentleman?"

Melisande's shoulder twitched, but she did not reply. Sick at heart, Caroline addressed Lord Thomas, "He speaks of El Puente de la Dama Blanca. Who could he be?"

"Miss Wendham, when you mentioned a Don Luis, did you mean Don Luis de Almarez y Santiago? He was the lord of that region."

Melisande's answer was her mute back.

Lord Thomas compressed his mouth, then said, "Don Luis has a son, Don Alessandro, who had been away with the Spanish Army of the Center. I never met him, although I ate at Don Luis's table often enough. He is frail, but immensely proud and stubborn. He would not suffer the loss of any piece of his heritage, valuable or not. He, and almost every other Spaniard, have lost too much already."

"Lost? Lost?" Melisande asked, turning around, frowning, eyes blazing. "Do not speak to me of loss. Did he lose his son? No. Did he know the chapel was there? No. He was as ignorant as any peasant."

Lord Thomas stiffened.

"He knows of it now," Caroline said, with some asperity, "if that is Don Alessandro we found by the roadside today."

Melisande twitched.

"How long have you and Mr. Bowes known it was he?"

But Melisande folded her arms.

"Had he been left there long, his injuries might well have proved fatal," Lord Thomas said.

Melisande pulled herself together. "I knew nothing of his being hurt, but he has been writing me, importuning me about what Peter may have had shipped. He had not before been seen in the neighborhood, however."

"This artwork is not yours, Miss Wendham. It must be returned to Spain."

"I will not give up Peter's legacy," she said hotly.

"It is not Wendham's legacy."

"He died for it, did he not?"

Caroline felt torn between wanting to shake her sister to make her see how unreasonable she was, or giving her whatever comfort she would accept. She knew Melisande was lost to her, but years of habit made her implore, "Melly."

But Melisande paid her no heed. "He died for it. That makes it his."

"No," Lord Thomas said sadly. "Blood cannot pay for everything."

"And you would know, would you not, high and mighty Major Lord Thomas Dashley? You, who took Peter's life? What do you know about sacrificing your very life for what you believe in?"

"Be still, Melisande," Caroline said, surprising herself with her own vehemence. "You have no idea of what you speak."

Melisande's expression took on a hooded, glittering aspect. "I have nothing else to say. You cannot do anything about Peter's legacy. It is done. I am going to retire."

"Tell me, Miss Wendham," Lord Thomas asked, "had you or your brother made any provision for the men endangered in this enterprise?"

Melisande passed out of the room without replying.

"I'm going to stand guard, sir," said Rowan.

"Very well."

"Miss Norcrest," Rowan said, nodding as he left.

Melisande's departure loosened something within Caroline. She sank into a chair, twisted her hands in her lap, watched Lord Thomas lean an elbow against the mantel, his back to her. He thumped the mantel with his fist. His other hand clasped and unclasped into a similar fist.

Was this regret and relief? Caroline wondered. It must be. For the first time in over a year he understood he was not responsible for what had happened to her brother. He did not have to marry Melisande. He could not want to marry Melisande anymore.

But he did not look happy. Had the lifting of that weight happened too quickly? Yes, that would be it. Doubtless he was trying to sort out what he should do next.

When Caroline could no longer bear it, she said, "What are you going to do?"

He whirled around to face her. "Do? *Do?* What choices do you expect me to have?"

"I do not know," Caroline replied in a small voice, embarrassed and hurt and alarmed. Why did he single her out so for his disapprobation? Had she not done everything she could to ease his progress here?

He took a few quick strides toward her, sat down on the opposing divan, stood up again. "What did you know of this?"

"I knew of the art. Lucy found it yesterday morning. But where it came from?" Caroline shook her head. "I did not imagine."

"But you suspected."

Caroline bowed her head. "Whatever my suspicions, they did not include this. There is a building full of crates. How would Peter have had the time to manage such an amount?"

Lord Thomas shook his head dismissively. "Likely he volunteered his company for picket duty. The army was the whole winter at Ciudad Rodrigo."

"But you were not. You were out there." Caroline waved her hand toward the windows. She imagined him cold, always on the edge of being captured, shot, finally captured. She remembered how Rowan had described Lord Thomas's escaping in an offal cart, his being placed under arrest, facing an inquiry, then coming to Norcrest Manor to apologize. "You were out there alone."

Lord Thomas flinched. Then his face hardened. "Do not pity me."

"But I do pity you. Did you not hear my sister? Peter went to the White Lady's Bridge because he wanted to protect art that did not belong to him, that he was stealing from its rightful owners. You have been made to feel this responsibility for something you were not responsible for."

"Of course I am responsible for it. He would not have gone if he had not heard that I had spoken to the enemy. He would not have met a French company if I had not been convincing to that accursed French colonel. I could have withstood more."

Caroline blinked, flabbergasted. She had been so certain that he would feel free. She could not imagine how anyone, learning what he had learned, could not feel freed. Unexpectedly, and out of all reason, Caroline lost her temper with the man she loved. "You, Lord Thomas Dashley, are a fool. Never would I have thought I would say such a thing to you, but there it is. You are a fool—a patent, unmitigated fool."

She did not realize she had stood until he loomed close to her, close enough for her to smell the forest upon him, and his own elusive scent. He looked as angry as she had yet seen him, and for a moment she feared for her safety. She turned her back on him, lest she continue to be afraid of him. Caroline hated the very notion of being afraid of him.

"A fool, am I?" he asked in a rough, rasping voice. "How so?"

"You chided me for arranging myself to fit the situation, so that I make people comfortable. You, though, are quite worse. You arrange yourself to take responsibility for every situation."

He touched her shoulder. Caroline gasped, and so when he turned her about, his mouth found hers open and waiting for him. The not-so-gentle pressure of his lips, testing, exploring her mouth, created a hot, liquid feel deep within Caroline. She was so startled by the feeling and the suddenness of it all, that she had not time to respond before he took a large step back from her.

Caroline stood there, abandoned, breathing deeply. So was he, and a wildness was upon him, as unlike the shuttered expression he would get when he would contain his feelings.

"I must take responsibility for that, certainly," he said, his voice hoarse.

He has not given up on Melisande, Caroline thought, despairing. He had kissed her, but he had not given up on Melisande, or he would not be speaking of responsibility. He would not be stepping away from her. "The heat of the moment, my lord. That is all."

The wildness faded from his face. "You *were* chiding me for my overweening arrogance. You have the right of it."

She could not unsay what she had said. Nor did she want to. Perhaps he had not had enough time to become accustomed to the idea that he no longer owed anything to Melisande. So Caroline softened what she had said. "I think you have too nice a conscience."

He was silent for several wild beatings of Caroline's heart. "And this makes me a fool?"

"It does if you do so regardless of whether you have had anything to do with arranging the situation. You had no authority over Peter. You cannot be responsible for what he did. You did not know about his precious secret. How could you?"

He compressed his lips, looked away.

"We can both change. I recognized the justice of your comments, and I tried, I tried hard, my lord, to commit my sin no more. Not," she added, and could not keep the bitterness from her voice, "that my efforts have received either gratitude or appreciation."

"You expected appreciation for questioning your sister about stolen art?" he asked. "Or gratitude from me?"

"Gratitude is the last thing I want from you, my lord." She cursed herself for showing him her weakness. She folded her arms and walked a few paces away, toward the windows. "I shall try to live with my mistakes."

At this, he frowned, his arms likewise folded.

Thus Mr. Bowes found them.

Chapter Nineteen

"Such a pretty scene I have before me," Mr. Bowes said, tossing a pair of soiled gloves upon a credenza. "Almost, but not quite, rivaling the one going on in my northwest guest room." Other than the gloves, he looked none the worse for wear, and confident of his position. Why should he not be, Caroline wondered? There was still no real proof that Lucy's patient was Don Alessandro, or that he had come to demand the return of the artwork.

"So," said Mr. Bowes, and went to pour himself a drink. "I am summoned and I come. Where is your sister?"

"Upstairs," Caroline replied. "She felt unwell. She needed to lie down. Your plan for the artwork is discovered, sir, and it has quite unnerved her."

Mr. Bowes frowned a little, then said, "Careful, Miss Norcrest, or the triumph in your voice will turn into crowing. Just what are you talking about?"

"I take no pleasure in any of what has happened. I am sickened by it. All those lives lost!"

"Just what are you talking about?" he said with exaggerated patience.

"Your northwest guest room inhabitant is none other than Don Alessandro de Almarez y Santiago," Lord Thomas said.

"Really? Has this gentleman spoken to you?"

"Not yet, but you know who he is, so there is no reason for you to proclaim your ignorance. Did you ask Lefty or Righty—excuse me, those were my names for your two tender ruffians—to bash Don Alessandro's head in, then roll him down the hill, or did you take pleasure in doing it yourself?"

"Tender ruffians, Dashley? My, how descriptive. Who?"

"Melisande has told us everything," Caroline said, losing all patience. "It is quite shocking. The shrine in the cave, the forged letter from Don Luis, Peter dying at El Puente de la Dama Blanca to protect his precious art."

"An interesting story, Miss Norcrest, with some elements of truth."

"Do enlighten us," Lord Thomas said.

"Peter did find artwork in Spain, but he found it all over the place."

"Then why did Melisande show me only the letter from Don Luis?" Caroline asked.

"Don Luis is the grandee of the land near El Puente de la Dama Blanca. Likely you were asking about artwork from there, since you both seem so consumed by the matter."

Lord Thomas's expression darkened, and Caroline protested, "Of course. Are not you, and Melisande as well?"

"We are speaking of art from all over Spain, my dear. It is a much larger subject."

"No, Bowes, you are bluffing," said Lord Thomas.

"No, Dashley, I am not. If the gentleman in my northwest guestroom is indeed Don Alessandro, can he say what piece is his? No. Whatever he has to say is immaterial. It is his word against mine."

Lord Thomas shook his head. "Maybe he cannot speak to anything but a small part of the larger issue. But what odds do you lay on Lord Wellington's resenting this looting? What punishment did he order meted out to looters?"

Bowes swallowed, then scowled.

"Are you not still commissioned, Captain?" Lord Thomas asked. "Would it not be better if we worked this out between ourselves?"

"If we returned everything, you mean."

"And apologized most profusely to Don Luis and Don Alessandro. Yes, that would be for the best."

"Best for whom?"

Lord Thomas gazed at Mr. Bowes in stony silence. Then he said, "What persuasion did Wendham use to enlist your help?"

Bowes smiled. "He had promised to sanction my marriage to Miss Wendham, and she took up her brother's promise. I had only to transport the art, and I would get what I have wanted these nine years."

"No, you will not marry Melisande," Caroline said. "And I think you know that, too. I think now that Melisande never had any intention of marrying. She has always had her art, and now she has Peter's memory."

Lord Thomas looked sharply at her. Caroline wished she knew what he was thinking, but although his eyes could have driven nails through her, the hammer behind them hid from her. His look made her straighten, square her shoulders, brush aside a lock of hair that had gone astray. Exasperated and angry at him she might be, but she could not help feeling proud of him.

Then he released her to regard Mr. Bowes again. "Miss Norcrest has the right of it, I do believe. What other persuasion did our friend Captain Wendham use, Bowes?"

"I have so enjoyed our visit. Good day."

"Have you not been looking for something brave to do," Caroline said to Mr. Bowes, "to make up for the time . . . the time you—"

"You ran, didn't you?" Lord Thomas asked. "You—"

"Peter forged those orders, did he not?" Caroline asked. "Peter could fake anyone's signature."

Again Lord Thomas gave her that inscrutable, searching look. Not, Caroline thought, because she had interrupted him. "From Colonel Gaddington, was it not?" Caroline continued.

"Nice slanders you mention to young ladies, Dashley."

"It is quite true, is it not, Mr. Bowes?" Caroline asked, stepping closer to him. "You had a moment's hesitation. I am sure such a thing has happened many a time before to many other men. Am I not right, Lord Thomas? Then Peter came to you, helped you. But was he kind about it? No, I am sure he was not."

She hung her head. "I loved my brother. Peter could be wonderful. But he also believed the world owed him favors. Now he had you in his debt, deeply in his debt. You would have repaid him in so many other ways, but he chose this way. Maybe he convinced you that embarking on such a dangerous venture would restore your faith in yourself. Maybe—"

"Maybe he said he could change Miss Wendham's opinion of me," Mr. Bowes said. "I have loved her all my life. I know nothing of art, but she is perfection itself."

"I am sorry," Caroline said. "I wish she would love you, for you have risked much for her. I would wish—" She broke off, bit her lip, then plunged ahead. "I would wish that no one who attaches their happiness to the behavior of someone else ever goes away unhappy. It is a wish in vain, however, I fear. We all have free will, given us by God, not our friends and family, and we are downright blind and stubborn in its pursuit."

Mr. Bowes looked to the side and away.

Lord Thomas rubbed his jaw with a knuckle.

Caroline wanted to stamp her foot and tell them both to stop being so downright blindly stupid.

Then Bowes said, "Do not grant too much nobility to free will, dear Miss Norcrest. It can lead us willingly in the wrong direction. Take Dashley here," he said, looking to Lord Thomas.

"Whatever do you mean?"

"You were involved from the beginning," Mr. Bowes said to Lord Thomas.

Caroline stared at Mr. Bowes.

So did Lord Thomas. "Explain that, sir," he said.

"Peter laughed himself silly over you. You would come in from one of your jaunts, and he would find out any number of things from you. You gave him the idea to look around El Puente de la Dama Blanca when you told him how the peasants would go there to pray, although there was no sign of any church.

"That pricked up his ears, I will tell you. He was mad to explore it, and it did not take him any great time before he discovered the shrine's entrance, for there was a narrow slit between fallen rocks. Superstition had kept the peasants back, superstition, and probably the blasted noise the opening would make when the wind picked up. Horrible moaning that was."

Lord Thomas appeared very still. "So I set him upon his course."

Oh, no, Caroline thought.

"He was looking to make his fortune. He told you so." Bowes shrugged, drank. "There was no mystery about it, and he would have used anyone to do it. How do you think he knew what you had said in a French prison?"

Lord Thomas looked dumbfounded. "You cannot mean?"

"A Spanish woman," Bowes said. "The last winter, in Ciudad Rodrigo. She was *afrancesada,* of course."

Caroline was stunned by the implication. "You would not—"

"No, he would not," Lord Thomas said. "There would be an inquiry, and Mr. Bowes does not want another inquiry."

Bowes shrugged.

A knock at the door made Caroline jump. It was Griggs, who bowed and said, "A note has come for you, ma'am, from Miss Bowes."

"Thank you, Griggs."

"Very good, ma'am." He bowed himself out.

Caroline broke open the note. "Lucy writes that the Spanish gentleman has recovered his senses. She asks me to come right away."

Lord Thomas stepped quickly between Bowes and the door. Then he said, "Miss Norcrest, may I ask you to bring Sergeant-Major Rowan here?"

"You would place me under arrest?" Bowes asked.

"I am not commissioned. I do not place you under arrest. But Rowan can persuade almost anyone to follow suggestions."

Bowes's lips curled in a sneer.

"Would you also, Miss Norcrest, allow me to borrow your landau?"

"I will ask it be readied immediately," Caroline said.

Lord Thomas bowed, and Bowes snorted.

Caroline gave the orders for the landau to be readied, then went upstairs, where she found Rowan standing before Melisande's closed door. "Lord Thomas desires you downstairs," she said.

Rowan raised his brows, but followed her downstairs, where he took in the tense scene before him with interest but no apprehension. "Yes, sir?"

"The three of us are calling on Mr. Bowes's houseguest."

"Yes, sir."

"It would be better, Miss Norcrest," Lord Thomas said, "were you to stay here, with your sister."

"I understand," she replied, although she wanted desperately to go herself.

"You will be all right?" he asked. He made no move toward her, and half a room separated them.

"Do not concern yourself with me, my lord," Caroline said.

He compressed his lips, nodded, and before Caroline could think anything coherent, he had gestured to Rowan, who gave Mr. Bowes a rather intimidating look. The three of them left.

The sudden quiet buffeted Caroline like a winter gale. She held out a hand to steady herself, set it down upon the falcon's abandoned perch.

It had been a bad omen for the bird to be gone, she thought. It had been a thing of beauty, like her love for a man who had kissed her and found her so wanting he had set her away from him.

And why should he not?

Caroline realized that even if he had given up on Melisande, did his spurning her not show a quite thorough reasonableness? Was she not sister to two people who had caused him nothing but pain and grief, who had conspired with his enemy and were no better than thieves? And Caroline had been loyal to them! He must be wishing her entire family to perdition.

Thomas paid little attention to the landscape flying by the landau. He was reliving the staggering impact to his senses delivered by his brief contact with Miss Norcrest's lips. If he had ever thought he loved her, he had known it then. Every fiber of his body had cried out, seeking more of her.

Then he had realized she did not return his kiss, and a cold wave of shame drenched him. Thomas had committed what he most feared. He had importuned a lady who knew he had pledged himself to another.

She had dismissed it as arrogant rashness. Likely she also thought every other horrible thing that could be thought of him. Had she not said he should not concern himself about her?

The landau pulled up before Bowes's house, and Thomas dragged his thoughts away from his personal gloom. He nodded to Rowan, who said to Bowes, "You'll behave yourself, eh?"

Although unhappy, Bowes did not demur. Presently they were upstairs, where the Spanish gentleman lay upon a bed. His eyes were closed, but his hands plucked at the brown coverlet.

Lucy Bowes sat next to the bed with an ewer of water and a tray of light broth and drink. She stood. "I expected Caroline."

Thomas shook his head. "She attends her sister."

The Spanish gentleman opened his eyes, saw Bowes, and drew in a breath. "*Dios!* Where have you brought me?"

"Don Alessandro?" Thomas asked. When the man nodded, he continued in Spanish, "You are safe, despite being in Captain Bowes's home."

"You may say that how, sir?"

"I am Lord Thomas Dashley, late a major in His Majesty's 43rd Foot. I have also been a friend of your father's, and am seeing to your safety."

"Yes, yes, I have heard my father speak well of you. How do you come to be here?"

"That, sir, is a long story. What is more important is that I know about the artwork you seek. Captain Bowes says you cannot prove your claim."

There followed a full minute of Spanish indignation, which pleased Thomas absurdly and lifted him from his grave thoughts. Rowan grinned, too, no doubt understanding more than he knew. Although neither Bowes nor his sister professed knowledge of Spanish, neither could mistake the tenor of what Don Alessandro must be saying. Miss Bowes raised her brows and looked pointedly at her brother, who suddenly found his fingernails interesting.

Finally, Don Alessandro pushed himself up on his elbow, groaning. Miss Bowes steadied him. Then Don Alessandro pointed to his waistcoat, which hung over a chair.

Miss Bowes shrugged. "There was nothing in the pockets."

Don Alessandro snapped his fingers at her. "Bring it to me," he demanded in English.

Miss Bowes did as requested, although she was not happy about being ordered around.

"A knife, sir."

Thomas handed him the knife from his boot. Don Alessandro slit the bottom right seam at the back, pulled out a piece of paper folded over closely. "This, sir," he said, handing it to Thomas and lying back, his hand pressed to the bandages upon his head, "is a copy of a page from the Almarez y Santiago family archives.

"Your other friend's interest," Don Alessandro said contemptuously to Bowes, "in El Puente de la Dama Blanca did not go unnoticed by our local peasants. They complained to my most admirable father's servants that it was a sin to have the English all over their peaceful site. Regretfully, Don Luis did not pay much attention to their complaints. He is old, sir, and become weak, and the English were to be our liberators."

Don Alessandro lapsed back into Spanish for a moment of invective. Then he said, "But when I came home, I listened and I went into the archives, and I found the original to the copy you have before you. It lists everything Captain Bowes there had removed from my land. What is more, he knows of this list, and that I had planned to bring it to your government. That is why I was attacked!"

"Rest easy, Don Alessandro," Thomas said in Spanish. "You are in good care with Miss Bowes. She is an honest woman. I will see to it that your family treasure is restored to you. You may have my hand on it."

Don Alessandro studied Thomas, then shook his hand.

After reassuring himself that Miss Bowes could continue her care of Don Alessandro, Thomas signaled to Bowes and Rowan that he would speak to them out of the room.

"You knew," Thomas said in the hallway, when the door closed behind him. "It *was* a bluff."

Bowes drew himself up, although it seemed to take him more effort each time. "You have a copy of a letter, Dashley. A copy. Who knows how long it will take to verify the original, if it exists?"

"As long as it takes," Thomas said, losing all patience with his evasions.

"No," Mr. Bowes said, regaining some of his swagger and sneer. "No. Sometime or later, Dashley, you will give up and let all this fall behind you."

"You do not know me very well, do you, sir?"

Bowes shook his head in mock amazement. "That you can still take responsibility for what Wendham and I did, knowing what you think you know now? Dashley, you astonish me, you really do, and I must admit, people I dislike so intensely rarely astonish me."

Thomas wanted to plant him a facer, saw that Rowan contemplated a similar move. Then Bowes's words penetrated, and Thomas thought, *Damn you, Wendham, and all your games. I do not like being manipulated.*

The thought and its accompanying anger and indignation hit him with the force of revelation. Was he finally free of El Puente de la Dama Blanca?

Yes, and no. Whatever Bowes said about his involvement in Spain, he was involved now. He could not walk away from this coil, not after Bowes had accused Wendham of consorting with the French. Did the least difficulty present itself, Thomas felt certain Bowes would publish that little detail far and wide.

Then what fate for Miss Norcrest? To be labeled sister to a turncoat and a thief?

No. She might have decided she wanted nothing more to do with him and his overweening arrogance, but he would not leave her vulnerable like that.

"Move along, Bowes, you're coming with us."

"And where would that be?" Bowes asked, losing a little of his composure.

"You, sir, are going straight into the hands of the magistrate. That artwork is on your property, and I want it all safe in one place while I'm gone. You and I, Sergeant-Major, are going to London. Horse Guards. If Annie can spare you."

Bowes paled further.

"If you're set on London, sir," Rowan said, "I'm thinking there's no point in my going home. At least, not yet? Hm. Not anytime soon, then. I see."

"There will be no more discussions on *that* subject, Rowan. Annie will not close the door forever."

"What are you talking about?" Bowes asked.

"Quiet," Rowan said. He cocked a brow. "Then what are we waiting for, sir?"

* * *

"How is Don Alessandro?" Caroline asked Lucy as they sat in the greenhouse behind Norcrest Manor. Warm and balmy even in the thinning autumn sun, the greenhouse also offered blessed privacy. With all that had gone on, Caroline had come to value her privacy. Even Peg Denbigh's visits had grated upon her. Lucy, however, understood.

"I liked him better when he was unconscious," Lucy said. "Or keeping to his rooms. Now that he is up and about, he spends much time speaking to himself while he writes letters—fortunately he does that mostly in Spanish so I do not have to *pretend* ignorance as to his subject—or playing up to my cousin. Sally has developed the rather unfortunate habit of giggling behind her hand."

"I am surprised they have stayed this long."

"After Jack escaped his house arrest, John thought it only fitting they should stay. It is kind of them, I suppose, although I should have liked some excuse to . . . well, put Don Alessandro from my house. While he remains, and there is no word from Lord Thomas, there is little to do but fret and look apologetic at the neighbors for having such relatives. *You* know."

Caroline did know, although that was all she wanted to say on the subject.

"How is Melisande?"

"She has kept to her room or her workroom."

"That is good of her."

From Lucy's perspective, Caroline supposed she was right. Caroline did not mention she had heard sobs coming from the workroom and the ringing of a chisel upon stone and left her sister be. Let Melisande work it out the way Melisande could. Caroline had realized Melisande would only push her away, and with that realization had come a certain freedom.

"Have you heard from him?" Lucy asked. "Lord Thomas, I mean?"

Caroline was playing with the broad, shiny leaf of a fig tree that encroached upon her chair. "I would certainly have told you if I had," she replied.

"Would you?" Lucy asked.

"What do you mean by that?" Caroline asked, more sharply than she intended, but she was not going to apologize. She had had to answer too many questions lately, to ignore even more. Her nerves were rubbed raw.

Why had Lord Thomas kissed her? She had dwelt on that question every available minute since he had left her. Had it been the heat of the moment, as she had suggested? It could not be love, or even desire, or he would not have said he must take responsibility for it.

Caroline knew what category of things Lord Thomas took responsibility for.

She remembered the rough, demanding, but heady feel of his lips and could come to no conclusion. Speculation she had aplenty, from his meaning to punish her for speaking her mind, to frustration over her sister's perfidy.

"Nothing," Lucy said. "I meant nothing by it."

"Yes, you did."

Lucy sighed. "Lord Thomas might have news of Jack. You might have decided not to tell me if it would give me pain."

Full of remorse, Caroline reached forward and took Lucy's hand. "Doing so would give you more pain. I know that about you, and I would not. I promise."

"Then I do wish the blasted man would come back and give us news. I shall go quite mad without something new to chew on, and it shall not be learning Spanish!"

Caroline smiled at her, and before they knew it, they were laughing and hugging each other.

"We are strange creatures," Lucy said.

"Better strange than Bedlamites," Caroline said.

A discreet cough startled them. Griggs stood at the greenhouse door. "Your pardon, Miss Norcrest, but Lord Thomas has come to call."

Caroline blinked.

"Has he indeed?" Lucy asked. "I shall leave, Caroline, so he may tell you the worst and you may soften it for me."

"But, Lucy—" Caroline said, frightened and desperately eager to see him again and incredibly annoyed at herself for feeling such disparate things.

Lucy pulled on her bonnet and tied her cape. "But nothing. Just keep me informed." Lucy swept past Griggs with a nod.

"He is in the Red Room, ma'am," Griggs said, "and I have taken the liberty of ordering refreshment for him."

Caroline wanted to ask Griggs if Lord Thomas could be placed anywhere else. She did not want to see him again where he had so recently rejected her. But she let her pride hold her tongue and went into the house.

Lord Thomas stopped pacing before the large fireplace, and bowed. "Please pardon my dust, Miss Norcrest. I thought you would want to know my news as soon as possible."

"You are all consideration," she replied coolly in her best imitation of Melisande. He *was* dusty, his Hessians speckled with mud, but her wicked imagination dressed him in regimentals and set him alone in the Spanish plain.

Reject her he might, stubbornly cling to a duty she did not believe he had to perform, even punish her with a kiss, but she loved him, and resented herself for it. "Would you sit down?" She herself sat down on a divan.

"Thank you. I have been to London, to Horse Guards,

and spoken to General Beresford, one of Wellington's most trusted officers. I wanted to speak with Wellington himself, but he is on the Continent."

"The general believed Don Alessandro's claim?" Caroline grimaced. "I have the story from Lucy."

"They believed me. General Beresford has dispatched an envoy to Spain to make some inquiries. Discreet inquiries. I want to reassure you that there will be no public mention of how the artwork came to be in England—at least, neither by the government nor the army. If the claims prove true, Beresford has promised to lay the whole affair before Lord Castlereagh and negotiate the relocation of the artwork to Spain."

"Did you know Mr. Bowes escaped?"

"Yes. The magistrate wrote me, and Horse Guards did not take it kindly. They are inclined to regard him as a deserter. So Mr. Bowes is hardly in the position to contact the press."

"So it is all over now."

"More or less. There is a detail on its way to guard those outbuildings until higher powers make decisions. Billeting soldiers to guard outbuildings will cause some stir."

"There has already been stir," Caroline said. "I must let Lucy know." She twisted her hands. "She has been frantic, and feels her brother's guilt most keenly. But you, Lord Thomas, this detail, will they cause you trouble?"

"No. The orders Beresford has written clears me of any responsibility for El Puente de la Dama Blanca."

They were such simple words, but Caroline heard a measure of relief in them. She thought she held her breath. "And you?"

"I would have ignored that part of the orders, taken it for pity, had not Bowes said so as well. It is funny, is it not, how we love our friends so well, but the words of someone who is patently not a friend sounds a truth we cannot ignore?"

He did not say anything about giving up Melisande. Caroline looked away, fearful she would betray the contemptible passion he did not return. She folded her hands, for they were shaking. "That must be a great relief."

He stood, seemed unsure what to do with himself. He went to the fireplace, folded his arms. "So Miss Bowes has been frantic. Has Don Alessandro given her much trouble?"

Caroline had to smile slightly. "The Spanish temperament does not agree with her."

"And you, how have you been?"

"Would it not be better to ask me how Melisande has been?"

The grandfather clock ticked out twenty-one beats before he answered. "Do you remember how I told you that you would always let a man know you were off to fight a villain?"

"Yes, and that I would carry a stick. Why?"

"The justice of that comment strikes me right now. I deserved that question about your sister."

Caroline frowned. "No, you take the wrong implication, my lord. I am sorry. Such a question was impertinent and rude."

He shook his head. "Truly you are a strong woman, Miss Norcrest. There were women in Spain, following the army. Even the wives of the officers had hard lives. You could have lived such a life. You doubtless may not have enjoyed it. I heard of only a few who did. But you could have done it."

"I must protest yet another unorthodox compliment. You give me too much credit when I was, really, being quite rude."

"I think everyone else gives you too little credit, although not for being rude. Even—" He shook his head. "Even myself," he went on.

"Lord Thomas—" she began, half daring to hope.

"Very well. How is your sister?"

Caroline's heart sank. She tried to smile, suspected it came out as a grimace. "Now that she no longer has the artwork—which she still calls Peter's legacy—Peter is truly gone for her. She is completely out of balance. Until this week I never realized that instead of looking up to Melisande, I was looking up to Melisande and Peter. My friends saw it, but I did not. More fool I."

"You must not blame yourself."

"But I do blame myself. I never tried to see how—" She stopped, realizing that Lord Thomas was working his customary magic on her again. Her cursed tongue always loosened around him, made her say things she had to apologize for.

"How what?" he asked, coming close to her.

Caroline felt so many contradictory desires pull within her. She wanted, still, to be the cool, gracious lady her sister was. She wanted to be the unorthodox woman Lord Thomas appeared to admire. She wanted to be herself.

What would *Caroline* say? She took a breath, and a risk. "How she had become until I saw how she treated you." She looked up at him, so close, but his expression was shuttered.

"From her vantage point, she treated me as I deserved."

The distance in his tone made Caroline cringe, and, in cringing, become angry. "You forgive her for that?"

"What else can I do? I see, you will accuse me of overweening arrogance again."

"I beg you to forget that I said that."

"You were right. You have reminded me of the other time you accused me, and you were right before, too."

"I do not understand you," she said, her yearning for him filling her with a curious emptiness. But she did not know what else to say, what other risks to take, and felt stupid and dull.

"I should not have kissed you. It was wrong of me, and I have not apologized properly for it."

"Lord Thomas, I want no more apologies from you."

A muscle in his jaw twitched. "I concede to your wisdom. The last apology did bring us to this point." He paced away, holding his fist over his mouth, one knuckle tapping his lips. "But there is something else I must say. Call it an admission, if not an apology. I have resented your loyalty to the one person I would be loyal to myself."

Caroline shook her head. "No, you must not say so. I bent my loyalty in so many ways. Your talk of my arranging myself to satisfy any circumstance—you could not be more right."

"I am come to see the circumstances," he said, smiling a little with self-mockery, "where such a trait has its merits. Solving the problem is infinitely preferable to merely taking responsibility for it."

"I solved nothing."

"No, Miss Norcrest, that shall not do, and I shall hear no more protests on the matter, for I am following your lead and solving the problem of my continued presence here."

"You would give up Bonwood House?" Caroline asked, stunned.

He nodded. "I have thought hard on the matter. What I cannot get around, you will understand, is that even while I found my honor cleansed of El Puente de la Dama Blanca, I besmirched it by imposing upon you, my good friend."

"Friends forgive each other," she said, desperate to find some persuasion that would keep him near.

"Perhaps you can forgive me for kissing you, but I do not know how you will forgive what I have to say next. Say it I must, however, although you will think very much the less of me—may think me dishonorable, even. I no longer wish to marry your sister."

"Poor Melisande," Caroline said. Her heart began its erratic beating again as hope surged through her. "But you are wrong—I would not think any less of you."

"I no longer wish to marry your sister," he said.

"You have said so," Caroline said.

"I did, didn't I?" he asked.

"Yes," she said, almost in a whisper. "Why?"

He sat down next to her. "Because, like your friend Miss Denbigh, I did not think I could look even higher. You accused me of arrogance, and I could think of few things more arrogant than of desiring to be your husband, rather than your friend. Caroline, dearest Caroline, I am far from perfect—"

"No. No," Caroline said, smiling and crying. "You are perfect to me. I thought, when you kissed me before, that I was repellent to you."

He took her hands, drew her to him. "Never. I shocked you. You thought I wanted your sister."

"Surprised me, yes, but you did not shock me. In truth, I never wanted you to want my sister. Not even from the first. Not even after I heard what Mr. Bowes said. I looked at you and could not believe you dishonorable."

He gently wiped away her tears. "You would see your stubbornness as a curse. I find it beautiful."

She gulped a laugh. "Another unorthodox compliment."

"Can you survive a lifetime of them?"

"If you are the one giving them, my lord."

He took a quick breath, as though he had taken a blow, then said, tenderly, "I am not sure I deserve you, especially since I will need to be reminded, from time to time, to let things go."

She slid a hand along his back, reveled in the sheer solidity of him. With her other hand, she brushed back his desert-colored hair. "And I, my lord, will need to be reminded, from time to time, to leave well enough alone."

"I will insist on taking responsibility for you, though," he said, drizzling little kisses along her neck.

"Only if I may take pride in you," she replied.

"I love you to distraction, you know," he said.

"As much as I love you?"

He smiled, kissed her sweetly, searchingly. As his lips found hers as eager, as urgent, as filled with yearning, and the passion built between them, Caroline felt that she had finally discovered what made any falcon soar.

"I have a Special License in my pocket, just in case," he said, his lips a delicious inch from her ear.

"You *are* competent. I always thought so," Caroline replied, and reveled in the shudder she felt going through him. That she had the power to overwhelm so splendid and honorable a man thrilled her.

"Competence had nothing to do with it. I was afraid you would change your mind. Can you live in Bonwood House? I have no desire to subject you to Dash's menagerie."

"I can live wherever you are," she said, her head against his broad, powerful shoulder, "wherever you go, but thank you for keeping me near Melisande, at least for a little while. She is my responsibility now."

"She is ours."

"Very well," Caroline said, much pleased.

"I have another admission to make."

"Thomas?"

"I am glad your brother never mentioned you to me."

"Good Lord, why?"

"He made your sister sound so wonderful, there was no way she could live up to his description. What I have learned, however, is that he combined you both into the perfect woman, and that woman is mostly warm, touchable, honest you."

"Thomas?" she asked, touching his face and thrilling to see how it affected him.

"Yes?"

"I do believe I am come, not only to accept unorthodox compliments, but positively embrace them."

"Ahem," Rowan said from the doorway.

Caroline jumped, but Lord Thomas held her firmly within his arms. Caroline knew he would never let her go, and she felt so complete she could not imagine ever wanting to be let go.

"All as it should be, Sergeant-Major?"

"My part of it, yes, sir."

"Then you may be the first to wish us happy."

"Thank God, sir. Now *I* may go home and sleep in my own bed."

"You go do that, Sergeant-Major."

"Yes, sir. Ma'am. Congratulations." And he closed the door behind him.

More Regency Romance From Zebra